THE FOUR HORSEMEN

END TIMES PROPHECY
BOOK 2

TOBY NEIGHBORS

MYTHIC
adventure
PUBLISHING

The Four Horsemen: End Times Prophecy Series Book 2

Copyright © 2023 by Toby Neighbors

ISBN: 978-1-952260-54-4 eBook

978-1-952260-55-1 Print

Mythic Adventure Publishing, LLC

Idaho, USA

For Jesus,
I have, and always will, lean completely on the promises you made.

CHAPTER 1

DO you really believe that aliens are responsible for the Vanishing? It may have seemed plausible at the time, but a lot has happened since then. Keep reading, and maybe you'll change your mind.

When millions of people suddenly go missing it's a pretty big deal. If you're anything like me, you were surprised at how quickly the world adapted. My head was still spinning when the news hit, and my former girlfriend tried to kill me. But that's a different story. You may have read that one, or maybe you just picked this book up wondering what the Horsemen of the Apocalypse are. I mean, people have long been fascinated with the end of the world.

No, I don't believe we're living in the last days of human history, just a major transition point, but we'll get to all of that in time. For now, let's focus on the millions of people who suddenly disappeared, including nearly all the children. The official explanation is that the Visitors took them. That's what we're calling the extraterrestrials who showed up right after the vanishings. The Visitors claim to be our forebears, a superior race that seeded life on this planet millions of years ago. I was always a skeptic I suppose, but there are legitimate problems with the idea of the earth as we know it being that old. What I can't wrap my head around is the concept that life just sprang up all on its own. Microbiology was the final nail in that coffin. Living cells, even in the most primitive forms of life, are just too complex to have arisen spontaneously. Everyone knew that, even though the old guard scientists refused to admit it. But now the Visitors have given the world a more plausible explanation—they seeded life here on earth, and people are buying it.

The truth is, with the big shake-up of millions of people vanishing into thin air, people are pretty desperate for anyone with answers. And the Visitors showed up at the perfect time to fill that void. They also claim to have taken the people that suddenly disappeared. The official reason is the removal of those who weren't ready to accept reality, or live in the new, harmonious unity provided by the Visitors. But it's just another front, a deception that many people are eager to accept. But not you. No, you wouldn't be reading this book if you really believed that our space cousins took millions of people in an act of cosmic kindness. And it's not just that the answers to our questions are vague. No, some of you know the truth because people you know and trusted told you what would happen before the Vanishing took place. And when the single most significant event in the last two millennia happened, you knew the truth instantly. The only question now is: what are you going to do about it?

My name is Henry Downes, but most people call me Hank. My introduction to the supernatural came well before the vanishings took place. Luckily, I found a mentor who walked me back from the darkness that threatened to engulf my life. Some of you may remember Lorenzo Maltza, podcaster, filmmaker, and expert on the supernatural. He was my friend, and I am so thankful for him. He's gone now, vanished like so many others. But I know he wasn't taken away by the Visitors. He wasn't removed for his safety or taken for retraining on some other, as yet unnamed planet. No, he was taken by his God to be spared from the difficulties that we are currently limping through. Oh yeah, I'm one of those old-time religious nuts, the kind that aren't welcome anymore. Which is why I'm writing this from a secret location. It's for my safety, because I know what really happened. And I also know what's coming. You probably want to know too, so I'll fill you in as we go.

Of course this story isn't for the faint of heart. If you'd rather just go along to get along, then you might want to skip this book. If you're one of those people who believe that the Visitors are who they say they are, you won't like what I'm about to reveal. But if you're anything like me, and you care about the truth, then buckle up because this story is going to be a real shock to the system.

CHAPTER 2

LET'S START WITH ME. You probably want to know how I supposedly have all the answers. Well, first of all, I don't have all the answers. I just know there are some bad days in our future. The Visitors are promising peace and safety, but that's just a front. The reliable source of information comes from the Bible. *That old book? Are you kidding me, Hank?* No, I'm not kidding. The Bible not only predicted the Vanishing–it predicted a lot of other stuff as well, and a bunch has already come true.

Your first question is probably something like: *if you know so much Hank, and all this Christian stuff is true, why are you still here?* That's an excellent question, and my answer is probably a lot like many of yours. Yes, I heard the truth, but didn't act on it. I heard about God's love, about Jesus dying on the cross for my sins, but I thought it was all just a story. Even when I was with Lorenzo, who was a true believer, and who shared the truth with me multiple times, I felt uneasy with the whole subject. So I put it off–sound familiar? I delayed making a decision about what I really believed, and so I missed out. You see, the people who Vanished didn't die. They didn't get moved to a re-education center in the cosmos– they were taken home. I'll explain that more later. At the time, I didn't fully understand it, but after studying and going through Lorenzo's old presentations I'm getting the picture.

While it's taken me a while to get my bearings, I did know pretty early on that I had a unique and important opportunity. I was in possession of thousands of hours of video that Lorenzo Maltza had made over the years. So I made it my mission to put as much of it out into the world as I could. That's why I'm in a secret location. The authorities haven't found me yet. I put a video online, and it usually gets in the neighborhood of a couple hundred downloads before the AI systems remove it. Obviously, I can't stay in one place. You've probably heard of the secret raids being carried out. Thugs in strange, all-black uniforms, with guns are arresting people like me. There is lots of conjecture about what's really going on, but no official explanation because the people being arrested aren't given due process. They're just silenced, one way or another. But I'm getting ahead of myself. Let me fill you in on who I am and how this all started.

Like I said, my name's Hank. I'm officially an orphan. My parents were killed when I was just eight years old. Car crash, although the facts are pretty fuzzy. I remember being in the car with them when it happened. How I survived is pretty miraculous. I was thrown from the vehicle when our car hit something. No one knows who or what they hit. I have an idea about all that now, but officially it was just written off as an automobile accident on a dark rainy night. I would have been killed too, except that my mother crashed through the window before I did. How does that happen, you ask? Well, it shouldn't. The airbags in our car didn't deploy. The seatbelts didn't work. And there was no trace of what crashed into our car. So, like I said, a real mystery.

My father was working for a government military contractor. I've since come to learn that he was involved with some very sensitive materials. As in, stuff not of this world. Whether or not that had anything to do with his death and my mother's, I can't honestly say. But I'm pretty sure that it wasn't just a random accident.

So, at eight years old I entered the foster care system. I was one of the lucky kids that got adopted pretty early on. My adoptive parents were Asian Americans, Peter and Nora Soto. As soon as I graduated high school I joined the Air Force. I was near the end of my enlistment period when I stumbled upon the remains of a giant.

Some of you can't keep reading past that last sentence. But let's be frank–there are flying saucers hovering over the nations' capitals, so we're living in a world where the supernatural can no longer be denied.

The giant was dead, but it was real. That sent me down a strange road, and by a stroke of good fortune when I was looking for work after leaving the Air Force, I was hired by Lorenzo Maltza. My job was organizing his copious amount of work. But I was unprepared for the supernatural forces arrayed against my employer. Lorenzo was more than just a boss; he was a mentor and father figure to me. In the course of working for him I was able to rub elbows with some of the biggest names in the field of ufology. I even spent a weekend with Arthur Doll at his cabin in northern California. Yes, the same Arthur Doll who is now the direct liaison between humanity and the Visitors. But like I said, I wasn't prepared to deal with the forces at work around Lorenzo, namely the dark spiritual forces. It was during that time that I started seeing things and hearing voices. A demon tried to take control of my life and very nearly caused me to commit murder. It's all in my book, *They Walk In Darkness*. If you find a copy you should read it. Of course anything that offers a different perspective on the Visitors than the widely promoted official version being put out by every government on the planet gets censored. So, if you haven't read it or can't find it, that's understandable. You don't need to read that to understand this book.

Shortly after being attacked and possessed by a demon, the vanishings took place. Lorenzo was among those who disappeared without a trace. I know, because I was living in his home at the time. I searched high and low. The man had been in a car accident not long before the vanishings, and just getting back and forth to the bathroom was difficult for him. So, I know he didn't just up and leave home on a whim. One minute he was there, and the next he was gone. I've seen enough of his interviews and videos from his conference appearances to know that he was taken in what Christians called the Rapture. That's when things got real for me. I made a decision right then, in Lorenzo's home, to believe in Jesus. I accepted that he was who he said he was: the son of God. I put my trust in his death to pay for my sins, and I believed that God really raised him from the dead. And that changed everything for me.

The next day I saw Arthur Doll on television promoting the idea that the Vanishing was the work of a race of peaceful extraterrestrials, which may have seemed plausible to you, but I remembered sitting at his dining room table when he told Lorenzo and a few other experts in the field that a group of wealthy power brokers were offering them money to say that an event such as that would take place. How they knew it was coming could only be the work of supernatural forces, and why they would want to hide it was simple. They don't want you to believe the truth.

CHAPTER 3

I MADE plans with my former girlfriend to take her back down south. I was living in Lorenzo's home in Spokane, Washington at that time. Her family was in Tennessee, and she wanted to get back to them shortly after the Vanishing. Of course there were roving bands of people looting stores and mugging people. So, after reaching out to her, wanting to help her understand what was going on, I offered to take her back toward her family. But by the time I went to pick her up she was fully on board with the alien theory. In fact, she and some of her coworkers at the Ruby River Hotel threatened me. That's when I knew how serious things were.

So I gathered as much of Lorenzo's materials as possible, loaded up the cargo van he used when attending UFO conferences, and got away from the city. I really had no idea where I was going, but I needed time to think and study. I spent over a week parked in the middle of nowhere. I spent every waking hour studying about the disappearances. Not everyone in the religious community believed in the Rapture, and in fact there were still plenty of priests, ministers, and pastors around. They claimed their presence was proof that the Vanishing wasn't an act of God. As you can guess that was pretty confusing for a new believer like myself. But, I had Lorenzo's materials–not just the videos, but his own Bible–and several of the books which I had organized for him that talked about the event. They also talked about what was to come, and that's where things get really, really interesting.

One of Lorenzo's friends was a former businessman who became a Bible teacher. He called the Bible an integrated message system whose origins are outside of space and time. Sounds a bit strange, but the idea was at the core of what I was after–authenticity. How could God write us a message that we would believe, especially knowing that his enemy would attack said message? The short answer is that he could tell us things in advance, so that when they happened we would know it was a real message from God himself.

I was fascinated right from the start. There were of course historical examples. The nation of Israel was what many Bible scholars called the super-sign. How does a nation survive for nineteen hundred years with no land to call its own, and under near constant attack by outsiders? No other nation, or group of people has ever done anything like that. But the Jewish people did, and in 1948 they pulled off the biggest miracle ever—the resurrection of their nation in the very heart of enemy territory. It's no secret that the Muslims hate the Jews. It doesn't make sense that the nation of Israel would come back to life in the very land where it had originated. And of course it was attacked several times. Against all odds, not the least of which were the overwhelming numbers of the forces arrayed against them, Israel survived. In fact, the nation thrived. It became rich, technologically and militarily advanced. Even more interesting was the fact that a tiny nation like Israel could become the center of geopolitics. But who can deny it? The Bible says, "On that day I will make Jerusalem a heavy stone for all the peoples. All who lift it will surely hurt themselves. And all the nations of the earth will gather against it."

If that weren't enough, the Vanishing was the second super-sign. Initial reports after millions of people around the world suddenly disappeared were varied. Some places reported that entire compounds of anti-government, ultra-conservative groups vanished. Convicted felons in maximum security prisons, prostitutes, politicians, and ordinary people were suddenly missing, but there were plenty of priests, rabbis, monks, and imams still here. It was a time of complete chaos for a while, even after the Visitors showed up on the scene. So what do we make of it? Once again, the Bible predicted it: "After that we who are still alive at that time will be gathered up with those who have died. We will be taken up in the clouds and meet the Lord in the air. And we will be with the Lord forever."

I know that some of you think this is just wishful thinking on my part, that the Bible is too vague and we're stretching to make it fit the situation. I admit, there were times when I feared that myself. But as you know, after the Vanishing, things got pretty crazy. And like I said, it was all in the Bible, predicted thousands of years in advance. Say what you like, but that's pretty strong evidence if you're asking me.

After my week alone, holed up in the old van, sleeping on an air mattress, using a solar generator that I had found in Lorenzo's garage to keep the electronics charged, I needed a shower and to restock my supplies. So I headed into the nearest town. That's where I met Flip and Lisa, and it's also where this story starts getting weird.

CHAPTER 4

THERE'S a small Walmart right off I-90 in the mountains of North Idaho. Officially, it's in a little community called Kellogg. By that time the government had frozen prices, but the store was still struggling to get the supply chain and transit systems back on a regular schedule. When I arrived the Walmart was open, but all they had were generic sodas, boxes of macaroni, and cans of soup no one wanted, like cream of mushroom.

I was able to get gas, which was a real blessing, and restocked with the meager supplies available. The Walmart was short-staffed, which was not a surprise. And there were people loitering in the parking lot. Most were gathered around handheld radios listening to the news. Some of the groups looked rough, like they might slit my throat if they thought I had something they needed. There were also beggars, like Flip and Lisa. They were twins and looked barely old enough to drive, although they later told me they were nineteen years old, after they tried to steal Lorenzo's van.

Just as I was approaching the store the twins stepped up in front of me. The boy had on blue jeans and a sherpa-lined denim jacket. His hair was messy and a little too long. The girl wore tights and an old sweatshirt she had cut so that it hung loose over her shoulder and showed some skin above her waist.

"Hey man," the boy said as I was entering the store. "You need someone to watch your ride. Those people out there are crazy."

"I doubt they're after my old van," I said.

"No, they want it," he insisted.

"For sure," his sister added. "They'll steal anything."

"Look, man, you buy us some food, and we'll watch your ride. Make sure no one goes near it," Flip said.

"We haven't eaten in a couple of days," the girl said.

I could have walked away, but after reading about God's love for me all week, some part of me wanted to help them.

"Sure, I'll get what I can," I told them.

That's when I saw the look. I've heard that twins can read each other's thoughts. I don't believe that, but I know when two people are close they can communicate a lot with a glance. And what I saw in Flip's eyes was dangerous.

I didn't take long getting what was available. The goods had been moved to the front of the store; empty aisles and discarded clothes racks were jumbled in the back. I got two cases of Dr. Thunder, a dozen boxes of plain macaroni noodles, and six cans of soup. That was the limit per customer. On my way out I saw people staring at me with haunted eyes. I didn't know if that was because of the shock of the Vanishing, or if it was from the loss of children. I've heard that losing a child is one of the hardest tragedies a person can experience. And some people lost more than one in the Vanishing. Of course the Visitors tried to explain that away too, and I know a lot of people seemed to not care in the least. But a lot of people were deeply shattered by the loss. I heard reports of suicides by distraught parents. So I tried not to look at the groups. Instead I pushed my half-filled cart out to the van. Flip and Lisa were there, just like they'd promised. Only they had a knife and wanted my keys.

"Just give us the food and the van," the girl said. "No one needs to get hurt."

Flip was holding the knife. It was a folding blade, maybe as long as his pinky. The handle was in his fist, the sharp metal sticking up past his thumb. He wasn't really threatening me with it. Instead, he sort of showed me that he had it, without waving it around where other people might see it. I was in Idaho, and nearly every one I saw in the parking lot had a gun either on their belt or over their shoulder. Normally, I wouldn't try to be a hero, but something inside made me feel sorry for the twins.

"You don't need to do that," I said.

"Look man, just give it to us," the boy warned.

"Or what? Are you really going to stab me?"

"I don't wanna, but I will," he threatened, but I didn't believe him.

"You get cut, you'll probably die," his sister said. "The hospital already got looted. There's nothing they can do for you."

"That goes both ways," I said.

"You ain't got a weapon," the boy pointed out.

"No, I don't," I replied calmly.

There's something about defiance that can make an assailant hesitate. Lisa was angry that I wouldn't do what they said, but I could see that Flip was scared. He didn't want to use that knife, and I couldn't blame him. In the Air Force we learned some basic hand-to-hand fighting techniques. I had played the part of an attacker with a rubber knife. Going toward someone with a deadly weapon is difficult. I suppose that's why guns are so popular. It's much easier to point and shoot from a distance, than to get close enough to use a knife.

"So give it up!" The girl demanded.

"How about I give you both a ride, and some food," I said. "Where are you headed?"

"Nowhere," she said.

"Come on man, we're serious," the boy added.

"So am I," I told him, still standing casually with both hands on the shopping cart. "You want my van, you'll have to kill me for it."

The boy with the knife looked like he might be sick. His sister on the other hand urged him on.

"Do it," she said. "Cut him if you have to."

The boy stepped toward me. I didn't move. The truth was I didn't want to make a scene. Part of me just wanted to run away, but I couldn't leave the food or the van, and it was locked up. There was no way to get the keys out of my pocket and unlock one of the doors fast enough to avoid the teenagers intent on robbing me. And despite the danger I had a sense of peace. It wasn't the only time such a feeling of contentment has come over me since that day either. It's like knowing everything will be okay.

"You can hurt me, or you can just come with me," I said.

"Where are you going?" the boy asked.

"Who cares, we aren't looking for a handout," the girl insisted, but there was a tremor of doubt in her voice too.

"No, but I can show you a way out of this," I said. "My name is Hank, and I know what's going on in the world."

"Aliens have landed, everyone knows," she proclaimed.

"They aren't aliens," I told them.

A group of locals had taken notice of the stand-off. I wasn't sure whose side they would come down on, or if they would just take the opportunity to rob me *and* the twins.

"I'm going to open up the van, stow this food, and leave," I said calmly. "Before this gets ugly."

"Fine," the boy said. "We'll come with you."

"Flip!" his sister demanded as he closed the knife and stuck it back in his pocket.

"If he tries anything I'll cut his throat," the boy insisted.

I was surprised at how calm I felt. My hands weren't even shaking as I pulled the keys from my pocket. In fact, I reminded myself of Lorenzo. I had seen him talk down people who had violent intent before, and I always marveled at how calm and composed he remained in those situations.

The back of the van opened with a squeak, and I put the drinks inside. Warm soda wasn't great, but it was better than nothing. The food went in next. All I had inside was an air mattress, a sleeping bag, a tent, a duffle bag of clothing, and the film equipment, including my laptop. There was a box of books too, and Lorenzo's Bible was right on top.

"He's a religious nut," the girl said. "We'll be lucky if he doesn't rape and kill us."

"I won't hurt you," I said. "But I don't want to stick around here."

They hurried to the front of the van and got in when I unlocked the door. The boy, Flip, sat in the passenger seat, his sister perched on his lap. I started the van, and we drove away—no one got hurt.

"Where's home?" I asked.

"Don't have one," Flip said.

"Me either," I told him. "Like I said, my name's Hank. What's yours?"

"He's Flip," the girl said. "I'm Lisa."

"It's nice to meet you both," I said, doing my best Lorenzo imitation. "Flip is an interesting name."

"It's really Phillip, but she's always called me Flip since we were little. It stuck."

"No family?" I asked.

They both suddenly looked nervous. I didn't think they would answer, but then Lisa spoke up.

"Foster care," she said. "They drum you out the day you turn eighteen."

"We've been doing okay on our own," Flip said, but his boast wasn't very believable.

"You're siblings?" I asked.

"Twins," Flip replied. "Been in the system since we were ten. They tried to split us up, but we wouldn't let them."

"Where are you headed?" Lisa asked.

"East," I admitted, "but nowhere in particular. I'm putting

together some information about the vanishings to post online."

"Why?" Lisa asked.

"Because I believe we're headed for some bad times," I said.

"Oh, you think?" she replied.

"I *think* that the Bible predicted all this," I said. "And it predicts what's coming next."

"Which is what?" Flip asked.

"War," I said.

"Told you this guy's a crackpot," Lisa said, speaking to her brother like I couldn't hear her, even though she was close enough that I could have reached out and touched her. "There won't be any more war. The Apkallu are in charge now. Everything's going to be different. We should turn him in. There might be a reward."

"Turn me in to who?" I asked.

"The authorities. They passed a law, you know. Fundamentalists and ultra-conservatives aren't allowed to spread hate anymore. They'll lock you up."

"Who passed a law?"

"The President," Flip said.

"The President doesn't make laws, he enforces them. That's the way the government is set up, so no one has too much power."

"Where have you been?" Lisa asked. "Seriously. Everyone knows the President declared a state of emergency. They sent soldiers to all the big cities. There are new laws."

"Okay," I replied, unsure what else to say.

"You said you knew what happened to everyone," Flip

said as I drove out onto the interstate headed east toward Montana. "So what's your theory?"

"About the people who vanished?" I asked.

"Yeah," he replied.

"They went to heaven," I said.

"Crackpot," Lisa whispered.

"The Bible teaches that before the final judgment of God, his church will be raptured."

"What's raptured?" Flip asked.

"Which church? There's lots of churches still around."

"Not the buildings, and not everyone associated with church," I explained. "Only the people who believed that Jesus was the Son of God and that he died for our sins, and was raised to life three days later."

"If that's what you believe, why are you still here?" Lisa asked.

"Because I didn't believe," I said.

"But you do now?" Flip asked.

"Absolutely."

"So all the good people went to heaven, and all that's left is us bad people?" Lisa asked.

"No one is good," I told them. "We're all bad in one way or another."

"This is completely bull crap," Lisa said. "Even the Vanishing couldn't shut up the religious wackos."

"So what now?" Flip pressed. "You said God's going to judge us, right?"

"The judgment of God isn't like a prison sentence," I said. "It isn't to declare us a lost cause, but rather to bring us back to him. It's like a parent laying down the law to a rebellious teenager."

"Sounds about right," Lisa said. "Told you we should have just taken his van."

Flip ignored her. "So then, what's he going to do?"

I didn't have the time to lay out everything I knew, which was still pretty disjointed. But I was certain about a few things. And they were the real litmus test, so to speak.

"Ever hear about the four Horsemen of the Apocalypse?" I asked.

"You mean the end of the world?" Lisa said.

"Actually, no," I corrected her. "But it is the beginning of God's judgment on the—"

At that exact moment the front passenger tire exploded. It was completely unexpected. I was coming down a pretty steep grade too, and the van veered hard to the left. I tried to correct our direction and hit the breaks. The back wheels locked up, and we did a complete three hundred and sixty degree turn, before going off the road and coming to a stop right beside a steep drop into a river. Lisa was slung hard onto the dash. My head hit the side window, opening a small cut above my eye. We all sat still for a few seconds, trying to get our bearings.

"What happened?" Flip asked.

"Oh, my side hurts," Lisa said. "You wacko, you nearly got us killed."

I reached up and touched the trickle of blood on my temple. "Maybe we should check on the van," I said softly.

My door opened easily enough. I turned the key, shutting off the van's engine, and left my door open while I walked around the front of the van. It was pointing toward the road. The rear tires were right on the edge of a ten-foot drop into the rushing water below. The river wasn't wide and didn't look all that deep, but it was impossible to tell for sure. The water was clear and running fast. I could see the rocks in the bed of the river below us.

The front passenger tire was shredded. The sudden accident made me think of how my parents died. Only they hadn't spun around. Their car had been driving down the road and was suddenly stopped by something in the middle of the road, something my father hadn't seen, something that left no evidence. Maybe it was Bigfoot. There were plenty of stories of sightings in the wilderness of the Inland Northwest, but not so much in the hill country of north Texas. Still, I was grateful to be alive.

"What happened?" Flip asked as he helped his sister get out of the van on the passenger side.

"Looks like a blow-out," I said, feeling an odd sense of fear. It was like someone was running a fingernail down my spine.

"Well, at least you didn't kill us," Flip said.

"Yet," his sister added.

"That shouldn't have happened. I had those tires checked a couple of months ago. They were in good shape."

"Maybe you ran over something," Lisa suggested. "Do you have a spare?"

"Yeah, there's a spare," I said. "But we'll need to pull forward to get it out of the back."

They waited on the side of the road as I eased the van forward and turned it parallel with the road. When I opened the back again I handed Lisa my last bag of Doritos and a warm can of Dr. Thunder. She opened the bag of chips and crammed a handful into her mouth.

"Been a while since you ate?" I asked.

"A couple of days," Flip said. "Hey, save some for me."

I pulled out the jack and unfastened the spare tire from the anchor on the side wall of the cargo bed.

"What is all this stuff?" Flip asked.

"Recording equipment," I told him.

"What do you need that for?"

"To get the word out, I hope," I told him.

"Your sermon to the masses?" Lisa asked skeptically.

"You're a preacher?" Flip added.

"No," I told them. "But I worked for one of the leading experts on UFOs and the supernatural. His name was Lorenzo Maltza, and I'm going to get his videos up for as many people as possible to see."

CHAPTER 5

WE WERE WORKING the jack when a pick-up truck came down the road. The driver pulled over and got out. He was a nice-looking man, clean shaven, his hair neatly combed, his clothes unstained, but there was a strange look in his eyes.

"Car trouble?" he asked.

"Flat tire," I told him, as Flip continued working the jack.

It was a type of jack that had a long, threaded bolt in the center and used an L-shaped tire iron to crank it up. All in all, a slow and intensive process. Flip and I had been taking turns with it when the stranger arrived.

Lisa stepped around the back side of the van. She was a typical teenage girl. She wore black high-waisted tights and a sweatshirt. The shirt had been cut into shortsleeves, with a low collar that showed a little too much of her chest and one shoulder. The bottom of the sweatshirt had been cut off too, so that it rose up in front and showed even more skin above the tights. The stranger's eyes locked onto her, and I felt a wave of fear.

"We're good," I said. "We've got this."

"I can give you a ride," he said, still staring at Lisa. "It's no trouble."

I bent down and took over the work of cranking the jack from Flip, who seemed relieved.

"Nah, we're fine. Thanks though," I said.

"Well..." the stranger said, and my body tensed as he pulled a small gun from the back of his pants and held it in our direction. "I guess I'll just take what I want then. Why don't you come over here, darling? What I have in mind won't take long."

"What?" Lisa asked.

"Hey man," I said, pulling the tire iron from the jack and standing up. I held the L-shaped tool close to my leg and raised my free hand, palm out, in what I hoped was a calming gesture. "We aren't looking for trouble."

"Neither am I," the man said with a sadistic grin. "But ain't a soul gonna know what happened if I put a bullet in you. The river will carry you far away. So just stay where you are, don't do anything stupid, and send the girl over here."

"Go to hell!" Lisa snapped.

"Oh I plan to, darlin'. But not before I get a little comfort." He waved the gun at her. "Come here!"

"Flip, aren't you going to do something?" Lisa asked.

"Like what?" he said.

"Let's all stay calm," I said. "Sir, you don't want to—"

When I think about it I'm pretty sure he meant to kill me. The gunshot sounded like a balloon popping. The mountains seemed to absorb the sound. The bullet flew past my ear, but it was close enough that I felt the air moving in its wake.

"Shut up! And do what I'm telling you to do!" the man screamed.

I recognized the look in his eye. You may not believe me, but I've seen that look of pure malice before, in the eyes of a demon. That foul creature haunted me and eventually tried to take control of me. Fortunately for me, Lorenzo had known how to deal with it. Part of me wanted to do what he had done and command the demon to leave the man, but I was afraid. He was pointing the pistol right at me and had narrowly missed just a moment before. I feared that if I spoke at all, he would put the next round right into my head.

"Now get over here, girl," the stranger said. "Do it, or your friends die."

Lisa was terrified. We all were. I could feel Flip shaking right beside me. Lisa obeyed, walking toward the man, her body stiff.

"Now, we're going to the back of my truck," the man said. "If either of you move, I'll kill you."

There are times in life when action is vital, but doing that action is difficult. I knew that if Lisa went with the man she would be raped and probably killed. There was dread on her face and terror in her eyes. The man with the gun turned toward her. She was still just out of his reach, her posture stiff. He had the gun pointed in our direction, but his head was turned, and his free hand was pointing for Lisa to walk in front of him. In that moment I felt the weight of the world on me, and fear held me in its icy clutches, but I did what I had to do.

In one quick motion I hurled the jack at the stranger. He saw it out of the corner of his eye and raised his arm to block it. The jack struck hard. The stranger's arm snapped, the gun dropped to the ground, and I charged forward. Fighting wasn't something I enjoyed. Some of my fellow Airmen spent time learning martial arts and sparring with one another. There was nothing about getting hit that I enjoyed, but I wasn't a stranger to fighting. You don't grow up with foster parents and avoid bullies. It's like they're drawn to orphans by some invisible force. I guess I know that it's a spiritual thing, but I didn't know that as a kid. I just learned that the best way to avoid getting beat up was to strike the first blow and make it really count.

I hit the man with my shoulder, doing my best imitation of a football player. The stranger was knocked back into the big, shiny grill of his pick-up truck. And then I hit him hard with the palm of my hand. One of the few things that Peter Soto, my foster father taught me, was never to hit with my fist. There are a lot of little bones in a person's hand that break very easily. Punching with a fist works in the movies, in real life not so much. Instead, I drove my palm straight up under his chin. The stranger's head snapped back, his eyes rolled up, and his body stiffened as he toppled sideways. His head bounced on the road, splitting the skin.

"Wow!" Lisa said. "You laid him out."

"That was so badass!" Flip said.

I bent down, picked up the pistol, and hurled it over the river and up the steep mountainside beyond. The fir trees were thick, and the weapon disappeared into the evergreen boughs.

"What are you doing?" Lisa shouted.

"We needed that gun," Flip added. "You can't just throw it away. What if he wakes up?"

The stranger was already moaning and starting to move. I picked up the tire iron, then walked back to the van.

"He's not going to bother us," I said. "Let's get this tire changed."

"You're crazy," Flip said.

"Okay, okay," Lisa spoke up. "Just do what he says."

Flip rolled the spare over, and we got the shredded tire pulled off. By the time we finished the stranger was sitting up, his back against the front of his truck, his eyes glazed. Lisa had searched his vehicle and found a short, wooden club, which she was brandishing a few steps from the dazed man. He hadn't said anything or tried to do anything other than sit up. There was a gash on the side of his head where it hit the paved road. Blood stained his hair and leaked around the back of his ear to drip onto his nice shirt.

"That should do it," I said, once the old tire was in the back of the van and connected to the anchor where the spare had been.

"Why aren't we taking his ride?" Flip asked. "It's a lot nicer than this old van."

"That's stealing," I said.

"So what? That creep tried to kill us. He was going to rape my sister."

"Don't say that," Lisa said, her voice low and trembling.

"He can't hurt you now," I told her. "And just because he meant us harm, doesn't give us the right to take his property."

"Dude, I don't understand you at all," Flip said. "I'm taking it."

"You don't own that truck," I said. "You could get in a lot of trouble for stealing it."

"I don't think anyone is worried about that right now," he said. "I appreciate your help, Hank, really. But no offense, I think you're a little crazy."

"We've all been through a lot," I said.

"Come on, Lisa. Let's get out of here."

I could have stopped them, or at least tried. But even though I believed what they were doing was wrong, I couldn't really blame them for it either. They were young and desperate. So I stood back and watched as they took the man's keys and his money. Flip got into the driver's seat, started the big truck, and backed away from the owner, who hadn't moved. Lisa still looked frightened, but she rolled the passenger window down so I could hear her.

"Thank you," she said as they drove past me onto the interstate and away down the mountain.

I felt a little guilty. I hadn't had a chance to tell them what I knew was coming. Maybe Lorenzo would have done a better job connecting to them. I watched them go until the truck was out of sight, then I turned to the stranger, who was laying down on the side of the road.

"Can't say you didn't have that coming," I told him.

The man didn't respond. I walked over and looked at him. He was holding his obviously broken arm across his chest. The tool had struck him on his forearm and broken at least one of the bones. It wasn't a compound fracture, but his arm was swollen inside the sleeve of his stained button-up shirt.

"Come on," I said, bending over and grabbing him by his uninjured arm to haul him upright. "Can't leave you out here in the middle of nowhere."

Before the Vanishing the interstate was a busy place, used by hundreds of drivers every day. But in the hour since my tire had blown out, the stranger had been the only other motorist on the road. Leaving him would have been cruel. He was clearly in shock and injured. He might have even died out there.

I got him into the passenger seat of the van, and we made our way through the mountains. I really had no clue where I was going, or why. The only thing I could say for sure was that I didn't want to go back to Spokane. There were nothing but painful memories for me there. The next community we came to was called Osburn. I pulled over, and the stranger got out of the van on his own strength. I didn't even have to ask him to leave, and he never said a word to me. I can't be sure, but he seemed familiar with the place. So, I got right back on the road, going east. I stopped in Wallace. It's an old mining town. That night I stayed in a hotel. It felt good to get a shower, and there was a hamburger place across the street. They were out of hamburgers, but still had hot dogs and french fries. The name of the place slips my mind, but it had a flying saucer that someone had fabricated as part of their sign. I remember thinking how odd and shabby it looked after seeing the sleek spacecrafts that were hovering over the major cities of the world on television.

After my dinner I went back to my room and logged onto the free Wi-Fi the hotel offered. It was the first time in over a week that I had checked the news. To my surprise, most of the stories I found were full of optimism and praise. Yes, there were accidents around the country from the vanishings. In some places cars had crashed, and even a few planes had gone down, but work crews had already done most of the clean up. And instead of stories of tragedy or national emergency, there were messages being handed down from the aliens. It didn't take long for me to feel a little frightened in the little hotel room. And after reading a few stories it was incredibly clear to me that the world was buying the idea that the Visitors were who they claimed to be. But I knew better. The so-called Visitors weren't aliens from another planet, and they certainly weren't responsible for seeding life on planet earth. As I lay in the dark, trying to sleep, it was as if I could feel the evil in the world. And it wasn't long until I had the familiar feeling that I wasn't alone in my room.

CHAPTER 6

IT'S FRUSTRATING to deal with something that you thought was part of your past. But our issues always come bubbling to the surface eventually, and old fears are hard to shake. For well over an hour I lay in the darkness of the hotel room in Wallace, Idaho, fearing that someone was in the room with me.

I know that was physically impossible, but if I had learned anything over the last year, it was that we live in a supernatural world. Eventually my eyes made out the figure in the corner of the room. I'm not sure who was watching who more; the shadowy figure seemed bent over. I think it was a woman, but again I can't be sure. It wasn't until the next day as I prepared to leave that I discovered the hotel had once been an active brothel for decades, and that several girls had died in the old building. Some from sickness, others from injuries sustained in the course of practicing their profession.

The shadow in the corner seemed to take on more

substance as the night wore on. And for a long time my mind was seized with fear, like an overworked car engine that suddenly locks up and will no longer function. Eventually, I heard a whispering voice, mumbling something over and over. In the back of my mind I thought that I was going to die. Scenes of hell had appeared to me in Lorenzo's home. The fear that I hadn't really done enough for God, that he didn't really love me, or forgive me of my sins, seemed at that moment to be obvious. I was too late, too bad, too broken to be one of his, and the dark powers from the underworld were coming for me.

I lay trembling in the bed, staring at the shadowy form, waiting for death to take me. Time seemed to stop despite the glowing red numbers from the bedside clock. It wasn't until the shadows became substantial that the thing in the corner began to move. And with that movement, my mind was shaken out of its paralysis of fear. The mumbling shadow was moving closer to me. I couldn't understand what it was saying, the words seeming like another language, and the only bit that was clear was that occasionally it said my name. Not Hank, but Henry. There was no doubt in my mind that it was coming to get me. I was about to die, and the shadow was going to drag me to hell.

But then I remembered how Lorenzo talked when I was under the control of the demon. And I had read enough of the New Testament to realize that demons were subject to the authority of Jesus. So, in a shaking voice I finally spoke up.

"You have no power here," I said, feeling weak and silly at the same time. "In the name of Jesus I command you to leave!"

The shadow stopped. It didn't leave, but it stopped, and

for that I felt a surge of gratitude. The inevitable had been postponed. And maybe I wasn't as helpless as I felt.

"I belong to Jesus," I said. "And you have to leave. Right now!"

Maybe it was the words, maybe it was the shock of hearing my own voice as I shouted in the dark hotel room. Either way, the fear began to ebb away from me. The shadow dissolved, not in a *Raiders of the Lost Ark* type of way, though it was too dark to see details. It simply ceased to be anything more than dark in that small room. I lay back on my pillow, breathing hard and praying. I asked for God's comfort, for help, for the angels to fight on my behalf, and for sleep.

There were no more nightmares, no more terrors in the darkness, just rest. I woke up at dawn, relieved to see light around the curtains. And I got a little more sleep before getting up around eight in the morning and hurrying down to check out of the room.

Part of me felt trapped in Wallace. I was so uneasy that I left without breakfast, which was dry cereal, so no major loss. Especially since they didn't even have real milk to pour over it. I did however see a book in a display called *Selling Sex In The Silver Valley*. It was written by Dr. Heather Branstetter, according to the summary on the back cover, gave the history of prostitution in the city of Wallace, which flourished there into the nineteen nineties. I didn't bother purchasing a copy–I just got out of town as fast as possible.

I feel at this point of the story I should point out that I do NOT believe in ghosts. I do, however, believe in the paranormal. The Bible is pretty clear there are fallen entities, demons, and spiritual powers at work in our world. We don't understand it, not even the experts like Lorenzo, from what I've read of his work and heard in his videos. We're not meant to understand it. But I believe that evil can take shape and gain a stronghold in a place, especially where evil was permitted and even encouraged. That said, I don't think the shadow in my room that night was a ghost of a slain prostitute or madam. But whatever foul spirit that was there in that place it had drawn on the past atrocities that had most likely taken place in that very room. Remodeling can change the appearance of a place, but there was something sinister remaining.

After Wallace, I drove until I got low on gas. I was also getting low on funds. My bank card still worked, and prices had been frozen by the government, but that didn't mean I could just go on and on in my quest without being careful. At Missoula I filled the van's gas tank and stopped for lunch at a little stand where a farming family was selling vegetables. There were signs around the little stand with Bible verses written in black marker, which made me feel a little better. There wasn't a lot of traffic around town. I didn't know how many people in Missoula, Montana had been taken in the Rapture, but it seemed that the rest were staying home.

I got out of the van and walked over to the couple selling onions, squash, and piles of green beans.

"Howdy, there," the man said. He was older, with white hair and a beard. "Looking for food?"

"Yes, sir," I said, falling back into my military training when addressing a superior.

"We're selling what we pulled out of the garden this morning," his partner said. She was younger and clearly related to the older man. She was older than I was, with some lines around her eyes. I guessed she was his daughter. "And we have fresh eggs too."

"Getting a lot of business?" I asked.

"Oh, hell no," the older man said. "Everyone's hunkered down, waiting for Armageddon. But they don't know their Bible."

"We've got those too," the woman said, pulling an old copy of the Bible out from under the stand where the baskets of vegetables were displayed. She held it out to me. "It's free for the taking."

"I've got my own," I told her, pointing to the van. "So you're believers?"

"Been a Christian since I was a boy," the old man said. "Lutheran, just like my parents. My wife and I raised Ruth in the church too."

"That's me," the woman said. "I'm Ruth."

"Hank," I told her. "It's a pleasure to meet you."

"And you," she said.

"So, if you don't mind my asking," I said.

"Take what you need, pay what you can," the man said. "No set prices on this bounty. And we'll throw in a half dozen eggs too."

"No," I said, "I mean, yes, I'll take some of the food and thank you for it. But I was going to ask why you're still here."

"Lived here all my life," the man said. "On this very farm. My parents and theirs before them, we've got roots here that run deep."

"I think he means why weren't we taken," Ruth said. "Like mom."

"Oh, well, who can say," the old man declared. "God's

ways are not our ways, and so on. He's left us here for a reason. Unless the aliens are telling the truth, in which case, they must have misplaced my ticket."

I felt a sinking feeling of dread. The older man clearly didn't understand that only those who were believers in Jesus got taken. And I had known plenty of people just like that old man. People who were religious, who knew the Bible, and considered themselves to be Christians, but they had never actually put their faith in Christ. I looked at Ruth and saw tears in her eyes.

"I guess we're all late to the party," I said to her.

She nodded, but didn't reply.

"You ain't from around here," the old man said. "I know just about everybody down this way. Never seen you before."

"No, I'm just passing through," I told him.

"Where are you headed?" the man asked.

"Do you have family around here?" Ruth added.

I shook my head. "No family. My parents passed away, and my best friend was taken."

"How'd you end up in these parts?" the old man asked.

"I was Air Force," I told him. "Stationed at Fairchild Air Base in Spokane. When my enlistment ended, I got a job there, but didn't want to stay after the Vanishing."

"Can't say I blame you," Ruth said. "When everything got turned upside down, I came straight home. Luckily Dad was still here."

"Interstate's closed east of here," the old man said, completely ignoring his daughter who swiped a tear from her cheek. "A couple of long-haul truckers were taken in the Vanishing. There was a big pileup. One was hauling timber, the other some type of heavy duty pipe. It's a mess, from what I hear. Won't be clear for a while, I suspect."

"That's okay," I said. "I've been camping, mostly. Just live out of the van for now."

"Where will you park it?" Ruth asked.

"I don't know," I told her. "I honestly haven't given it much thought."

"Well, we've got plenty of space," the man said. "My name's Leo."

He extended his hand, and I shook it.

"That's very generous, sir," I said.

"I was Army from seventy-eight to eighty-six," he said. "Thought about staying in, but they had me in Germany and I absolutely hated it. Be nice to have another man around the place. Maybe you wouldn't mind helping out a bit in exchange for some food and clean water."

"Not at all," I told him.

"Good," he said. "Park your rig down there by the creek. Plenty of clean water there. We'll be here or in the house if you need anything."

So I took their advice, parked the van by their creek, and made camp. It was a nice little farm. The house looked old but well-maintained. There were two barns. One had chickens and a few sheep, with lots of hay and an old horse. The other was a more modern building, steel construction on a concrete slab. Inside was the farm equipment, a tractor, and all the different implements used to plant, water, and harvest crops. But the fields were empty, and the weeds had grown tall where corn, vegetables, and wheat had once grown. The area I parked in was shaded by a large maple tree. I put up my little tent near an old fire ring made with stones from the creek. And it wasn't long before I saw Ruth escorting her father back to the house. He walked with a cane and moved slowly.

Late in the afternoon Ruth walked out to my campsite, followed by a little Russell Terrier dog she called Shep. She had a bag full of vegetables from the small garden at the rear of the farm house and a couple of old folding lawn chairs. I had already gathered fallen sticks from the trees that grew near the creek, but hadn't started the fire. It was cooling off some, and the water in the creek was cold, so I put some of the generic soda pop in the water to cool it off. I was sipping from a can when Ruth came out.

"Hello," I said as she approached.

"You mind some company?" she asked.

"Not at all," I told her. "How's your father?"

"Napping," she said. "He would never admit it, but he's struggling without my mother."

I took the folding chairs and set them up between the van and the fire ring. We sat down with a view of the creek, and I offered her a Dr. Thunder.

"Where on earth did you get that?" she asked.

"Kellogg," I told her. "That's about all the Wal-Mart was selling."

"There was a run on all the stores right after the Vanishing," she said.

"Yeah, it was that way in Spokane too," I said. "It's a good thing you've got your own food supply."

"For now," she said. "The garden was my mother's. I don't have a green thumb, and Dad's too..." she struggled to find the right word, "... tired."

"I noticed you didn't use the word rapture when talking about the Vanishing," I said.

"Oh, no," she replied. "Not in front of my father. He won't hear it. He's never believed in taking the Bible literally."

"But your mother?" I asked.

Ruth nodded. "She was a true believer. Taught me all about God's love, but I was too much like my father I suppose."

"And now?" I asked.

"And now I know she was right," Ruth said. "Dad doesn't admit it, but he knows deep down. I just hope he isn't so stubborn that he ends up in hell."

It was a shocking statement to make. I wasn't sure what to say. We don't like to talk about people that we know are going to hell. It makes us uncomfortable, and I for one fear it. I remember all too well the visions of hell that the demon who called himself Salzaman showed me, and the many torments there.

"You mean..." I asked.

"He won't accept it. I've tried to convince him that he's wrong, that we were both wrong, but he refuses to listen. Stubborness is one of our family values. It's like owning this farm. He hasn't worked it in over a decade. Whenever he needs to pay the taxes on the land he sells something. I don't know what he'll do now."

"Could be worse, I guess."

"It will be worse," she said. "We're all pretty much doomed."

"You mean the judgments?"

She nodded. I knew what she meant, and I tried not to

think about it too much. The Bible was pretty clear that until Christ returned physically to the earth it was going to be difficult and dangerous, especially for believers.

"You keeping an eye on the news?"

"Every day," she said. "The whole world is buying into the lie that the Vanishing was the work of the aliens. How can people be so naive?"

"People believe what they want to believe," I said, thinking of my old girlfriend. She didn't want to believe in the supernatural and jumped at the chance to believe the official version of what happened in the Vanishing. Better alien Visitors than an Almighty God who people had chosen to slander and mock.

"They do," Ruth said. "I know I did. Forty-two and such a fool. I'm a two-time divorcee who was working sixty hours a week as an associate manager of a Best Buy in Spokane."

"Kids?"

"None," she said, with a shrug before turning away. "Got pregnant my senior year of high school, and again in the first year of my first marriage."

"What happened?" I asked, not realizing we were wading into the deep water with the conversation.

"I did," she said, her voice trembling with emotion. "I aborted them."

She had to wipe the tears from her cheeks. I looked at the river without a clue what to say. I wasn't the type of person to judge. In fact, I didn't even have an opinion on what I thought were political issues like abortion. Yes, I'm a believer, but up until that point in my life I hadn't really considered what the Bible taught about the value of life.

"I was such a fool," she said. "You want to know the first sign that a person is a fool, Hank? It's their unwavering belief that they know everything. And I thought I knew..."

Her voice trailed off.

"I'm sorry," I said, wishing I knew what to say or what to do.

"I believed all the wrong things," she said, her voice barely a whisper. "I believed it was just about me, that my babies were just a clump of cells, but deep down I knew it wasn't true. I was so smart, so progressive, that I sacrificed my babies so that I wouldn't be bothered with them."

I wanted to say it was okay, but in that instant I knew it wasn't okay. My former apathy wasn't okay either. I hadn't gotten a woman pregnant, or even voted for politicians that made abortions legal, but I hadn't done anything to stop it either. In that moment I felt the weight of my lack of action settling on me, more guilt to add to the burden I already carried.

"After the second one there were complications," she continued. "I couldn't have children. That's what ended my second marriage. So here I am, alone, looking after my father, regretting every choice I ever made."

"We sort of all are," I said, meaning every word.

"You have regrets?"

"Absolutely," I told her. "Lorenzo Maltza was my mentor and friend. Have you heard of him?"

She shook her head.

"He was an expert in the field of the supernatural. He tried to tell me about Jesus, but I didn't understand. I...I was..."

Telling her about my past was difficult. The sun was almost down, and so I knelt down by the fire ring.

"Do you mind?" I asked.

"Not at all. That's what it's here for."

I pulled a lighter from my pocket. It was just a cheap plastic lighter, and I had waterproof matches and a flint striker in the van, but the lighter was much more effective at starting fires. The wood was dry and kindled quickly. I sat back in my chair as the flames began to grow among the pile of firewood.

"You were saying," she prompted.

I felt silly and ashamed, but all the books I had read about the time after the Rapture gave weight to the idea that our testimony–that's our personal story of how we came to faith in Jesus–would be powerful. It also said we would be hunted down and martyred for it, but that hadn't begun to happen yet. So, I took a breath and plunged right into the deep end of the pool.

"Ruth, do you believe in Satan?" I asked.

She sat up and looked at me hard before answering.

"I guess so," she said slowly. "It's in the Bible, and I know that's true now. So, yes, I guess so."

"Good, because if you didn't this story would make no sense."

I told her everything, from my parents being killed, seeing the giant at Fairchild Air Base, the alien encounter in my hotel room, and the attacks by the demon Salzaman. I didn't hold back. I told her how the demon had taken control of me, tempting me to hurt myself, and eventually to kill Lorenzo. She sat and listened to every word. When I finished, she exhaled.

"I would have said you were certifiably insane two weeks ago," she admitted.

"That was my problem too," I said. "Even when it was happening to me, I didn't want to believe it. So yeah, I've got regrets. Lorenzo was taken not knowing how much he meant to me, or how much I valued what he shared with me. I wish, more than anything, that I could have made my decision before he was raptured."

"And then you could have gone with him," she said in a kind voice.

"Yeah, I guess so," I said. "I was such a fool."

"But you're here now, and it sounds like you've got a mission," she said. "I probably can't do much to help, but I would be interested in taking a look at some of those books you mentioned."

"Of course," I said. "And you are helping. It's great to have a peaceful place to work. And the food, thank you for the food."

"It's not much. I was a vegetarian for a long time, and now I wish I had meat."

"I've got some Spam in my van," I told her. "It's meat...sorta."

"Are you offering to cook me dinner, Hank?"

"I'm suggesting we cook it together if you want to be able to eat it."

She laughed, but rolled up her sleeves, and we went to work.

CHAPTER 7

IT WAS the best meal I had eaten since the Rapture. Peppers, onions, garlic, squash, all cooked in a cast iron skillet with the grease from the Spam, which we sliced up and fried in the pan over the fire. It wasn't filet mignon, but it was pretty darn good.

I slept in the little tent in my sleeping bag on an inflatable camping pad. It was a warm night and quiet. The sound of the creek running over the rocks was so peaceful. There were no unwanted alien visitors or demonic shadows. I slept in peace that night, with a sense of happiness that I hadn't felt since I was in Northern California with Lorenzo.

Early the next morning Leon came shuffling with his cane toward me. Shep barked and ran ahead of the older man. I was up and brushing my teeth. There was water in a pot over a small fire I had lit to boil drinking water. Leon said the creek water was clean, but my survival training during my Air Force days had taught me to always boil water before drinking it from an unknown source. I finished up and hurried over to where Leon was leaning hard onto his cane and breathing hard.

"Morning, sir," I said.

"I 'preciate the respect, but you can call me Leo," he said. "What'd you do in the Air Force?"

"A little bit of everything," I told him. "I was a logistics specialist."

"Logistics, eh? What's that entail?"

"Counting things and moving them from one place to another," I said with a smile.

"Okay, yeah, there's a lot of that in the military," he said. "Help me with this door."

I slid up the big overhead door on the side of the metal barn. Inside I saw his tractor, a planter, and harvester. They were clean and lined up inside the space. There were gaps too, which made me think of what Ruth had said. He was selling things to pay his bills.

He lumbered past the tractor and toward a small room in the far corner. He took out a key, unlocked the door, and flipped on a light.

"I'm gonna be honest with you, Hank. I didn't invite you to stay on our place out the kindness of my heart. We both know things are gonna go from bad to worse. I'm not worried about myself. But I've finally got Ruth back at home again, and I'll do anything to keep her safe."

"I understand that," I said, seeing the various rifles mounted on a pegboard on the wall inside the small room.

"She won't touch a weapon," he said. "Won't even consider learning self-defense. I need someone beside a broke down old man on our place who can use a firearm. Tell me right now, Hank. Is that you?"

"I'm not a soldier," I told him. "But I know how to shoot."

"What did you train with?"

"An M4 carbine in basic, and a nine millimeter pistol, although I wasn't allowed to carry it on base."

You still have it?"

"No, sir," I admitted. "When things got crazy in Spokane, I didn't go back for it."

"Crazy, huh?" he asked, pulling a rifle down from the wall and checking the breech. "Want to share what that means?"

"There was some crime in the area. I was staying with my mentor. He was taken in the Rapture. I went to help a friend and was pretty close to getting attacked by a mob. So I took what I could from Lorenzo's home and got the heck out of Dodge."

"Alright, I can respect it," he said. "Take this."

He held out the weapon. It wasn't anything I had seen before. It was a stripped down, highly modified AR-15. I checked the magazine, which slid out easily. The mag was empty, and I pushed it back into place. The rifle was light, with a foldable stock, and a wide-barrel sheath with holes for air flow.

"This is how I've made a living for the last two decades," Leon said, waving at the room.

There was a solid workbench with gunsmith tools, a metal bender, a small arc welder, and a mounted bullet reloader. There were canisters of gunpowder under the workbench and bins with gun parts inside.

"Farming doesn't pay the bills," he said. "Hasn't for a long time. I kept up appearances for a while, but when you get to a certain age people stop paying attention to you. That's got a thirty-round mag and a bump stock. You familiar with those?"

"I know what it is," I said. "But I've never used one."

"Takes a little adjustment but in a lot of ways it's more stable than a traditional auto. You just have to learn to use the movement like a shock absorber. Take it and this Beretta," he said, handing the familiar-looking pistol over to me. He pulled out a black duffle bag and started putting boxes of ammunition inside. "I've got a range set up on the back forty. We'll head out there on the RAZR and let you reacquaint yourself with these tools."

The RAZR was an all-terrain vehicle with four bucket seats and a very solid roll bar over top. We stowed the gear and settled in. I drove, and Leon gave directions. Behind the farmhouse was a water tank and a windmill. There were a few solar panels on the lawn next to the small garden. There was a tiny wellhouse and a greenhouse; past those was a long open field.

"I've got good lines of sight in all directions," Leon said. "The windmill powers the well pump. Those solar panels can keep the freezer running and recharge a few small devices. Of course those aren't so useful come winter time, but then we don't really need the freezer when it's twenty below zero."

"It gets that cold here?" I asked.

"Oh, yes, we get that arctic flow from Canada. Not as bad as they do on the far side of the continental divide, but it gets cold enough to kill a man, that's for sure."

We drove down dirt roads between overgrown fields. Eventually we came to a field where the weeds had been cut down and a tall, earthen berm had been built up at the far end. There were wooden targets and a few metal devices that would spin when hit.

"This is us," Leon said. "Let's load up a few mags and see what you've got."

We got out and loaded four magazines with shiny bullets from his duffle. I checked to make sure the safety was on, loaded one of the magazines, and pulled back the lever that pushed the first round into the firing chamber.

"Any advice?" I asked.

"Don't press it hard into your shoulder," he said. "Focus more on holding the weapon steady, but don't fight the movement from the recoil."

I brought the weapon to my shoulder, flicked off the safety, and took aim. The trigger had the lightest pull I had ever felt in a weapon. It rocked straight back into my shoulder, but it didn't feel like a kick. It bounced forward and fired again. It was almost as fast as a fully automatic rifle. I went through six rounds on a single pull of the trigger pull. The front of the gun wanted to rise upward as it continued to fire. I took Leon's advice and held the front end steady and let it rock against my shoulder.

"Not terrible," Leon said, looking through a set of binoculars at the target, which was easily a hundred feet away from where we stood.

"Just getting a feel for it," I replied, silently praying that I would never need to use the weapon.

When I fired the second time it was easier. I kept the bullets moving down range and into the target. I fired a ten-round barrage.

"That's it," he said, sounding relieved. "Keep it up."

I emptied the first magazine, then checked the breech. I could feel the barrel heating up through the shroud, but it was honestly the smoothest firing weapon I had ever shot.

"Thoughts?" Leon asked.

"It's...amazing," I admitted. "I've never fired anything like it."

"That's what I like to hear," he said. "She ain't built for the battlefield. But for home defense, there's nothing better. You have to take care of it, but if you do, it will do the job and then some."

"You sell these to hunters?" I asked.

"Sure," he said with a grin and wink. "The bump stock is outlawed in a lot of places. But people who know firearms want a custom-made weapon with the capacity to hold up to a real gun fight. If you're in a shooting war, the last thing you want is to be outgunned."

"How much do you charge?" I asked.

"That rifle is a full custom job and sells for forty-five hundred dollars."

"Takes a lot of corn to make four grand," I said.

"You can say that again," he replied. "Run another mag through, and then you can move up and check the pistol."

Our marksmanship practice only lasted half an hour. I didn't want to need the weapons, but they were sweet to use. I had never fired custom weapons. The Beretta 9 millimeter was a standard pistol, but Leon had cleaned up the firing components and shortened the trigger pull. It was what gun enthusiasts called a hair trigger, but the action was so smooth and the recoil so dampened that it felt like I was almost cheating. I had tighter groupings with the pistol than I ever had in basic training after practicing for ten straight weeks.

We went back to the barn, parked the RAZR, and I took the weapons to my van. It was easy to hide the rifle among the light stands. I made sure it was easy to get to. The pistol went into the back of my pants, with my shirt pulled over it. I didn't like the idea of carrying a loaded weapon on my person, but Leon insisted. And I had to admit after the stranger on the road had threatened us with a pistol, I didn't want to get caught without one again.

Maybe God was providing for my protection, or maybe I was leaning on the firearms for safety when I should have been leaning on God. But I was more than happy to be well-armed when war erupted in Israel.

CHAPTER 8

"YOU'VE GOT to come see this," Ruth said. "They're attacking Israel."

"Who is?" I asked.

The truth is I'm no geopolitical expert when it comes to the Near East. But my studies over the last week were in many ways focused on Israel. Most Bible scholars agree that before the Rapture the world was in what they called the church age. In that time period God's focus was on people all over the world, while his nation–Israel, the people chosen to bring God's love and redemptive plan to fruition–were in rebellion against His Son. But once the Rapture removed the church from planet earth, God's focus returned to his people. And the judgments to come were all about bringing as many of the Jews as possible back into a proper relationship with God.

Ruth was on the porch of the farmhouse as I jogged toward her from my little campsite. She was holding an iPad and looked worried.

"They're attacking from everywhere. It's not clear who is involved, but there's a lot of them."

She held the iPad out to me and looked at the video on screen. It was dark in Israel, but missiles could be seen shooting up into the night sky. The reporter was off screen but giving a running commentary.

"... intent was to overwhelm Israel's Iron Dome defenses. So far, the system is holding up, but if the threats are true we'll be lucky to make it through the night. This is Marcus Heston, reporting live, for Politico."

The image changed to a map with red arrows pointing toward Israel. If you know much about the area you know that Israel is just a strip of land, no bigger than New Jersey, running along the coast of the Mediterranean Sea. Over the short span of its recent existence, the nation has fought in several wars and in some cases been overwhelmingly victorious, leading to a few peace treaties with its neighbors such as Jordan and Egypt. But according to my studies, the agreements were always tenuous at best, and those same countries often harbored terrorist groups whose sole purposes were to wipe Israel off the map.

"Is this part of it?" Ruth asked. "Part of the Great Tribulation?"

I knew it wasn't, but there was no time for a long explanation. I just shook my head and followed her into the farmhouse. Leon was in a recliner snoring. In front of him was a large television. It was on Fox News, which was running a story on the attack as well.

"I think this is probably the Psalm 83 war," I said. "Have you read it?"

Ruth shook her head, looking a little embarrassed. "I'm reading the Bible, but it's hard to understand."

"Yeah, well, Psalm 83 lists a bunch of groups of people who are colluding to destroy Israel."

She sat down on a sofa. A coffee table was pulled close. A small iPad stand was there, next to her open Bible. She started flipping pages.

"Psalm eighty-what?"

"Eighty-three," I told her.

It turned into a long day of talking about Bible prophecy and watching the news. Somehow, against all odds according to the newscasters from both sides of the political aisle, Israel survived through the night with its Iron Dome defense system in place. But the attackers weren't content to just shoot rockets, as they had done so many times before. Groups were mobilizing, and with the light of day various reporters and locals using the video capacity of their mobile phones identified the assailants as various terrorist groups.

"This is bad," Ruth said.

"War always is, but at least we can point out that this is another prophecy coming true," I replied. "It's more proof that the Bible is real, and God is who He says He is."

"I wish I had your kind of faith," Ruth admitted. "I'm just so scared."

After an hour or so Leon woke up. He watched the reports in silence, and eventually lumbered off to the bathroom for a shower, but not before giving me a knowing look. I was starting to worry about what I was doing on the farm. I didn't want to give anyone false hope, but if I stayed around long I might bring more trouble than we could possibly handle. At some point I went out to the van and brought in my computer and the handful of prophecy books that I had taken from Lorenzo's extensive library.

For the next three days the living room of the farmhouse was where the three of us resided. Leon spent most of his time either in his recliner or bedroom. I wasn't shocked to discover the older man was drinking a lot. He kept a bottle of bourbon in his bedroom and a little flask in his back pocket. At one point he showed me where he kept weapons in the house just in case we needed them. It seemed that having a young man around the place was enough security for Leon, and he seemed to fade into the background.

Ruth was a voracious reader. She went through the prophecy books like a starving man who discovers a feast. I made posts of Lorenzo talking about Israel from his archives and uploaded them to the internet using a VPN so my location wouldn't be obvious. I was sure a determined IT expert could find me, but the persecution of dissenting voices hadn't begun yet, and so I felt pretty safe.

In Israel the war raged. The Israeli army is no joke, and they proved that in several key battles. Commandos swept through enemy territory and showed no quarter to their enemies. On the fourth day of fighting the Iron Dome faltered, and the various terror groups renewed their missile attacks. Strangely enough, ninety percent of their rockets either backfired, fell on their own positions, or hit Palestinian communities. The other ten percent reached Jerusalem, but instead of slaughtering the Jews living there, the rockets hit the sacred temple mound. The Dome of Rock was destroyed, and the Al-Aqsa Mosque was completely obliterated. Psalm

83:13 says, "O my God, make them like whirling dust, like chaff before the wind."

It was an undeniable blow to the terrorist groups and the larger Muslim world. One of their own holy sites was completely destroyed by their own rockets. There was plenty of video of the event. Missiles from every direction came flashing overhead and somehow converged on the holy mountain. It was a shocking display, one that we watched from various news crews and people in Jerusalem who had filmed the attack with their mobile devices.

Fire broke out in the Hezbollah strongholds to the north of Israel, perhaps from sabotage or maybe the work of God Himself. Their arsenal of weapons and rockets added to the destruction of their base of operations. More than the fighting, the fire wrecked their ability to exist and in a matter of days the entire group was essentially wiped out.

At the same time a hurricane struck Yemen with virtually no warning. The entire country was devastated by the natural disaster, and the terror groups located there were wiped out. The Israeli military fought hard, and after the unexpected destruction of their holy places in Jerusalem, the Muslim fighters lost heart.

In some ways it was amazing to see. The news didn't attribute the victory of Israel to God, but I felt that it was undeniable. And the people interacting on Lorenzo's website and social media were vocal in their belief that the war was both prophetic and a genuinely divine encounter.

Ruth was convinced, and growing in her faith, but Leon remained skeptical. He was stubborn and opinionated. No one would have ever considered him to be woke, and political correctness simply wasn't tolerated in his house. I did my best to be a polite guest. They fed me and allowed me to use their bathroom. The weapons Leon had gifted to me were worth thousands, and yet the older man wasn't ready to give up his self-reliance or admit that he needed anything, not even God.

And that's where I was when the first Horseman of the Apocalypse rode into the world of men.

CHAPTER 9

IF YOU'VE READ this far you know I'm not an expert on anything, but even I was taken by surprise when the first Judgment of God, the sign that marked the beginning of the seven years of tribulation on planet earth, broke. It centered around a guy that almost no one had heard of: Paul Eon. He was, up to that moment, just a young member of a European-based peace organization. Yet somehow he managed to get a seat in the negotiations between Israel and the surrounding nations.

I believe that he was there because the force behind the evil in the world wanted him there, but there were other theories. No one even knows what this guy's nationality really is. Some say he's Syrian; others say he's Italian. What we do know for certain is that he has money and connections. He was part of the Near East peace settlements, and he accomplished something people have been trying to do for over seventy-five years–he brought peace to Israel and all the surrounding Muslim nations.

In the media this guy became an instant rock star. He was lauded on every magazine cover, from GQ to Time. Newsweek called him the Savior of the World, I kid you not. You can look it up online. Paul Eon was the face of a new era in world politics. He had not only the backing of most of the civilized world, but according to Arthur Doll, he was hand selected by the Apkallu to help usher in peace. And we know he is one of the few people who has met the alien Visitors in person.

"Is this what I think it is?" Ruth asked when the news of the sweeping peace accord broke on national television.

"I think so," I said.

Paul Eon was on a stage with the leaders of a dozen countries, including the PM of Israel. The peace broker was a handsome man with thick, black hair, tan skin, a chiseled jaw, and mesmerizing green eyes. I couldn't stop looking at him. He wore a conservative business suit that was molded to his muscular frame. And on his lapel was a small, but noticeable rainbow ribbon.

"Who is he?" Ruth asked.

"The rider on the white horse," I said.

Now I don't know about you, but it does seem strange that the first in a series of judgments from God is a peace treaty. That doesn't sound like judgment so much as a blessing, but the truth is the judgment isn't the peace accord, it's the Antichrist himself coming to power. And that's what we witnessed. Every news agency in the world and most streaming websites covered the historic peace agreements. The terms were pretty clear: Israel would give up land in Judea, Samaria, and the West Bank, creating an independent

Palestinian state that would self-govern with financial and material aid from Israel. Including a percentage of the funds obtained from the exports of natural gas from the Leviathan gas mines off the coast in the Mediterranean Sea. In return, Israel would have sole control of the temple mount and permission to rebuild their temple in the historic location.

In the days following the treaty the world settled into a strange peace. There were still tensions between nations, but no fighting took place. It was, in a sense, the closest mankind had come to global cooperation. The peace was accentuated by two key events that came from the Visitors. You probably already know my personal opinion of the aliens, that they are the return of the old gods, the *bene ha'eloheim* or sons of God, also called Watchers in the book of Enoch. I won't get into all that here, except to say that we got our first glimpse of these so-called space men shortly after the peace accord in the Near East. The Visitors were not the grays that so many people have encountered, including myself. Nor where they lizard people that are occasionally seen by people who claim to be abducted. They were tall, beautiful people, what some people call the Nordics. There was an unmistakable look of divinity about them, a supernatural glow that emanated from their skin. They all dressed in bright white robes and had no discernible flaws. They were taller than the humans who were seen around them, and while there were nearly a dozen that allowed themselves to be captured on video, which was beamed around the world and watched billions of times, only one spoke. His name was Shemi Hazah, and he introduced what came to be known as Divine Nectar because it cured almost any disease.

This short era of peace was quickly hailed as a new golden age. Religious leaders joined in the euphoric celebrations taking place around the world by merging their faith into the collective new religious expression called Pax Divino or "Divine Peace." They spoke of the need to seek peace among the races, in our relationships, and of course, inner peace. The world seemed to come back to life. Food was suddenly available everywhere and in abundance. Medical care for the sick was provided freely. And lavish parties were the norm.

For nearly a month I stayed with Ruth and Leon, but my sincere belief that the second judgment was imminent was not a welcome topic of discussion. I couldn't blame Leon. He was in his seventies and infirm. What could he do when war broke out? Did I mention that the second of the four Horsemen of the Apocalypse is a rider on a red horse who brings war to the whole world? It's not a happy message, and eventually people turn against the one who bears it.

That meant trolls on all of Lorenzo's social media and online platforms. There were still views, but the comment sections were filled with people calling Lorenzo every horrible name in the book. They came after me as well, since I was posting new videos and interviews every day. They were actually old videos and newly edited clips from conferences, and I didn't use my name or any pictures. The VPN was under attack, not just from the trolls, but also the governments who proclaimed that anything meant to hide a person's identity was a tool for criminals. Soon, hackers were corrupting Lorenzo's social media accounts and crashing the website. I was still able to post to online forums and set up clandestine websites to give people access to his materials, but the audience was dwindling, and the opposition growing.

Leon changed after the peace accord. His faith, if it had ever really been in the God of the Bible, shifted to his new saviors. He was a vocal supporter of Paul Eon and the Visitors. Needless to say I stopped spending time in his home and kept to my little campsite by the creek. At first Ruth was on my side, but her support began to wane as people came out of hiding and started to join in the celebrations. Even in the small towns there were parties with drinking and people carousing. I won't go into all the sordid details, but these supposed Pax Divino parties were filled with all sorts of debauchery. Nothing was off-limits. It was a blessing that the children of the world had been taken, otherwise they too would have been abused.

On the one hand I understood that Ruth just wanted things to be normal again. And spending all day long studying Bible prophecy is a difficult chore for most people, especially when everyone around them is celebrating how great the world has become. It wasn't long until she was gone every night of the week and only returned to the farm to shower and change clothes. I didn't know where she went and didn't ask. Part of me wanted to stay and help them through the difficult times I knew were coming, but the truth was I had worn out my welcome.

So I packed up my gear, gratefully accepted the two metal ammo cans full of bullets for the rifle and pistol that Leon gave me, and set out for someplace safe to ride out the global war I knew was on the horizon.

CHAPTER 10

BY THAT TIME I had been a Christian for around six weeks. Fortunately, I had copious amounts of video teaching by Lorenzo Maltza to help me grow in my faith. You may wonder what that means, and the best way I can explain it is to say that when I put my faith in Jesus Christ I didn't join a religion or a set of rules for living a certain way. No, it's more like I was introduced to God, and I was getting to know Him. I didn't hear His voice. I didn't have visions or feel Him take control of my body, but I was learning about Him and how incredible His love for us truly is.

So when I tell you that I set out from Ruth and Leon's farm with no real direction in mind, you can imagine what that was like. I knew war was coming. It's a strange way to try and live. War is so devastating, so horrible, and while I knew it was unavoidable, I had no way of knowing how widespread it would be, or where I could go to be safe from it. Fortunately I was able to buy food and fuel. But I quickly learned to avoid people as much as possible. My beliefs weren't just contrary to what most people had quickly accepted as hard facts, but they were seen as hateful, backward, and cruel. So of course the response when people found out that I was a Bible believer was to be hateful and cruel, sometimes even violent.

On the streets people were in high celebration. There were no underage individuals left, so everything was deemed acceptable. Drugs and alcohol were sold openly, people paraded completely nude in full public display, and sex of every variant was practiced right out in the open. I not only felt threatened around other people–I was extremely uncomfortable. It's no wonder I found myself choosing old, narrow dirt roads in my wandering. I like to think I was guided by the Holy Spirit, but eventually I found myself halfway up a mountain in the middle of the national forest. And there I discovered something that was truly miraculous.

Some of you may know that before satellites orbited the globe and provided free access to the internet worldwide, there was a system of fire watch stations to keep tabs on the larger forests in the northwest United States. They were essentially one-room cabins, built on stilts with large windows on three sides. From inside, a person could keep watch over hundreds of acres of forest and report the first hint of fire so that the blaze wouldn't grow out of control and threaten the towns and communities nestled in the mountains.

Fire watch station ID 2873 was in the northeast corner of Idaho, in the Bitterroot Mountain range. It was unmanned, but well-stocked with provisions, including solar power, a hand-pumped well, and about six months of survival rations in big plastic buckets. There was also a water filtration system and medical supplies, including iodine in case of radiation exposure. I don't know who owned the cabin. It was no longer part of the national forest system. Most of the old fire watch cabins were abandoned or sold. Whoever had purchased ID 2873 had been a Christian, and I believe from the state of the cabin, they were raptured in the middle of washing their clothes in a metal tub on the deck that surrounded the cabin on three sides. I parked the van beneath the cabin, right next to a snowmobile and a four-wheel ATV.

There was a lot of thanksgiving that took place in the cabin as I settled in. The previous owner had installed a HAM radio, as well as a Starlink internet dish. There was no television, but I could keep tabs on world events via my computer. I also found a full bookshelf of books, from novels to guide books on edible plants and medicinal herbs found in the wild. It wasn't really off-grid with the Starlink internet connection, but it was about as far off the beaten path as a person could get. And I felt right at home.

That's not to say that I didn't get lonely. I wasn't in love with Ruth; she was at least fifteen years older than I was, but I did miss her friendship. Leon had been a grumpy pessimist until the Visitors unleashed the plan for a new golden age, and we had never really gotten along all that well. He tolerated me for a while, and I tolerated his attitude. While I didn't really miss him, I did sometimes think that his company would be better than none at all. I began to pray that God would send someone to befriend me. It might have been what the Bible describes as the most terrible age of human history, and that if it weren't cut short no one would survive, but still, I wanted a friend. No, that's not really true. What I wanted was a true companion. So that's what I prayed for.

Weeks passed, then summer turned to fall, and with each passing day my doubts grew. I'd like to say I was stalwart in my faith, but let's be honest...I had major doubts. Sure, the Bible says a lot about this specific seven-year period, but it isn't exactly clear. The second Horseman of the Apocalypse was war, and every day I checked online for reports of fighting. And every day I grew a little more discouraged. People weren't fighting. The celebrations were growing. Racism, crime, poverty were all disappearing. The faith in Divine Peace seemed to be growing at a record-setting pace. Was I wrong? Had I misunderstood? Most of all I feared that Lorenzo hadn't been taken to heaven in the Rapture, but really had been removed from planet Earth by the Visitors. Despite the proof right in front of me, I had fears and doubts in my ability to understand the Bible. There was a constant nagging feeling that if God existed he wouldn't love me.

And then one beautiful day as I wandered through the forest collecting chicory, whose leaves can be eaten raw, and the roots can be dried and used as a coffee substitute, I saw her. Or actually, she saw me. Her name was Mira Jones, but she called herself Wild Cat, or just Cat when she posted to YouTube about her off-grid adventures. She was a self-proclaimed primitive skills enthusiast and subsistence hunter. Imagine my surprise when a woman in animal furs, her hair tied in a messy braid, hands dark from working in the dirt, with a recurve bow and a quiver full of stone-tipped arrows, strolled out the woods and spoke to me. At first I thought maybe I was imagining her, but Cat was real.

"Hello there," she said. "Mind if I harvest some of that chicory?"

I stepped back, blinking in surprise. I must have looked stunned, because she smiled.

"I didn't mean to startle you," she said. "My name is Cat."

She extended a hand. After a moment I got myself under control and shook her hand.

"I'm Hank," I said.

"Nice to meet you, Hank," she replied as she started digging up some of the chicory plants. "Good foraging here in this part of the forest."

"Yeah, I guess so."

"Old man Burton used to live in the fire watch cabin. I'm guessing you're there now."

I nodded.

"Funny how fast the world fills up," she said.

"Who are you again?" I asked.

"They call me Wild Cat. I'm a primitive skills subsistence hunter. I kind of roam around all over the mountains here before winter sets in. I'll have to build a good shelter soon, then when the snow comes I'll run a trap line, do some hunting, maybe shoot an elk or moose with my bow if I'm lucky."

I was mesmerized by the strange woman. She lived off the land like a native American during the hunter-gatherer days.

"I hate to ask this, but old man Burton always let me get cleaned up at his place. It's the only warm water in fifty miles. Would you mind?"

The cabin had an outdoor shower, with an elevated black plastic bladder that when filled used the sunlight to heat the water. It had become my habit to fill the bladder first thing in the morning on sunny days, and by mid afternoon I could enjoy a lukewarm shower.

"Of course," I said. "Yeah, the shower should be ready by now."

I had a little basket full of chicory flowers, leaves, and roots. It was enough for me. I could have hunted with the rifle that Leon had gifted to me, but I still had plenty of food from my travels, including cans of tuna, pork, beef, and Spam. Most of the vegetables I had brought to the cabin were gone, but there were plenty of wild edibles growing on the mountainside to supplement my diet. I had even collected some and hung them to dry.

"How long have you been living off grid, Hank?" Cat asked me.

"Not long," I said. "I came out after the peace accord."

"The what?" she asked.

"The end of the war in the Near East?"

She just looked at me with a blank stare.

"Israel was attacked. Surely you heard about that?"

"I don't really keep up with world events."

"You know about the vanishings, right?"

"Yeah, I've heard something about it. And some claptrap about aliens or something."

"Okay, so after the vanishings a war broke out, but it's over now," I explained. "The world is at peace for the time being, but..."

"You know, that sounds a lot like the story old man Burton was always on about," she said. "Every time I came by this way he would tell me about God."

"He was a believer," I said, knowing that from what he left

behind, from Bibles to his personal journals, which I had skimmed through. "So am I."

"So, he was taken in the vanishings?"

"Yes," I admitted.

"And you think this peace isn't going to last?"

"No, I don't."

"Well, you should be pretty set at Burton's old place. He had plenty of supplies set back for that."

"But you don't believe him?" I said.

"I don't know," she said with a grin. "I don't keep up with the modern world, Hank. Things are simpler here and now."

She waved her hands at the trees and boulders as we walked a well-worn game trail on the side of the mountain. I had heard of people like the man who lived in the cabin before me. From doomsday preppers to people who preferred to live off-grid. Some of my favorite television shows before the Rapture had been about people living off the land in Alaska and different places around the world.

"How long have you lived like this?" I asked her.

"I don't know. Ten, maybe eleven years now. I used to just do trips, a few weeks at a time, but eventually the pull to go back to the modern world just sort of disappeared and I stayed."

"You're happy here?"

"The happiest," she said. "Just me and Mother Earth. She provides for all my needs."

Part of me wanted to argue with that, but it was neither the time nor the polite thing to do to question another person's beliefs. So, I kept my mouth shut, but all the time I was wondering if she was the answer to my prayers.

CHAPTER 11

THE OUTDOOR SHOWER was built into the side of the cabin deck. The previous owner had even built a wooden screen that could be pulled out to wrap around a person for privacy. I stayed in the cabin until Cat was finished cleaning up. When she appeared on the deck she had on different clothes, a buckskin shirt, and a long wool dress that reached her ankles.

I admit that I was lonely. I hadn't seen another person, much less a woman in several weeks. But Cat was attractive. She had a round face, her skin tanned dark, her lips full. And she carried herself in a way that I wasn't all that familiar with. She had confidence. Here I was, a total stranger, and yet she wasn't afraid of me or awkward around me. It was like she was comfortable in whatever surroundings she found herself in. And I know that a buckskin blouse and long skirt isn't the latest fashion trend, but Cat made the simple outfit look amazing. I was mesmerized and had to work to hold myself together around her.

"Feel better?" I asked, opening the cabin door.

"A warm shower does work wonders on the soul," she said. "Look at this place. You've been busy."

I had a lot of plants hanging from the rafters in various states of being dried out. She walked around, naming most of them.

"You plan on staying the winter?" she asked.

"Yeah, I guess so," I said. "I don't have long term plans yet. I'm just waiting to see what happens."

"Well, I can tell you that in the winter it gets pretty snowy," she said. "The hunting is good. Do you hunt?"

"Never have, but I've got a rifle."

"You'll want some meat with good fat on it come winter time," she said. "The survival food will keep you alive, but your body needs good, healthy fat to stay warm up here. That little wood stove will keep it tolerable in the cabin, but you better get used to being cold."

"Thanks for the advice," I said.

"Thank you for the shower. I'll be getting on. There's still a few hours of daylight left."

"You're leaving?" I asked her. There was no reason for my shock other than I had it in my head that she was going to stay.

"Yes," she replied. "Like I said, it's about that time of year to start preparing for winter. I wouldn't want to crowd you."

I was at a loss for words. Fortunately for me, at that very moment, the emergency alert tone on my old cell phone went off. The blaring sound startled us both.

"What is that?" Cat asked, as I hurried over to the small desk where I had my computer set up.

"Not sure," I said.

The tone stopped, and an automated voice spoke from the phone's speaker.

Warning, this is an alert from the emergency broadcast system. Nuclear weapons have been deployed. I repeat, nuclear weapons have been launched toward the United States. Please take shelter where available. Stay off the streets. A nationwide curfew had been issued. I repeat, nuclear weapons have been detected. Seek shelter and wait for further instructions.

"It's happening," I said.

"What's happening?" Cat asked in shock.

"World War Three."

I dropped into one of two chairs in the cabin. One was a swivel desk chair, the other a wooden-framed rocking chair with thick cushions tied to the seat and back. I powered up my laptop and checked the first news site on my browser. A video feed from outside New York City was showing a dark mushroom cloud over what had once been a familiar skyline. Most of the skyscrapers were already gone. The audio picked up car horns and alarms sounding in the distance, along with what could have been rolling thunder.

"That's New York," I said. "At least it was."

"Who would do that?" Cat asked.

"Depends," I said. "Russia's been threatening for a while now. Ever since they invaded Ukraine, I suppose. North Korea has threatened nuclear war. China has been building their arsenal for years now. And any number of terrorist groups would set off a bomb if they could manage it. But that looks like a high-yield blast. A suitcase nuke wouldn't take down so many buildings."

"How do you know that?" she asked. "Are you a soldier or something?"

"I was in the Air Force," I admitted. "But more recently I've been studying the effects of nuclear weapons."

"You knew this was coming?"

"The Bible predicted war. It's the second seal judgment in the book of Revelations."

"I don't know what that means?" she said.

"For now, it means we wait and watch," I told her as I switched to a different window on the computer where a reporter was standing outside the Pentagon giving a report.

"I'm told the administration has moved to a secure location, and military forces are being mobilized. Our orbital defense system has taken down eighteen ICBMs as they crossed over the Arctic Circle, but dozens more are being launched from North Korea and from naval vessels in both the Atlantic and Pacific oceans. We are at war, and at least for now, we are surroun—"

The feed blinked off suddenly.

"What happened?" Cat asked.

"Either they lost power or..."

"Or what? They got hit by a nuclear bomb?"

"An intercontinental ballistic missile," I said. "China, Russia, North Korea all have them. And that reporter was outside the Pentagon. Washington, D.C. would be one of the first places our enemies would target."

"I can't believe it," she said.

With shaking hands she pulled a small pouch from the

pocket of her long skirt. The pouch was made from some type of leather, with a thong woven around the top to cinch it closed. She pulled out a pipe made from bone and started filling the bowl with marijuana. I didn't pay her much attention until she lit it up and smelled the skunky odor.

By the time I turned and looked at her, she had already taken a long draw on the pipe and was holding the smoke in her lungs with her eyes closed. I turned back to my computer, too excited and in some ways relieved to want to zone out with Cat. She was dealing with her fears, and I had plenty of my own, but I was also relieved because the Bible had once more proven to be true.

"Looks like it's not just us," I said. "Russia hit the UK, and China launched against Japan and Australia. India and Pakistan are fighting. Turkey is scrambling to launch assaults against Greece. Finland was hit with a nuke from Russia, I'm guessing. There's fighting breaking out all over."

"It's the end of the world," Cat said.

"No, it isn't the end," I said. "This was predicted in the Bible. There's going to be very hard times ahead, but in seven years Jesus will return and set everything right."

"Seven years? Hank, we're not going to last the night."

"Maybe, maybe not," I replied. "We aren't near the big cities. As long as nothing too close gets nuked we should be okay for now."

And we were. The US launched counterstrikes. North Korea was for all intents and purposes obliterated. Unfortunately, South Korea suffered heavy losses as well. Russia was taken out after the first volley of missile launches, but China kept the fighting going. They had been preparing for war and had more ships at sea than the US, plus cells already set up in America that began to sabotage our attempts to get back on our feet militarily.

For three days we watched the news, and I had a chance to explain what was really happening to Cat. Nuclear war is a very pervasive object lesson, but she needed time to process things. She took long walks in the forest, and a couple of times I feared that she might not come back. But every evening she showed up again, sometimes with a small animal or two, which she roasted outside over an open fire.

The invasion came on the third day. We didn't see them, but we heard the airplanes. They came in over Canada which had declared itself to be neutral, then quickly capitulated to China's demand to let them stage an invasion into the United States from the north. Tanks and armored troop carriers rumbled down our own interstates. Los Angeles, San Francisco, Portland, and Seattle were all taken out with nukes. New York, Boston, DC, Atlanta, and our military bases on the east coast were all hit. The President of the United States was alive but hidden in a bunker. Denver, St. Louis, Dallas, and Phoenix were all hit with aerial bombing raids before Chinese fighters parachuted into those areas. The US military was fighting back, but many of our bases had been taken out in the first wave of fighting. The world was in chaos, yet through it all the internet still worked, and reports of the war came in from all over.

"Do we win or lose?" Cat asked.

"You mean the United States?" I asked her. She nodded, pulling her pipe out and checking her nearly empty pouch of marijuana. "The Bible doesn't say. You know that stuff isn't helping you."

"I gotta do something to keep my nerves in check, Hank. How is that you aren't terrified right now?"

"Who says I'm not?" I replied.

"Look at you...solid as a rock," she said. "I don't get it."

"I guess it's because I know what's really happening," I told her. "I know who's behind all this. And I know what's coming next."

"Do I want to know what's coming next?" she asked.

"It's a famine," I said. "But we're okay with food. We've got plenty here in the cabin and access to what the forest has to offer."

"Unless they drop a nuke and we're killed instantly."

"Nothing to nuke out here," I said. "Besides, they haven't fired nuclear weapons since this started. It's a shooting war now."

"So what's to keep an army from showing up on the mountain?"

"The fact that there's no one to fight here would be a good reason," I pointed out. "We're in a pretty good position right now. We can stay put and ride out the storm."

"And then what?"

"I don't know," I said. "But I'm glad you're here."

"You're glad not to be alone," she said.

"That's true, but I'm also glad you're not alone. I'm glad you are safe, Cat. I'm glad for this time together."

I won't lie–my feelings for her had been growing since the moment she appeared in the forest. She had long, dark hair and brown eyes. There was a little scar on the side of her chin, and she moved with a gracefulness that I had never seen besides that of a professional dancer. But I had kept my distance. I didn't want her to feel threatened or coerced into something because she was afraid I would kick her out. Of course, that's how little I really knew her. Wild Cat was probably stronger than I was and didn't fear being alone in the forest the way I did. The truth was, she could have kicked me out of the cabin, and I would have been in big trouble.

But she didn't push me away, and I didn't push myself on her. We came together–two weary, frightened people–watching the world rip itself to pieces.

CHAPTER 12

A WEEK into the war the outcome was inevitable. China had dominated America and Australia, after obliterating Japan. (I'm sure entire books are being written about the war, but this isn't one of them.) Fighting was rampant everywhere. In Central America, all across the continent of Africa, among the nations of Europe–it was a bloody, devastating travesty. All the pent-up aggression, combined with the perceived slights of every people group in the world, created a powder keg of violence the likes of which no one had ever seen before.

In the United States militia bands were waging guerrilla warfare on the Chinese invaders, but there was also violence between blacks and whites, Latinos and Asians, as the survivors from the big cities looked to take whatever they could from anyone and everyone in their path. The death toll was staggering. Casualties in the United States alone were in the fiftieth percentile range, and over a hundred and fifty million people were unaccounted for.

And somewhere, far away, a group of individuals, aided by the Visitors, were essentially laying claims to entire regions of the world. Eight days after the bombs first dropped, a Global Council for Peace announced that they were taking control of the entire world and dividing it into ten regions.

If you know much about Bible prophecy, you know that all of this was predicted first by the prophet Daniel and later by the apostle John. In the Bible it says ten kingdoms, but the GCP called them Economic Prosperity Regions. They said nothing about the fighting going on. And there was no agreement made between world leaders. In the US, rumors that the President and most of the elected government were already dead were hard to refute. No one had seen them or heard from them. The GCP didn't care what we thought of their plan from the ground. They simply took control while no one was looking.

"They can't do that," Cat said. "I mean, who gave them the right to just take over?"

"You know what I think," I told her as I stacked firewood near the little stove in the corner of the one-room cabin.

Dark clouds had filled the skies since the bombings. Somehow the internet signals got through, but the autumn days were noticeably colder. I had begun cutting wood for the winter. There was plenty of timber, and finding standing trees that were dead and dry wasn't difficult. I used the four-wheeler and a pull-behind wagon to move the bucked-up wood to the cabin. After moving Lorenzo's van, I started stacking wood for the long cold season ahead. All the while my mind shuffled the puzzle pieces of what I knew was coming. Two more seal judgments, the last two Horsemen of the Apocalypse.

"Yes," she replied. "I know what you think, I'm just venting. I mean, you can't just decide to take over a place and have everyone just agree."

"But they will," I said. "They'll agree because they want someone to tell them everything is going to be okay."

"Well sure, I'd love that, but you never do."

"I say that all the time," I argued playfully. "In seven years."

She wrapped her arms around me the moment I stood up straight from stacking the pile of wood. I wrapped my arms around her, and we stood that way for several minutes, neither of us speaking. We needed that human touch, that true connection with one another, and neither of us was in a hurry to let go.

Some of you are going to object to the fact that two people were lovers outside of marriage. If that bothers you I'm sorry, but the truth of the matter is that pretty much since Cat had arrived at the fire watch cabin, the entire world had been at war. We had no opportunities to go to town and find someone to marry us. And we were both frightened. So we did what people do. I'm a man, she's a woman—we fell into each other's arms for the comfort they provided.

"I thank my lucky stars for you, Hank," Cat whispered.

"And I thank God for you," I replied.

That was the way it was for a few weeks. We divided up a list of chores and did what we could to get ready for winter. I didn't push her to accept Jesus as her savior. That was a decision she needed to make for herself, but I prayed for her every single day.

For her part Cat focused on hunting, but there were noticeable effects from the heavy bombing. At one point ash drifted down like dirty snowflakes. The animals were less active and more skittish. Cat insisted on hunting with her primitive bow and only managed to get a small deer before the weather turned bitterly cold.

I'll admit I'm not a mountain man. I grew up in Texas and never spent more than six months in any one place while I was in the Air Force. We were over halfway up the mountain when the snow came. It fell heavily, maybe as a result of the nuclear bombs, which kicked up a lot of debris into the atmosphere. We had nowhere to be, and the snow actually helped to insulate the fire cabin, so I didn't mind too much. But I made sure to keep the Starlink Internet Receiver Dish swept off so that we didn't lose connectivity. We watched as the cities in America became warzones, and in places that weren't active battlegrounds there were bread lines. People were starving. Food was actually plentiful, but the supply chains had been severed. There were images of food in vast warehouses rotting and of ships with food that were sunk before reaching shore.

The highway systems in America, Europe, Australia, and Eastern Asia were destroyed by the fighting, and the result was catastrophic. Of course, not everyone was suffering. There was no fighting in Israel, and most of the surrounding nations were able to keep things under control. Videos of the new Jewish Temple being built were on all the media sites. It was as if people believed seeing the magnificent building being erected so quickly was a sign of hope.

And it wasn't just the building of the temple either. The lost Ark of the Covenant, the gold-covered chest with angels on the lid, was discovered in a chamber deep inside the temple mount itself. It was the final holy instrument that was needed for the priests to begin reinstituting animal sacrifices.

"I don't get it," Cat said one evening as an announcement of the grand temple's opening was made.

"What don't you get?" I asked.

"They're going to sacrifice animals? Why?"

"The Jews still follow the Old Testament laws," I pointed out. "Those laws lay out the reason and the administration of animal sacrifice."

"Buy why?"

"Because without the shedding of blood there is no forgiveness of sin," I said, quoting from one of Lorenzo's lectures I had watched.

"That seems a little cruel, doesn't it?"

"You kill animals," I pointed out.

"We kill to eat, not just as a religious ceremony," she said. "That's the natural way of things. We may be at the top of the food chain, but we're still part of it."

"Well, I don't know everything about it," I said, leaning back in the desk chair while Cat sat with her feet up in the wood frame chair with thick cushions and a blanket over her legs. "But this is how I've heard it explained. God gave the Israelites the law to show them their need for a savior. The law was sort of like God's standard. If we can't live up to it, then we need some other way to be made acceptable. From

THE FOUR HORSEMEN   83

the time of Moses until Jesus, that way was by making a sacrifice at least once a year for the forgiveness of sins. The procedure is laid out in detail in the Bible and requires an innocent,
spotless lamb."

"So far, you're not making it better," Cat frowned.

"Stay with me," I told her. "God was giving us an example
of what was really required to make us right in his sight. It was
part of his plan all along to send Jesus to be the sacrifice for
our sins. He is the blameless lamb of God, who went willingly
to the cross and bore the punishment for our sins. Everything
we've ever done wrong, and everything that we ever will do
wrong, was poured out on him, and he paid the debt."

"Okay," she said nodding, although at that point in time
Cat hadn't put her faith in Jesus yet. "I see what you're saying.
It's a beautiful story."

I didn't push her. She knew what I believed, and she
watched some of Lorenzo's lectures and interviews with me,
but she hadn't made a personal connection with God yet. She
believed deeply in a creator, but in her mind she equated the
earth with God. She found acceptance with him by living in
harmony with nature. But she also couldn't deny that the
prophecies of the Bible were coming true. Every day there was
some new thing that made us stand in awe. Probably the
biggest was the group of elites, the same people who had arbi-
trarily set themselves up as world rulers, began building a city
near the ancient site of historical Babylon, and were calling it
by the same name. If the Jewish temple was being constructed
in record time, it was nothing compared to the grand city's
rate.

And the wildest thing of all wasn't the accomplishments

of Babylon, or even the alien technology being used to construct it. The real shock was the beings that were constructing it. They say every story comes full circle. Mine did the day I saw video footage of Babylon's construction. The builders were giants.

I remember the body of the first giant I ever saw. It was at Fairchild Air Base, in a crate that I was never supposed to see, but the Airman driving the forklift had had a heart attack. I was ordered to put the crate into cold storage; only I had an accident along the way, which cracked open the big wooden box. When I looked inside, what I saw was so shocking that it upended my entire worldview. Up until that moment I didn't believe in anything supernatural. And after that I didn't know what I believed. Without Lorenzo's guidance I would have been lost. There was a time when I was struggling under the influence of some very menacing voices who strongly suggested I hurt myself.

Since the Vanishing, the supernatural was becoming more and more common. Shemi Hazah was showing up at peace rallies all over the world with Paul Eon. While Paul preached a message of inclusion and acceptance, Shemi Hazah performed miracles. That may sound weird, but there's no other way to describe it. People were healed, and not just in a good con job way–the alien being actually caused severed limbs to grow back and healed bullet wounds for people on the verge of bleeding out. There were tons of videos of these miracles, but Shemi Hazah was never seen apart from Paul Eon, and he rarely spoke about anything other than peace and harmony.

Together, the pair of them held meetings with religious

leaders from all around the world. Press conferences after these meetings were full of announcements of various groups joining what was being hailed as the Peace Initiative. But it wasn't just a movement or affiliation–it was actually a new religion. People were giving money and joining new congregations all over the world, especially in areas hit hardest by the war. There were videos of soldiers throwing down their weapons and joining the religion.

Of course all these things were predicted in the Bible. And things were only going to become more and more strange. But I think the strangest thing of all was actually getting very little media attention. It was what the Bible called the Two Witnesses in Jerusalem.

CHAPTER 13

YOU WON'T FIND the witnesses without doing some serious searching online. Whoever is monitoring the internet takes down any post or video where they can be seen and revokes the accounts of the people who post them. It was something I was already familiar with, since keeping Lorenzo's videos and interviews online was becoming more difficult with each passing day. But the two witnesses have been in Jerusalem since the peace accord that allowed the Israelites to rebuild the temple. No one knows where they're from, and they never talk about themselves, even though they regularly answer questions.

What's really crazy is that people from all over the world report hearing the witnesses talk in various languages. For instance, many of the initial videos posted were from Israelis. You can hear the person filming ask a question in Hebrew, which I can't speak or understand, yet when the witnesses reply it's in English. At first I thought it was strange that they always answered in English, but then people in Spain said they were speaking Spanish, and people in Russia claimed to hear their answers in Russian. Impossible, you say? Well, nothing seems impossible anymore.

Whenever I found a video of the witnesses I immediately downloaded it. And it's a miracle that I haven't crashed my laptop from some virus or Trojan horse program hidden in the video, but any footage of the two men gets scrubbed from the internet so quickly that I don't want to risk losing it. I'll admit I'm fascinated by the men, and so is Cat.

"Why do they wear those clothes, I wonder," she asked after the first few videos surfaced.

"Beats me," I said. "Can't be comfortable."

"It looks like a burlap bag," she said. "I know poor people used to use them for clothing when nothing else was available."

She wasn't wrong. The witnesses wore black outfits, sort of like robes but simpler. Just a long, black rough-looking garment with holes for their heads and arms. And speaking of their arms, both men were muscular. They didn't appear to have an ounce of fat on them. They didn't have bodybuilder arms though, just tough, sinewy muscles with protruding blood vessels. One had shoulder-length gray hair; the other was completely bald. Both had thick, gray beards, and their skin was darkly tanned. Often they just stood at the foot of the temple mount, or sat on one of the ancient stone blocks that had once been part of the old city of David's protective walls. They usually spoke one at a time, sometimes preaching, other times answering questions. One video went like this:

"What's your name?" someone in the video called out.

"Our names aren't important, but His name is all that matters," the bald witness said. "He is called Wonderful Counselor, Mighty God, Everlasting Father, Prince of Peace."

The other witness rose up, as if he were inspired by his partner, "Keep on hearing, but do not understand; keep on seeing, but do not perceive. Make the heart of this people dull, and their ears heavy, and blind their eyes; lest they see with their eyes, and hear with their ears, and understand with their hearts, and turn and be healed."

Some people in the crowd laughed and mocked the men. I couldn't understand them, but their attitudes were clear enough. But others fell on their knees and raised their hands like children longing to be picked up.

The bald witness spoke to them. "Repent and be baptized every one of you in the name of Jesus Christ for the forgiveness of your sins, and you will receive the gift of the Holy Spirit. For the promise is for you and for your children and for all who are far off, everyone whom the Lord our God calls to himself."

The camera shifted, and there was shouting as a band of policemen came hurrying through the area.

The video ended, but it made me long for more. The two men weren't charismatic; they weren't pleasant to look at or even very clear in what they were saying. Yet whenever they spoke, it was as if they were talking to me. Cat felt the same way too—we were mesmerized.

"What did they mean, 'keep on hearing, but do not understand; keep on seeing but do not perceive,'" she asked.

"Well..." I said, thinking about the question. "When Jesus came the first time it wasn't like the Jews were expecting. And even when he started his ministry and declared that he was the Son of God, many of his own people rejected him."

"Why would they?"

"Maybe because he looked like a regular guy," I said.

"But he did miracles," she said.

"That's right."

"So, doesn't that make him more than a man? Doesn't that validate what he says about himself?"

"I think so. Do you?"

She sat back in her chair. She had a pile of what looked to me like weeds right beside her, and she was carefully peeling the tough inner layer out of the stiff stalks. Her hands worked diligently, but almost of their own accord, pulling the fibers free and then twisting them skillfully into twine.

"I think I'm interested," she said eagerly. "I want to know more."

"That's good," I said.

"But the Jewish people didn't?"

"Some did. There were a lot of people who believed him and followed him. His disciples carried on after he returned to heaven and started churches that have shaped the beliefs, morals, and culture of western civilization."

"But some didn't?"

"No," I admitted. "Some rejected him. Partly because he wasn't what they wanted, and partly because, like the witness said, they had hard hearts."

"Hard hearts," she repeated. "What do you mean by that?"

There were times when I missed Lorenzo so fiercely that it was difficult to breathe. I wished he could have been there with me and Cat. I wish she could have heard him explain things. He was so eloquent, so compassionate and understanding. And I think she would have loved him the way that I did.

"I mean, they refused to even consider the idea that Jesus was the Son of God. The religious leaders not only rejected him, but they prosecuted him. Claiming that he had broken their laws and was worthy of death."

"And that's why he died on the cross?"

"No, that's why he was sentenced to die," I tried to explain. "It's what the enemy wanted. It's what Satan had been plotting since Jesus was born, but it was ultimately God's plan for Jesus to die on that cross."

"Why would he want that?"

"I don't think he wanted it. Jesus didn't want it either. The Bible says he prayed that if there was any other way to please take the cup of sacrifice from him. But he followed that request with the words, 'nevertheless, not as I will, but as you will.'"

"He would do it God's way," Cat said.

It was simple, yet profound, and I couldn't help but wonder if I was strong enough to let God have his way with me. What if God decided to take Cat from me? What if I had to watch her die? Could I do it? What if I had to sacrifice myself to save her? I like to think of myself as a pragmatic person. My feelings can run deep, but I've never been one to rush into danger. If a bully was looking for me, I wouldn't wave my arms around to get his attention. Did that make me a coward? I didn't know, and I wasn't sure that I wanted to know.

"That's right. And he did. He went willingly to the cross,

took our punishment. Then the Bible says some interesting things happened."

"Like what?"

"Well, we know there was an earthquake. They've even found evidence of it. The Bible says the sky grew dark and that people rose from the dead."

"Oh, man, that's kind of creepy."

"I bet it was shocking," I admitted. "It also says that the curtain that separated the Holy of Holies from the inner chamber was split in two from top to bottom."

"The Holy of Holies, like in the new temple where they plan to put the Ark."

"Yes, the same one. Only the high priest could enter the Holy of Holies, and then only once a year on the day of atonement. Lorenzo said they would tie a rope around his ankle so that if he did something to offend God and was killed they could pull his body out without having to go in themselves."

"Wow," she said with a grin. "Who needs movies when I've got such a great storyteller right here?"

"It's not a story though; it's real."

"I know, but you tell it with such enthusiasm, Hank. It's one of the things I like about you. What else, tell me more."

"Well...there are a couple of passages that indicated that Jesus went into the abyss, or Tartarus, when he was dead."

"He went to hell?"

"No, not hell like we think of it. In fact, Lorenzo would say that people who die don't go to hell they go to Hades, or the concept in Hebrew is Sheol. That's the underworld, the place of the dead. But there's another place that is reserved for the fallen *bene ha'elohim*, those divine beings who left their positions in heaven and came to Earth, took wives, and set themselves up as gods. That is who the ancients worshiped, not just made-up idols, even though they carved idols to connect to these beings. Anyway, I'm getting off-topic here. There's a place that is sometimes called the abyss in ancient texts, the Bible calls it the pit or the bottomless pit, but in 2 Peter he called it Tartarus, which in Greek belief was the place where the gods banished the Titans."

"So you're saying that Greek mythology is true?"

"I'm saying it's based on truth," I replied. "It's how those fallen divine beings, the sons of God, tried to justify their existence and their place in the world. It's not truth, because they are led by a being that Jesus called the Father of Lies."

"And Jesus was sent there when he died? He was sent to Tartarus?"

"No, he wasn't sent there, but he went there. The Bible says he proclaimed the gospel to them. See, the powers of darkness thought they could overthrow God's rule by killing his son. But it was Jesus's plan to die for our sins all along. What they meant for evil, God meant for good. By crucifying Jesus, they sealed their fate. We don't know exactly what Jesus told those beings that are locked up in gloomy chains of darkness—maybe he declared his victory, maybe he explained that their time was coming to an end, or maybe he was making a formal announcement that what had been theirs, namely authority over the various parts of the earth, was officially revoked."

"It's all so fascinating," she said. "How come I never heard about any of this in Sunday school?"

"You went to Sunday school?" I asked, more than a little surprised.

"Oh, yes, as a child. My family was in church every Sunday right up until my parents divorced. I'm not sure why we quit going, but I always had the feeling they were embarrassed or maybe judged."

"How old were you?"

"Twelve," she explained with a grin. "It was a time of change, a lot of change. We moved into a little mobile home on the edges of the woods, which was hard enough. My father took off. He tried to see us about once a month for a while, but that didn't last long. My mother was a wreck and working a job she hated just to pay the bills. It was better to be somewhere else when she was around; otherwise there was a lot of yelling and crying. That's when I discovered nature. I spent hours in the woods alone at first, just exploring. Then I saw that movie, *My Side of The Mountain*. Did you ever see it?"

"Yes," I replied. "And I read the book."

"That changed everything for me. I was obsessed with the idea of living off the land. Which is pretty much what I did for the next few years. I built a little shelter in the woods, started reading all I could on foraging and hunting. By the time I was sixteen I had some pretty serious skills, so I dropped out of school and went out on my own."

"Wow, sixteen?" I asked.

"Yep. I took off and never looked back."

"Your mother was okay with that?"

"I don't know. I didn't ask her permission. She was probably relieved to have one less mouth to feed, you know?"

"Where was this?"

"Tennessee," she replied. "It took me a few years to make my way up here."

"How old are you?" I asked.

"I don't know," she said. "Don't care. This is the last true freedom a person can find, Hank. My only calendar is the seasons. I live in a place where the resources are abundant, and when that changes I move on. Everything I own I can carry on my back. That's the way we were meant to live."

"Come on, you can't really mean that," I said.

"Sure I can. Everything in the world is just a bigger, glitzier version of that simple truth. Only people get caught up in the need for more things, or nicer things, and they become slaves to the system."

"The system?"

"You know, like they're little cogs in the machine. They don't really own things. They spend money they don't have, whether it's a mortgage to buy a house, or a credit card to buy a designer handbag. Once they sign on the dotted line their lives aren't theirs any longer. They don't get to make their own decisions or do what they want to do. They have to work, like it or not, to keep making payments on all the things they've convinced themselves they can't live without."

"So what's the solution?" I asked.

"I don't have a solution. I'm not trying to convince people of anything. I just made the choice a long time ago that whatever I did it would be for me. I don't want to work for someone else, or get trapped in a system where I can't pull up stakes and head somewhere else whenever I want."

"And what do you believe about God?" I asked.

"I believe in a creator," she said with a smile. "You can't see what I've seen and not believe in a creator."

"But you don't believe in Jesus?" I pressed a little.

"I don't really know," she said honestly. "I'm not a Bible scholar like you."

I wanted to argue that I wasn't a scholar by any means. I was just a believer eager for the truth, so I was reading and watching as much as I could to try and understand it all.

Cat continued thinking and voicing how she really felt. "I feel like there's good in the world. You're a good guy. I'm happy to be here with you. But there's also evil. Anyone who would use a nuclear bomb has to be evil. We've done so much harm to the planet, and we were doing it long before the war. Even in the middle of nowhere I could look up and see the planes spraying who knows what into the sky. And I've met a lot of people like me, people who depend on the land to survive, who have seen the damage we're doing. From toxins in the water, to trash piled in heaps that clog up the oceans and the wild places."

"So where does that leave you?" I asked.

"It leaves me in a cozy cabin, safe in the mountains, with a handsome man," she said. "Honestly, in my book, I'm in heaven."

But it wasn't heaven, and things were about to get much, much worse.

CHAPTER 14

IT SEEMED like we were hidden in the forest, far away from the chaos of the world, but the truth was the fire watch cabin was at the end of an old logging road that wound up the mountainside. And we weren't the only people who knew it was there. Food had become incredibly scarce in the cities, which meant more and more people were resorting to hunting for food. Cat was one of them, although she was struggling to get in range of any sizable game that she could bring down with her primitive bow. She did have a trapline set that often produced a rabbit or two. She walked the line every day, while I scoured the internet for news, and uploaded videos of Lorenzo teaching about the end times.

I'll admit that the weeks alone with Cat were wonderful. We were different people, with completely different world-views, but somehow we got along so well. And not just because we avoided difficult topics. In fact, we talked about everything, from religion, to politics, to sports. Somehow we managed not to fight. When we disagreed we laughed. And when things got scary we found comfort in each other's arms. Cat taught me about living off the land, and I taught her about what the Bible predicted for the days ahead.

I should have been ready for the attack. I should have known it would come sooner or later, but I was too lost in what I was studying. My focus was on the big picture, and I neglected to consider how the hardships the world was enduring would affect me.

The gunshot was startling. I had heard gunshots from hunters before, but those were far away. The shot that rang out that early October morning was much closer, and some instinctive part of me realized something was wrong. Cat was already out checking her traps. It was cold outside, and there was a thick layer of snow on the ground nearly a foot deep. I had been reading about a new edict from the Global Council for Peace. They were doing something to try and stabilize the digital currencies of the world, which had crashed as a result of the wars that raged around the globe. But the gunshot shook me from my study and made me nervous. It was hard to see out of the windows of the cabin. We packed snow up to about chest height against the glass to help insulate the structure, and most of the upper portions were either iced or fogged. I stepped out onto the porch, looking for Cat. Part of me wanted to shout for her attention, and another part felt afraid to. The cabin was elevated to give the occupant a view over the nearby trees, but the forest was thick. I could see the trail that Cat used to run her trapline. She preferred to walk rather than use the snowmobile. Her handmade snowshoes had packed down the snow along the trail she used every day. Still, there was no sign of her, and no sound since the sudden crack of the rifle shot.

I felt exposed outside on the wraparound porch, so I went down the wooden stairs to the open space under the cabin. I was lucky that the former owner had left behind a good winter coat. It was a bit small for me, but much better than anything I had in my little duffle bag. I stuffed my hands deep into the pockets and paced beside Lorenzo's van. There were tire chains hanging from a peg on one of the cabin supports. It crossed my mind for the very first time that maybe it would be a good idea to make sure we could get down off the mountain if the need arose. So I made myself busy while I waited for Cat to come back, even though I felt afraid that something was wrong. Call it intuition or maybe prompting by the Holy Spirit, I'm not really sure, but I felt certain the gunshot was a harbinger of something bad.

I spent two hours getting the chains on the tires of the van and loading several boxes of emergency rations inside. It was all dry goods, mostly pasta and dehydrated foods that we mixed with water when we needed it. The cold wouldn't hurt them, and it gave me something to do while I waited for Cat to return.

But she didn't come back. Her trapline normally took an hour to walk. Sometimes when there was game in one of the traps it took her longer, but never more than two hours at a time. So when four had passed, I retrieved the Beretta 9 mm and fired up the snow machine. It was loud and stank of gasoline when the engine ran, but I didn't want to wait any longer to go searching for Cat.

The trail through the trees was narrow and not very

straight. I went slow, sweeping my eyes back and forth for any sign of her. The first clue was a mile from the cabin. I didn't see Cat, but there was blood on the snow. A little farther down the trail I saw her tracks leading off course. I followed, the snow machine making quick work through the trees and brush. She was moving downhill, and I was thankful to have the snow machine when I found her.

"Cat!" I screamed when I saw her body laying prone beside some bushes. I jumped off the snow machine and waded through the snow to reach her. It would have been much more difficult if the trees didn't catch a majority of the snowfall. "Cat! What's wrong?"

I knew she was hurt and cursed myself for not going after her sooner. Tears flooded my eyes as I dropped to my knees beside her.

"Please, God! Please don't let her die."

There was blood all across one side of her skirt. She lay on her stomach, her face turned toward the bushes. I rolled her toward me, and she groaned in pain, her eyes fluttering open.

"What happened?" I asked her. "Cat! Hang in there. Please!"

Her eyes closed, but she was breathing. The folds of her skirt made it hard to tell where the blood was coming from. I had to hike it up on the bloody side and eventually found a bullet wound in her upper leg, just below her hip. Blood seeped from the hole, which made me feel sick. I checked the back of her leg, but there was no exit wound. Dread flooded through me. My Air Force training had covered basic battle-field first aid. And I remembered that a bullet wound that stayed in the body had the added threat of poisoning the body.

I hastily recovered her legs and then picked her up. Cat screamed, but there was nothing I could do for her pain. She was hypothermic and losing blood. Getting her back to the cabin was my highest priority.

The snow machine was still running. I put her on the seat sideways, then climbed on behind her. I wrapped one arm around her body and used the other to steer. It wasn't smooth, and Cat groaned and cried the entire way back, but I covered the two miles back to the cabin in less than ten minutes.

Carrying her up the stairs was difficult. I was out of shape and she wasn't dainty, but I managed it. My breath was coming in hard gasps by the time I reached the top. The cold air made my lungs burn, but I didn't care. I carried her in and dropped her onto the bed.

"Han..." she moaned. "Ha...nk...hel..."

"I'm here," I told her, stoking the fire in our little stove before adding more wood. "I'm going to help you."

"Hurtsss," she moaned.

I shut the door to the stove and stood up, looking around. There were plenty of blankets. And we kept a tub of freshly filtered water. I got some and tried to delicately clean the wound using one of the rags that had been washed a few days before.

"Cold," she said.

"I know," I replied. "I'll get you warm soon."

I had to remove her wet clothing and wrap her in blankets, but I left her wounded leg exposed. Then I gave her a shot of whiskey that had been in the cabin when I found it. The previous owner probably wasn't a big drinker, but he had a bottle next to a few first aid supplies and over the counter pain relievers. She drank the whiskey, sputtering a little, but got most of it down.

"This is going to hurt," I told her, right before I poured some whiskey into the wound.

She screamed, then to my relief she passed out. It was better that she was unconscious for what I had to do. I'm no doctor, but I knew it was imperative that we get any foreign matter out of the wound before I attempted to stitch it up. I poured a glass of whiskey, folded open my pocket knife, and put the blade into the liquid. From the box of tools under the desk where my laptop and several books were spread out, I got a pair of needle nose pliers and added them to the glass of whiskey. The last thing I needed was a headlamp. It was late afternoon, and the light from outside the cabin was fading fast. The frost and fog on the windows diffused most of the light anyway. So I powered on a lantern and set it on the bed next to Cat's leg. Then I strapped on our headlamp, turned it to the high beam setting, and adjusted it so that I could see into the wound. I didn't want to tear her flesh, and so I cut her with my pocket knife. It was a small, straight cut, just enough to open things up a little so that I could use the pliers.

There's a reason why surgeons have special rooms set up specifically for their work, plus nurses who help them with every procedure. I couldn't see much past the blood that seeped into the wound and out onto her leg. Maybe if I had suction and better lighting, perhaps some type of magnification I could have done the work. As it was, I had to go in pretty much blind. Cat groaned in pain as I stuck the pliers into her leg and tried to get the bullet. Eventually I managed it, and also some of the wool from her skirt, but I couldn't be sure that I had gotten everything. Still, all I could do was pour whiskey into the wound, pinch it together, and use butterfly bandages to hold the wound closed. I pressed gauze pads onto the bloody gash and wrapped her leg with an ace bandage that I pulled tight to help staunch the bleeding. After that, I cleaned up and prayed like I had never prayed in my life.

CHAPTER 15

I WISH I could say that everything turned out great. It did not. My intervention was rudimentary at best, but the real threat came the following day. Every single thought and my entire focus was on Cat. She woke up in the night in terrible pain. I crushed up eight extra strength ibuprofen tablets, mixed them into a shot of whiskey, and helped her drink it down. But that barely took the edge off her terrible pain. And she was still in shock. At one point she vomited, and afterward was wracked by intense chills. But a few hours before dawn she was able to sleep again.

I napped beside her in the old, wooden chair, which was surprisingly comfortable with its thick cushions. I was in a daze a couple hours after dawn, not fully asleep, but not conscious either, when the shooting started. And it wasn't a single hunter either, but a group of people with high powered rifles, firing into the cabin from the tree line.

"What the..." I saw, waking up.

I saw Cat's eyes open, and I flung myself across her body as one of the windows shattered.

"Hey!" I screamed. "There's people in here!"

Of course, that was why we were being shot at. I can say that now that I'm thinking clearly, but at that moment I was in a state of complete panic.

"Hank," Cat whispered. I looked at her. "You have to go," she said.

I could barely make out her weak voice over my own heavy breathing and the gunshots.

"Leave... me."

Her words were like a shot of pure adrenaline.

"The hell I will," I said, before rolling off the bed and crawling across the cabin floor.

My hands and knees were cut by the shards of glass that seemed to be littered everywhere. Another window exploded, raining shards down around me. I was oblivious. My complete focus was on the rifle that Leon had given to me. It was propped next to the desk and loaded with a full thirty-round magazine. I grabbed it, rose up on my knees, and flicked off the safety.

Nothing in my Air Force training had prepared me for a gun fight. And even though I was by the window that had shattered, I couldn't see the assailants, who were hidden in the trees. But I could return fire and did so. The AR-15 rocked back and forth on the bump stock, rattling out a cadence of death. I joined it with a roar of my own.

"You want me?" I shouted, blazing away. "Come and get me you cowards!"

I emptied the magazine and hit the release. The mag

dropped onto the floor, and I pulled the only other one that was loaded from the ammo box nearby. I rammed it into place and fired another short burst. The shooting from the trees had stopped. Maybe I hit one of the assailants, I don't know. All I cared about was getting away and getting Cat somewhere safe.

By that time my mind was clear and focused. Of course people had come with bad intentions. I should have been expecting it. They shot first because that's what the world in the grip of the tribulation period was like. It was a brutal place. No law, no order, and almost no hope. I got to my feet and moved over to the side of the shattered window. The walls of the fire cabin offered no protection, but they did hide me from the eyes of the attackers.

Looking out, all I could see were trees and snow. The once magnificent view had morphed into one of terror and fear.

"Are you hit?" I asked Cat while still standing and staring out the shattered window.

"No, just cold."

"Yeah, that's not gonna get better any time soon," I said. "We can't stay here."

Cat didn't respond. I can only imagine how she felt. It would be horrible to be so terribly hurt and then told that you would have to flee into the cold. I was internally raging at the people who had opened fire on the cabin. Perhaps they were desperate and had no idea that Cat and I would have gladly shared what we had with them freely. Instead, they put us in mortal danger, and I wouldn't have hesitated to shoot each of them.

Fortunately, I didn't have to do that. I grabbed my computer and books, stuffed them into my duffle bag, and slung it over my shoulder. The AR-15 went over the other shoulder, and I stuffed the Beretta 9 mm into the waistband of my pants. Cat didn't have a duffle bag, but she had a satchel made from buckskin and decorated with porcupine quills. I put everything of hers inside, along with handfuls of dried herbs and all the first aid supplies. Then, taking a deep breath, I opened the cabin door and dashed down the stairs. I expected another volley of shots, but there were none. And when I reached the ground, I was thrilled to see that the tires on the van weren't damaged by the shooting. In fact, it seemed that the attackers were downhill, and in shooting up at the elevated cabin, had missed Lorenzo's old van completely.

I yanked open the driver's side door and flung our things in, including the rifle. Putting it down could have been a huge mistake, but I still had to carry Cat down from the cabin, and there would be no way to wield any kind of weapons while I was holding her. I raced back upstairs, my breathing coming in powerful blasts, and hurried to her side. Her eyes were barely open.

"Come on," I said. "Don't quit on me. Please God, heal her."

Cat's eyes closed tight as I slid my arms under her. And then she groaned, and tears seeped from between her long lashes as I lifted her up.

"No," she sobbed as I lumbered toward the door. "Please."

"Sorry," I said, angling her out of the door and starting down the steps.

At some point she passed out again. I managed to get the passenger door of the van open and sat her in the seat. I reclined the seat back as far as it would go, and then strapped the seatbelt over her body. God was surely protecting me. If the assailants in the woods had wanted to shoot me they had plenty of opportunity. Somehow I made it to the driver's side and got the van started. The wheels turned, the chains I had put on them the day before mashed into the soft earth, and then the snow. Gravity and the grace of God got us away from the fire cabin. I never saw who attacked us, never knew if my angry barrage had hit them or merely driven them back. Perhaps they weren't expecting someone with an automatic weapon to shoot back. I hadn't found any weapons inside the cabin except for an old .45 caliber revolver in a fancy holster that would have been right at home on the set of a western movie. In the weeks of my stay, I never touched that gun and never saw anything else. If the people who were shooting into the cabin were expecting the former occupant and his six-shooter, they would have been very surprised to find me instead.

The nearest town was nothing but a gas station convenience store and a post office. I didn't even bother slowing down. There were times when the van slid in the snow and other times when the wheels spun without much traction. But the snow thinned as we dropped in elevation, until we were driving on wet roads without snow. I stopped long enough to pull the chains when we got onto the first paved road. We wound our way through the backroads until we reached the community of Saint Maries. There was a little hospital there, and I took Cat to the emergency room. It was a sad, desperate place. A few doctors were still making rounds, but with almost no medicines and dwindling supplies, there wasn't much we could do.

I rolled out the gurney by myself, got Cat on it. She was weeping again, in so much pain that she had turned white and was sweating despite the cold. I rolled her inside. A nurse took over, checked the wound, and apologized for not having any pain killers.

"The National Guard took almost everything," the nurse said. She had a nametag pinned to her scrubs that read *M. Smith*. "A local pharmacy was supplying some pain relievers but they've run out. There's been a lot of stupid people doing stupid things."

"I'm sure," I said.

"How'd she get shot?"

"A hunter maybe," I said. "She was walking her trapline."

"People are desperate. A lot of the elderly haven't survived. At least the Visitors got the children out before the world went crazy."

She left, and all I could do was watch as Cat struggled with the pain. Eventually a gray-haired doctor came in, inspected the wound, and gave me instructions on cleaning it.

"If it turns colors or starts to smell, get her back in to see a doctor," he said. "She needs antibiotics, and I'll give her a shot, but it's not a full course of treatment."

"I understand," I said.

"You from around here?"

"No, sir," I admitted.

"Well, find a good, warm place to let her rest. The more you move her the more pain she'll be in."

"Okay," I said, wondering what I could possibly do to help her.

We spent the night. The nurses kept tabs on Cat, and I

slept in the van to make sure no one tried to steal it or the supplies we had inside. The next morning I went for gas. The prices were outrageous. It cost me nearly four hundred dollars to get ten gallons, which was the limit allowed. When I got back to the hospital, Cat was awake.

"How are you feeling?" I asked her.

"A little better," she said. "As long as I don't move."

"What's the doctor saying?"

"That I have to leave," she said. "They need the bed."

"Well, that stinks, but I made up the air mattress in the back of the van. Blankets, my old pillow, it isn't four stars, but it will get us out of here."

"I'm used to sleeping on the ground," she said. "An air mattress in the back of your van will be an improvement."

Nurse Smith was back. She helped me get Cat into a wheelchair, which I maneuvered out to the van. Getting her inside wasn't easy. Cat couldn't put any weight on her injured leg, and hopping around was so painful as to be impossible. What she could do was stand up on that good leg, pivot around and then sit back into the van, where I pulled her inside. The old vehicle wasn't built for luxury, but it was warm and she could lay down. Looking over my shoulder I could see her.

"You okay?" I asked.

"Yeah," she said, despite obviously being in great pain.

I pulled over and took some ibuprofen from Cat's bag. The bottle was dangerously low, especially with her need for the maximum dosage. Still, it was better than nothing, and she was grateful.

"Where are we going?" Cat asked.

"The doctor said you needed a warm, safe place to recover. So I'm taking you to the only place I know of."

"Where's that?"

"Lorenzo's house, in Spokane."

Cat wasn't a city girl, but she was in no shape to object. I could only hope that Lorenzo's home was still there. After all I had been through, and all we had lost, it was the only place that still felt like home.

CHAPTER 16

THE DRIVE to Spokane took more than two hours. We went slowly through the winding landscape. As we approached the border we had to climb some pretty big hills. The highway department was no longer a functioning service, and there were places where the roads were covered with slush and snow, but the old van handled them better than I dreamed possible.

Back on Interstate 90 there was evidence of fighting. We passed a lot of cars that had been rolled off the road or knocked off in a collision. A tank and two armored vehicles were also left behind, both having taken enemy fire that left the road cracked and in some places crumbling. There wasn't a lot of traffic on the highways. Fuel was insanely costly, along with everything else. We had just enough gas to get to Lorenzo's home.

You've probably seen footage after a tornado of the path of destruction that's plowed through a neighborhood. Homes are leveled, the streets filled with debris, cars flipped upside down, trees uprooted, and then there's one home that seems completely untouched. How that home was spared the destruction when all those around it are damaged or destroyed is always anyone's guess. I like to think that God spared those homes for a reason. Lorenzo's neighborhood reminded me of those tornado scenes. In fact, Spokane, Washington was more like Beirut than an historic American city. Buildings were leveled; others were left with gaping holes where bullets and explosions had ripped through them. The streets were filled with craters and debris, and cars were left burnt out, nothing but blackened shells. Worse still, there were bodies left out in the streets, parking lots, and alleyways. Packs of roving dogs ripped and tore the bloated corpses. There were lines of people outside the grocery stores. Big signs displayed what was available and the audacious prices.

The Bible says that when Jesus breaks the third seal judgment, a rider on a black horse emerges with a scale in his hand. A voice cries out that a loaf of bread will cost a day's wages, and that was on full display in Spokane. Not that there was much bread to be had–that food item label had already been struck through. What people were left to buy were instant potatoes. A box of dehydrated ones cost seventy-five dollars. Powdered milk was fifty dollars a canister, and individual cans of soup were thirty dollars each.

I drove past people who stood destitute on the streets. Some had signs that said they would work for food. Others, believe it or not, were giving themselves away for just a single meal. Once again I was glad that there were no children to be bartered by desperate parents.

And I was glad that Cat was able to doze in the back of the van. She didn't need to see the scenes of desperation on the streets. I saw people with wounds and others with what could only be radiation sickness, looking for help that would never come. We passed churches that were burned down to the ground and others that were boarded up. I saw poverty, hunger, and absolute hopelessness everywhere I looked.

But when we reached Lorenzo's neighborhood, I was stuck with a sense of fear. Several houses were burned down, those around them damaged by the intense heat of the flames. Others looked like they had been broken into. Doors hung on busted hinges, with windows shattered and bullet holes in the walls. Likewise, cars in the street and in driveways were damaged. I felt sick. My bank account was nearly empty, and the gas tank of the van was down to the fumes. If we had to find another place to stay, I wasn't sure how I would get Cat there.

But, like those homes spared from the storm, as I approached Lorenzo's house there was no sign of damage. The windows were intact, the door closed, the garage door down and undamaged. I pulled into the driveway, feeling a sense of relief.

"Hang on," I said softly. "I'll be right back."

Cat was dozing and didn't respond. I was tempted to get the rifle out, but I hadn't seen anyone in the neighborhood. If people were watching from the damaged homes they hadn't been visible. The last thing I wanted was to parade the rifle, which was probably worth its weight in gold, for the whole neighborhood to see. Instead, I kept the Beretta 9 mm under my shirt and made a quick circuit around Lorenzo's house.

The backyard fence was intact. The sliding glass doors on the walkout basement weren't touched. The deck above, undamaged. I made a complete pass around the home and still saw no sign of damage or intruders.

Among the items on the ring with the van keys was Lorenzo's house key. I unlocked the front door and went inside. It was dark, no power, no beeping alarm system. I did a quick walk-through of the main floor. It was empty. In the garage, I pulled the handle that unlocked the garage door from the electric opener. It rose easily on the well-oiled hinges. Then I drove the van inside where Lorenzo kept it parked beside his daily driver. That had been a Lincoln Aviator SUV before I crashed it on our way back from California. That crash had led to the rest of my life falling to pieces, but of course, that's in my other book and I won't bore you with a recap.

Once we were inside the garage with the door closed, I helped Cat out of the van and carried her into the house. I probably should have changed Lorenzo's sheets, but there was no time. His bed was one of those adjustable models. I plugged it into the solar generator, which had been sitting unused in the van for weeks. It had just enough juice to get the bed adjusted comfortably for Cat.

"That's better," she said, with her legs elevated and her head angled up. "This is nice."

"Beats an air mattress in the back of an old van," I said.

"Yeah," she agreed.

I was thrilled to find Lorenzo's pain pills still in his bathroom. He had several different pill bottles: some were narcotic strength pain relievers, others were muscle relaxers, and even a prescription to help his bowels keep moving while under the influence of the powerful drugs.

"Jackpot," I said, coming out with a bottle of pills. "Lorenzo had some Vicodin left, and if that doesn't help, he's got some Oxycontin too."

"Why did he have this?" Cat asked, holding out a hand for the pills.

"Broken hip," I said.

She knew the story and nodded. I grabbed a bottle of water from the little micro fridge we had put in Lorenzo's room. It wasn't cold without working electricity, but that didn't matter. I unscrewed the top and handed it to Cat.

"I hate these," she said, looking at the bottled water.

"At least you know it's clean," I said.

She swallowed the pills and sipped on the water while I got her covered up. She fell sound asleep for the first time since leaving the cabin right after getting shot. While she rested, I made my way through the house. There were canned goods in the kitchen. The fridge was worthless, and the electric appliances wouldn't work, including the oven and stove top, but according to the prices I had seen on the way to Lorenzo's home, there was a small fortune in food supplies.

Downstairs, among his many artifacts and his recording equipment, there was a storage room with Lorenzo's travel gear. He had water filters and camping supplies from his expeditions in Central and South America. That would come in handy, I thought. The one thing we didn't have a lot of was water, but there was enough bottled water in the kitchen and garage to last us a couple of weeks. After that we'd need to find more, but it could wait while I nursed Cat back to health.

That night, after triple checking that the doors and windows were all locked, I propped Lorenzo's sitting chair against the door of his bedroom. It was the same chair he had made videos in after the accident–a nice, heavy sitting chair. The door was close to the wall, and with the door pushed up at an angle, there was no way anyone could open it wide enough to get inside. I put the rifle on the far side of the nightstand, and the pistol within easy reach on top. Finally, I laid down beside Cat. She was breathing easy. The sun had set; the room was dark. I had a lantern on the bedside table that I had found with Lorenzo's camping gear. It ran on a battery, and I kept it on the lowest setting so that it didn't bother Cat. After checking her bandages and seeing that she hadn't bled through them, I turned off the lights and went to sleep.

Cat woke me up in the wee hours of the morning. I helped her use the bathroom and gave her more pain meds. Then we slept until well after sunrise the next day. Light flooded in through the window, despite the fact that I had closed the blinds. I got up slowly, trying not to wake up Cat. Then I checked outside. There was no sign of anyone. I moved the chair from in front of the door and checked all around the house again. There was a part of me that would never feel safe again. But it felt good to be back in a familiar place. And I was so thankful that God had saved it for us. Still, I had no illusions. We couldn't just buckle down and ride out the tribulation period. The winter was going to be terrible–really, really terrible. And that meant we had a lot of work to do if we were going to survive.

CHAPTER 17

NOT EVERY HOUR of the tribulation was filled with fear. The calamities of war and famine were terrible, but they came in waves. The Chinese military forces seemed intent on destroying the United States, and air raids were a regular occurrence. Bombs exploded across town, but attacks focused mainly on the downtown and industrial sites. Fairchild Air Base was gone, a smoking crater, that much I knew. It had never been more than a logistical storehouse at any rate. Still, the fuel and other chemical tanks kept on the base had been a primary target at the start of the war. Once that was gone, the city of Spokane became a more tempting target.

I was just glad the city wasn't large enough to have been hit with a nuclear bomb. Seattle was a radioactive heap, and I knew it was only a matter of time before the poison of nuclear radiation reached across the state. We couldn't stay at Lorenzo's forever. Food was going to be an issue before long, and water was already on my mind. Before the Rapture, getting food and water was simple. Turn on the tap and out poured a seemingly unlimited supply of water. Need food? Just run to the grocery store. No transportation? That's okay, just make an order right from your phone and have whatever you want delivered to your front door. We had no idea how easy we had it.

And I was certain things were only going to get worse. So while Cat recovered from her gunshot wound, I spent my days preparing. Lorenzo had given me access to his bank accounts after the car wreck. In my mind that money belonged to his children, but their relationship was strained by Lorenzo's study of the supernatural, which brought a certain amount of ridicule from mainstream religious leaders, and even more scorn from kids in school. His children had suffered, but moved on when they reached adulthood. And to my knowledge they hadn't made any attempt to reach out to Lorenzo, even after the accident. They were probably taken in the Rapture, I told myself, although I had no way of knowing for sure. Either way, I had no idea how to reach them with the news about their father. So, I used some of Lorenzo's money.

Banking had been taken over by the government. All funds became Central Bank Digital Dollars. People still took cash locally, but with inflation so high, it was becoming scarce. Bank debit cards still worked, so I used Lorenzo's to fill up the van's gas tank. But even with enough money to get what we needed, you couldn't buy what wasn't available. Food was becoming scarce. Fortunately, I still had a month's worth of emergency food rations, and the canned goods from Lorenzo's home. So we ate, but with an eye toward the future knowing that we only had a finite supply. Water was the more pressing concern. I found a plastic barrel in the garage, and after scrubbing it out, set it up under the rain gutters. It was a wet time of year, and the barrel began filling up. I knew better than to think the rain water was clean. But Lorenzo had plenty of wood stacked under the deck in the back yard for his fire pit. It was a fancy, stainless steel pit that was supposed to minimize smoke. He had purchased a cast iron cooking attachment which mounted over the top of the fire pit. I used that to heat food and boil water. And before I boiled it, I ran all the captured rainwater through Lorenzo's portable filtration system. It was time consuming, but allowed us the luxury of having not just drinking water, but the ability to bathe and wash our clothes too.

In the evenings we lay in bed together, talking about what was happening in the world. The gunshot had changed Cat. She had lost some of her fearlessness and her easygoing attitude about the world. We were both pretty young, but stress wears on a person. Cat had lost a significant amount of weight, and the skin around her eyes grew dark. She developed deep lines across her forehead and at the corners of her eyes. Gray strands of hair became visible in her dark braid. Most of all, she grew hungry for information about God, the Bible, and especially the events foretold about the seven year tribulation period.

"Seven years," she asked. "Is that from the Vanishing?"

"The Rapture," I said. "No, the tribulation was kicked off by the peace treaty in Israel."

"That's been a few months, right?"

"Yeah, they signed that in June," I said.

"And it's November now, right?"

"Yeah, just turned November. We had that candy bar on Halloween."

The candy had been in Lorenzo's pantry. I bought it for him. He enjoyed chocolate and popcorn when we watched a movie. That had been such an idyllic time, but I wasted it. I was too busy moping over my lost love and tormented by a demon. It may seem strange to say, but it's true. For years we lived in blissful ignorance. The supernatural had long since been banished to myth in the civilized nations of the west. Yet, that didn't make it any less real. And being in Lorenzo's home brought back the horror of that oppression to me in ways that were at times frightening. I didn't like going downstairs where Lorenzo kept the artifacts from his expeditions around the world. Many of those items were linked with the strange beings from the past, creatures that Lorenzo called hybrids, the offspring of the Nephilim.

"So what happens now?" Cat asked.

"According to the Bible, the next judgment is the rider on the pale horse," I told her.

"Which is death?"

"Death and Hades, yes."

"So what does that mean, Hank? Are you saying that people die?"

"The Bible, as I understand it, is saying that the spiritual entities connected with death and the underworld are set loose on planet Earth. They will kill a quarter of the world's population through war, famine, pestilence, and wild beasts."

"Wonderful," Cat said. "I don't know how this is supposed to make people turn to God. It doesn't make any sense."

"God isn't causing this," I told her. "He doesn't want war

or famine, or death. For thousands of years he's been holding back the forces of darkness, giving us time to turn our hearts toward him."

"But he's not any more?"

I shook my head. "Not anymore. People have rejected him. They have loved evil and sought only to do what they wanted for a long time now."

"If it feels good, do it," she said sadly.

"Yeah, so those people, under the influence of the powers of darkness, are getting what they want."

The proof of that statement was on the news each night. There was no electricity in Spokane. But I already had Lorenzo's portable electric generator. They were common before the Vanishing. Essentially they were big batteries that could be recharged using solar panels. There wasn't much sunshine, but among Lorenzo's camping gear was a wind turbine. It looked like a little windmill, and with a little work I got it set up on the deck. There was plenty of wind as autumn turned to winter. The power generated wasn't enough to do much. We couldn't run a refrigerator, but we could charge the laptop. And while there wasn't electricity in the city, the Starlink signal was strong. So each night as we lay in bed together, we caught up on the news.

There were plenty of stories about people running out of food, but there were nearly as many videos that showed the wealthy from around the world who seemed to have more than enough. Nowhere was that more evident than with the new Regional Administrator who lived like a king in a newly built complex outside of Toronto. There were videos of the lavish meals that were served to the Administrator and his underlings. Fresh meats, vegetables, wine, baked goods, and sumptuous desserts were prepared while the people they supposedly governed went hungry. Of course, there wasn't much governing going on, not while the United States and China continued fighting.

There was no real strategy to the war itself. Isolated military units fought both in America and in mainland China. Missile bombardments and air raids did damage to any place where people gathered. In the States, militia groups formed to fight back against the soldiers who had invaded from the north, and with great success at first. But the famine had put a hamper on the fighting. Even the Chinese troops were starving, their supply lines either cut by militia forces or simply running out of supplies all together.

Death tolls were still being reported from bombings and battles, but it was hard to keep up with. In the United States alone, we went from nearly three hundred and fifty million people down to less than two hundred million in a matter of months. The vanishings had taken a toll, but the nuclear bombardment had been worse. And somehow, the famine was going to claim even more than both the war and the Rapture put together. It was hard seeing the images of people in the United States who looked so frail. But there were similar scenes from around the world. Russians, Germans, South Africans, Brazilians, and Australians all looked the same–gaunt, hollow-eyed, emaciated, and weak. Saddest of all was the fact that so few were turning to God and calling out for his help.

While I continued posting interviews and videos online, for every question I got in response, there would be dozens of nasty replies from trolls. Some pushed the new religion of global peace and called Christianity a cult or myth. But most of the negative responses were visceral rants full of hate and perversion. I knew that soon it wouldn't be safe to openly talk about God or Jesus. The Four Horsemen of the Apocalypse were only the beginning of the judgments that were being set loose upon the earth. The seven years of tribulation are described in the book of Revelations in the Bible. It starts with a scroll, and upon that scroll are seven wax seals. Each of those seals is a judgment, or a disastrous consequence of the evil at work in the world. The first was the rider on the white horse, the Antichrist. He appeared as a savior of the world, bringing what had for decades seemed impossible–peace in the Middle East. God sent his son, Jesus, to save us from our sins, but we rejected him. Instead, we cried out for a savior who would deliver us from God himself, and so He gave us what we asked for. Only the peace that the Antichrist delivered was a short-lived illusion. It lead to worldwide warfare, because when people have the freedom to do whatever they want, they end up stealing, and raping, and killing one another. It happened between individuals and between groups, as well as nations.

In the streets people fought and killed one another over the slightest perceived offense, or to get something that one person had and another person wanted. The illusion of safety was shattered. There was no safety. Reports came in of abuse from every corner of the globe. And the newly formed government was the worst of all, taking whatever it wanted and leaving the people destitute.

All the anger and loss was building to what would become

a fever pitch, and just before the cauldron of humanity boiled over, a scapegoat would need to be given. I knew that we would be blamed. Anyone who didn't adhere to the new religion of peace, still being hawked by Paul Eon and the supposed alien who called himself Shemi Hazah, would become a target. Christianity would be blamed for the war, the corruption, and the famine. Billions of lives would be lost, and God would be to blame. Anyone who still believes in him would be slaughtered. And that meant I had to be ready for the storm that was coming.

CHAPTER 18

"SO WHAT ARE WE LOOKING AT?" Cat asked me as I helped her slowly move her leg.

One of the benefits of still having the internet was access to articles on physical therapy. The muscles and tendons in Cat's upper thigh had been damaged by the bullet. So as it healed we slowly began the process of exercising her leg so she would be able to walk again.

"Five more minutes," I told her.

"Not that," she said. "I know how long I need to work on my leg. I'm asking, what is next for the world?"

"You believe now?" I asked her, in a light, almost joking tone.

Only I wasn't really joking. I didn't want to push Cat into doing something she didn't really believe in or feel good about. But I was desperate for her to do more than just learn about God–I wanted her to believe. Still, all my hoping and praying wasn't enough. I knew Cat believed me when I told her what the Bible said was coming, but she hadn't put her trust in Jesus for the forgiveness of her sins yet. She was like me, the way I had been with Lorenzo. I used my ignorance as an excuse, looking to learn but not really accept the truth.

"You know I'm interested," she said. "So, what's next?"

"I can't predict it all with perfect clarity," I admitted. "What I know is that if a lot of people die, then there's a period of persecution for anyone who believes in God."

"So why would anyone admit to believing in God?" Cat asked. "It seems stupid to me. If the world is out to kill Christians, why would anyone admit that they were one?"

"Because we can't help but tell people that God still loves them," I said.

"That's what you're doing with Lorenzo's videos?" she asked, with a note of trepidation in her voice.

We had talked about it before, and I knew how she felt. What she wanted was to find a place that was safe and for me to give up posting about God. In her mind, we should just lay low, and who was I to argue? She was the one with a bullet wound. She knew the reality of nearly dying, and I was a mere spectator. But like I told her, I didn't feel like I had a choice.

"That's what I'm trying to do," I said. 'I know that it might sound crazy, but I know what's really going on."

"The spiritual war?"

"That's right," I said. "This fight isn't really east versus west, or communism versus capitalism. It's the fallen children of God in rebellion against him. People need to know that."

"Even if it gets you killed?"

That was the million dollar question. What was the message worth? Did it really matter that people knew the truth, when so many would reject it no matter how much evidence could be produced to back it up? Was I brave enough to give my life for what I believed in? That was the question that haunted my soul.

"How can I not tell people?" I said. "God still loves us, despite everything we've done."

"If he loves us, why doesn't he save us from all this?"

"We had plenty of chances," I said. "The Bible warned us what was coming."

"But you didn't believe it," she pointed out. "Not when Lorenzo told you. Not even when you were haunted by a ghost."

"I was attacked by a demon, not haunted by a ghost."

"What's the difference?"

"It doesn't matter," I said. "The point is that we still have a chance to do the right thing."

Right and wrong were in a state of flux. Even in my own mind I was trying to balance what I felt compelled to do with Lorenzo's materials and my desire to keep Cat safe. She wasn't my wife, and I had no claim over her. Maybe she didn't expect or even want me to try to keep her safe, yet I felt the obligation. Not that it was a chore or hardship. I had strong feelings for Cat, partly from the trying times we had been through, and partly from the way we connected. She was a quiet woman with a kind soul, and she was completely different from anyone I had ever known. Under normal circumstances I doubt we would have been together. She loved the freedom of being on her own in wild places, and I didn't think I could adjust to that lifestyle. The tribulation, and specifically the war in the United States, had changed everything for the both of us, and I was really happy to have her in my life.

"But it's dangerous," she pointed out. "If you know there are going to be people who will want to kill you for uploading the videos, why do it? Surely it would be better to wait and see what really happens. When things cool down, you can start sharing them again...maybe."

It was a logical way to look at things, but only if one opted not to think about God. Having Jesus in my life changed everything for me.

"That would be like someone telling me to hide my feelings for you," I told her. "I'm not looking for trouble, but I feel like I've wasted so much of my life already. I don't want a day to go by that I don't do something for God."

"Even if it costs you your life?"

"Even if," I replied. "I should be dead already. God chose to save me when I was firmly in the enemy's clutches. He's got a reason for why we're here right now. I believe that the message from Lorenzo's teaching is more important than ever. It's just one point of view about the things going on at this moment in history. There are other great theologians out there, but Lorenzo's legacy is my responsibility. I can't hide it."

"But you can be smart about how you disseminate it, right?" Cat asked.

I had just finished stretching her leg, and the look in her eye was deadly serious. There was more behind the question than just the topic at hand. I think maybe she was trying to decide if I was someone she could trust for the long haul.

"Yes, of course," I replied. "I'll always be careful."

"Okay then," she said, relaxing for the first time since we started her therapy. "That's good to know."

An hour later Cat was asleep. She was already weaning herself off Lorenzo's pain pills. She was down to a single pain pill, after her stretches, and a half pill at night. The muscle relaxers were only being taken as needed. There were times when her legs and back cramped, so the muscle relaxers were invaluable, but she didn't like the way they made her feel afterward. She described it as a mental fog. Still, even though she was being strong, I had plenty of time on my own to prepare for what I knew was still to come.

The United States of America was no longer the world's superpower. In fact, with the collapse of our economy, and the devastating effects of the war with China, we were barely existing. The world had been split into ten regions. The North American region consisted of Canada, the US, and Mexico. No big surprise there, but what had once been the beacon of freedom and prosperity to the world had radically shifted. Europe was another region, but it too was plagued with war. Russia from the West Asia region attacked Great Britain, and old rivalries had sprung up among the countries in Europe. The Southern Asia Region that included the Near East and Arab nations was quickly becoming the dominant world power. India and Pakistan had quickly renewed fighting once China initiated what people were calling World War III. But otherwise, the Southern Asia region had been relatively untouched by the carnage of war. Even Israel, which had known conflict since being reintroduced as a nation in 1948, was at peace.

If I was surprised by anything, it was the fact that Paul

Eon was not made the Administrator of the SA Region. Instead, the man who brought peace to the most hostile region in the world had been given a ceremonial position in the new government. He was a figurehead, with no real power among the leaders of the ten new global regions.

Yet it was the city most linked to him, the new Babylon, that was fast becoming the world's most famous city. Everyone with means took up residence in Babylon. The architecture was both ancient and modern. The city was a reflection of its heritage, with massive gates and huge walls made of massive blocks of stone which were carried and set in place by literal giants. The Visitors, or Apkallu as they also called themselves, designed massive, interlinking skyscrapers that were made of glass and steel. In a matter of months, since the signing of the peace accord in Israel, the city had taken shape. At the center of the new Babylon was the Temple of Global Peace, a massive building shaped like a serpent–I kid you not. The base was round, but with undulations almost like a viper's coils. And from those rose a tower with a serpentine shape. The top of the tower was wider than the rest and looked like a cobra's hood. The lower portion of the exquisite building served as a place of worship. What people worshiped there was anything but God. People from all religions came and set up shrines within the temple, as well as people who worshiped nature, or claimed that the concept of peace was in fact, a deity to be worshiped. There were chambers for cere-monies of all kinds, from deep pits used to call up the dead, to lavish bedchambers where temple prostitutes sold themselves as an act of divine worship.

The upper floors comprised a training center for priests of

the new global religion, as well as storerooms for the lavish gifts that were sent there from all over the world. The most surprising offerings came from the Vatican, from where priceless treasures from thousands of years of collecting were handed over. And actually not just a few items, but everything from the Vatican and from cathedrals around the world, were gifted to the new temple. The polished exterior of the massive building hid what I thought of as pure evil within. Paul Eon, along with his counterpart the alien being called Shemi Hazah–or as he was more often called, The Prophet–took residence at the very top.

The world's richest people moved into the city. They invested billions into the World Bank, which had its headquarters in the business district and was quickly nominated by the ten leaders of the world's regional government to be the control unit for each region's Central Bank Digital Dollars. The famine plaguing the rest of the world didn't touch the elites in Babylon, which was overflowing with the finest foods and wines from around the world. There were gardens in Babylon, but no produce was grown there and no products manufactured there–it was just another playground of the rich and famous.

Ships brought in goods to the port at the northern end of the Persian Gulf, and were shipped over land to the city whose spires and glistening walls were visible from the sea. It was odd to see the entire world pivoting away from the west and turning their attention to the ancient city that was rising to new life in the desert. The Near East was once again the center of the world.

We had been in Lorenzo's home for nearly three weeks

when the announcements of new festivals were made. Paul Eon, with the towering alien Shemi Hazah, The Prophet, at his side, gave a short speech, which Cat and I watched live on my laptop.

"The world is changing," he declared, pausing for effect.

"You think?" Cat mocked.

She knew exactly who the head of the Peace Initiative really was. And we both saw through his false humility.

"War has touched us all, but that too is changing. We will not fight forever. Old rivalries and ancient feuds must die in order to give life to new traditions. We will fling off the yokes of exclusionary thinking and embrace unity, equity, and inclusivity. These are the pillars of the new age and will be the bedrock for the new peace and security that will arise from the ashes of the past. I know each of you will join me in this monumental shift for our fledgling world. And we will begin with the week-long Peace Festival and New Year Celebration. Out with the old, and in with the new. Peace is all about doing what you love, and you are encouraged to go all out. Embrace the reason for the season, as we all manifest the peace that we deserve."

The well-dressed members of the crowd cheered. They were wealthy citizens of Babylon, or pilgrims who traveled to worship at the serpentine Temple of Global Peace. All wore rainbow-colored emblems of peace, an upside-down broken cross in a circle, a throwback to the 1960s. All other religious iconography was being removed, although no official order had been given to my knowledge. I mean, I wasn't privy to the workings of the new powerbrokers in their glistening city of extravagance. Cat and I were huddled in a dark house in

Spokane, which was fast becoming a ghost city. Still, in the videos we watched from around the world there were priests who no longer wore the crucifix and imams who had given up the crescent moon of Islam. Outside of Israel, even the Star of David was gone, all replaced with the rainbow-colored peace symbol.

Of course it was impossible not to long for peace. We heard gunshots and screaming on a daily basis. Fortunately, nothing was close enough to make us feel threatened, but we longed for times when a person could feel safe and at ease. Instead, we struggled daily with fear and anxiety. If the people in the city knew what we had in Lorenzo's home they would try to kill us for it. People were starving in the city, and it seemed almost obscene that we were eating two meals a day.

"So, Christmas is out," Cat said, after watching the video of Paul Eon announcing the new Peace Festival, and listening as news pundits declared how brilliant he was.

"Looks like it," I said.

"And here I was thinking we could get a tree and decorate it," she said. "Maybe wrap up a few canned goods like presents."

"I suppose we could," I said.

Cat shook her head. "We've got enough to do."

"Yeah, winter's almost here."

"Which means we need to find a way to stay warm," she said.

"Or head south," I pointed out.

The cold was quickly becoming a problem. It was warmer inside than out, but we had no real way to heat Lorenzo's home. It had a gas fireplace, but there was no gas to burn. I never burned the fire pit for long, and always at night, when the smell of the wood smoke was masked by other campfires around the city. I would also hang some old towels around the fire pit to hide the light. The last thing we wanted was for the fire to attract unwanted attention, so I only burned a little of the wood—enough to boil a gallon of water and heat some cans of soup.

Despite having food, we were both losing weight. And while I had gone out and stood for hours in the cold, waiting for food from one of the few stores still getting the occasional supply, it was pretty clear that the famine was hitting everyone hard. I've never seen such despair in my life. The people in Spokane were completely without hope.

There were a few people preaching the good news of hope in Jesus, but their sermons fell mostly on deaf ears. And while the outright persecution of Christians hadn't begun yet, those few bold souls who proclaimed the gospel were usually shouted down and threatened. It might have been good for Cat and I to join with other believers, but she was hesitant. We both knew the dangers, not just of publicly declaring one's faith in Christ, but in the inevitable betrayal that would strike and scatter groups of Christians in the days to come.

Occasionally I felt like I should try and tell people about Jesus. Mostly when I stood in the food lines and heard people crying in despair. But I knew my purpose was to keep Lorenzo's voice alive online. That responsibility had fallen to me, and I knew it was important. No one else could do it, and there were thousands that could be reached with a single video, so I didn't risk my life trying to persuade people to put their trust in Jesus or that we were living in what the Bible called the Tribulation. Instead I stayed quiet and watched the world around me grow darker and darker.

In my free time, I prepared. Not just getting the van ready to travel, but collecting things we would need, from sleeping bags and survival supplies, to things we could trade down the road. Staying in Spokane wasn't a long-term option. Eventually we would have to face the dangers of the open road if we wanted to survive, and when that time came I wanted us to be as prepared as possible.

CHAPTER 19

BY CHRISTMAS, which was no longer a recognized holiday in the new ten-region global government, Cat was on her feet and walking. She had a limp and was using a cane that Lorenzo had picked up on one of his many trips around the world. I found the cane in the closet, and it was pretty obvious that it had been hand-carved somewhere. It was a bit tall for Cat, but I sawed a few inches off the end, and it worked perfectly for her.

The first real snows had hit the mountains around us, which would make traveling even more difficult, but we had to do something. The house was still above freezing, but just barely. The sky was covered in thick, gray clouds day after day. There was no chance of things warming up for months, and even though we had blankets and winter clothes, it was getting harder and harder to stay warm.

We weren't the only ones migrating in hopes of finding warmer weather. The North American Regional Administrator was setting up aid camps in Texas, New Mexico, and along the gulf coast. In the online forums I monitored daily, the only places left for new believers who had missed the Rapture, the consensus was that these new camps would be the only places getting food in the very near future. I was glad that we weren't in a highly populated area that would be a target of the Chinese—yes the fighting between isolated groups continued despite the stalemate between the two former superpowers—but the downside was the scarcity of food. Lorenzo had done well financially, and the government-controlled bank had converted his savings into digital dollars, but hyperinflation was running wild. And the truth was, money or not, you couldn't buy what wasn't available.

I had managed to get a couple of five-gallon fuel cans and filled them up with gas. But unless we could find more supplies and something valuable enough to trade with, we could only get four or five hundred miles in the van. The aid camps were at least twenty-five hundred miles away, assuming the roads weren't destroyed or blocked by snow. It would be a difficult journey, but staying where we were wasn't an option.

"Glad we're driving," Cat said as she settled into the van. "Never thought I would say that."

"Do you ever wish you were still in the wilderness?" I asked her.

"No," she said, but there was a note of sadness in her voice. "I miss it. But I'd already be dead if it weren't for you, Hank. The world has changed and..."

"And..." I prompted her.

"And you're not so bad to be around," she said.

"Hey, I'll take that," I replied. "Not so bad, kind of has a nice ring to it."

I would say and do anything to make her smile. She favored me with one as we backed out of Lorenzo's driveway. I couldn't imagine owing anyone a greater debt than I owed Lorenzo Maltza. He had helped me through a radical paradigm shift into knowledge of the supernatural world we lived in, rescued me from demon possession, led me to faith in Jesus, and left me with life-saving supplies, shelter, and a purpose for enduring as long as I could in the tribulation period. But as I backed the van loaded with supplies out of the driveway, I couldn't help feeling sad about leaving his home. Maybe it would shelter someone else, I thought.

"You okay?" Cat asked.

"Yeah, just a little sad about leaving," I admitted. "The kindest man I ever knew lived in that home. And even though he's been gone for months, he's still taking care of me."

Cat didn't reply. Instead, she reached over and put her hand on my shoulder. It felt good, and I put the van in gear and drove away.

When I say the van was loaded down, I mean that literally. From the outside it just looked like an old cargo van. But behind the two front seats there was room for an insulated, inflatable sleep pad. I rigged shelves above so that we could stow as much gear as possible, from tents and extra sleeping bags, to the extra fuel and the weapons to defend ourselves. I kept the Beretta 9 mm pistol in the center console between my seat and Cat's. It was easy to reach at a moment's notice, and I planned to keep it on my person at all times. The rifle was tucked into a sleeve that was tapped to the back of Cat's seat. I could reach over and pull it free without leaving the driver's seat. And I had taken a laundry list of items that I thought might be valuable enough to trade. There were old coins that had been part of Lorenzo's collection of artifacts. They were made from silver and gold, which was becoming increasingly valuable as a trade good. In the back of Lorenzo's closet I also found an old shotgun and several boxes of shells. It was a hunting rifle, not a tactical weapon–single-shot breech loader that had to be reloaded after each shot. I knew the weapon was pretty useless for self defense, but it was a great weapon for killing birds and small game. I also got a collection of ritual daggers. They gave me the creeps, but they might be worth a tank full of gas somewhere down the line. I had books, several pairs of prescription glasses, and some well-used, but still rugged boots. It seemed to me that Lorenzo must have bought a new pair on every excursion he took. So I had a dozen pairs of decent boots that would be good for trading, along with extra coats and a well-stocked sewing kit that had once belonged to Lorenzo's wife. I even packed cooking utensils, frying pans, pots, silverware, kitchen knives, and meat forks.

We kept all the food for ourselves and hid it in various places inside the van. I had no doubts that at some point we would meet desperate people who might try to rob us. It was no different than dividing your cash into different pockets just in case you got mugged walking through the city at night. But we did collect a large box of spices. We had salt and pepper in large containers, thanks to Lorenzo's preference for buying things in bulk from the local Costco. There also baking powder and baking soda, along with yeast and a big bag of sugar. But maybe the most valuable thing in our collection of trade goods were two old coffee pots, extra filters, and some large cans of ground coffee. In my mind, people would probably be willing to trade quite a bit in exchange for something that reminded them of how life used to be.

We took the side roads from Spokane and headed south on Highway 195. It didn't take us long to see groups of people. Some walked right down the middle of the road, armed and menacing. We gave them space, thanks to a pair of good binoculars that we had found among Lorenzo's expedition supplies. In addition to my phone and the laptop computer, which we could charge using the van's power outlets, we had an atlas of the United States. It was old and well-used, with out-of-the-way sites marked on it, like the serpent mound in Ohio and the best route to Roswell, New Mexico. Cat was an excellent navigator, and we drove for nearly six hours before making a stop at Le Grande, Oregon, where we were able to buy fuel and, to our pleasant surprise, a bag of corn chips and a can of bean dip. They were generic, of course, and cost over four hundred dollars, but they made for a perfect road trip snack. We washed them down with warm soda that we had taken from Lorenzo's pantry.

That night we stayed in the van, which was parked off the road with a stand of evergreens between us and any people passing that way. The temperature got down into the teens according to Lorenzo's old mercury thermometer, and that was inside the van. Fortunately, we each had sleeping bags rated to ten degrees below zero. We zipped the two of them together to make one big bag that we both squirmed into. We slept that way, combining body heat inside the sleeping bags to stay warm. But by morning we were both grateful to get the van started and the heat blasting on high.

We skirted Boise, turning south on the side roads and hitting the high desert. Eventually we ran into I-80 and headed east toward Salt Lake City. It had been hit hard by Chinese bombardment, although not nuclear. Still, it was a wasteland, and the suburbs were battlezones. So we moved as quickly as possible through the outskirts and only got shot at a few times. Fortunately none of the shots hit the van or us. We spent the night in Salina, where we managed to trade for fuel. Ten gallons cost us a pair of boots and a box of shotgun shells, which the gas station owner immediately loaded into a short-barreled, semi-automatic tactical shotgun. He then used a manual hand pump to get the fuel out of the tanks. There was no electricity to run the place, and he was friendly once we had traded goods.

After another frigid night, we reached Albuquerque, but found that it was in the throws of active fighting. The Chinese had set up a base at the regional airport and were using it to launch bombing raids. The reserve military forces, along with several militia groups, were busy harrying the enemy, but the Chinese had set up strong defenses. Unfortunately, the town around the airport had been devastated by the fighting. The military didn't need roads for their tanks or humvees, but the old van needed a good, flat surface to run on. So we were forced to double back and go around the city. At Las Cruces we turned northeast, driving past the White Sands Missile Range, and then Holloman Air Force Base. I had spent three months there during my time in the service, but didn't remember much about it. When we drove past there was nothing but debris and craters. It looked like a scene from a post-apocalyptic movie.

Eventually we reached Roswell and spent the night behind a little restaurant with a pair of green aliens on the billboard. They were shot full of bullet holes, and the cinderblock building was clearly burnt out, but it made a good place to hide the van. At least we thought so, until a group of locals showed up sometime around midnight.

CHAPTER 20

WE WERE ALL TEENAGERS ONCE. That's what I told myself after the incident behind the alien diner. Cat and I were trying to sleep. We had made a small fire in a barrel behind the restaurant as the sun went down. We kept the flames low and heated some water for a meal of chili-mac made from emergency rations. It was bland and pasty, but hot food in your stomach is a luxury that we often take for granted. After eating we made sure the fire was out. It was cold in Roswell a day or two before New Year's. To be honest, the days had sort of run together.

So, we went to bed early and planned to be up early. Not because it was easier to travel in daylight so much as it was difficult to sleep very long in the cramped sleeping bag. It always felt good to stretch out after a long day of slow travel and constant worry. I would lay on my back, my right hip crammed against the wheel well and our supplies. Cat would lay on her side next to me, her head on my chest, her wounded leg on top so that the pressure wouldn't make the pain worse.

We were long out of Vicodin by that point and nearly out of ibuprofen, but each night I convinced her to take a couple. She needed the rest; it was the best time for healing. And even though the wound itself had closed up, it was still painful, with plenty of deeper healing needing to take place. The muscles around the wound often cramped at night and spasmed, making sleep for both of us difficult. I could complain, but it was that light sleep and uncomfortable conditions that saved our lives.

We heard the locals coming. They didn't know we were behind the building and went inside to get out of the cold. I heard them laughing and yelling. By the time I untangled myself from Cat and the sleeping bag, they had decided to bring in the barrel we had built a fire in. They probably had the same idea. I was kneeling behind the driver's seat, getting my pistol, when they saw the van.

A wild animal backed into a corner is deadly, but so is one on the verge of starvation. There were six boys and three girls. They were all dirty, their faces drawn and dark from sleepless nights, lack of food, and probably drug use. They all had weapons, hammers and long wrenches mostly, just things to batter another person with. When they saw us parked behind the diner they knew instantly that we were travelers. It didn't matter what we had; it was more than they had. And like wild animals they rushed the van.

"Cat!" I said. "Take this!"

She was only half-awake, but took the pistol in both hands. I had just enough time to pull the AR-15 free from its sheath and draw back the charging handle that pushed a bullet from the magazine and into the breech when the back doors of the van were wrenched open. The metal groaned, the locking mechanism only holding for a few seconds. One of the locals had a crowbar as his weapon, and he used it to get the van open.

"Stop or I'll shoot!" I shouted.

There was a moment when we realized what was happening. The locals heard my threat, but they were already committed. It wasn't fear that stopped them, but the shock from our gear. Not that they could make much out in the darkness, but they could see the racks of goods stowed to help us get down south. It probably seemed like a gold mine to them. I was on the verge of offering to give them some food if they would leave us alone, but I never got the chance.

The local with the crowbar was short and skinny. It wouldn't be until later that I saw his face was pockmarked from acne and that his cheeks still held baby fat despite the lack of food. If any of the locals was old enough to legally drink alcohol I would have been surprised. Most teenagers were taken in the Rapture. I hadn't heard of anyone under the age of sixteen that was still around. The locals in Roswell reminded me of Trip and Lisa, but their fate was completely different.

The guy with the crowbar raised his tool over his head, and I knew I couldn't hesitate. I pulled the trigger and waved the rifle from right to left, releasing a barrage of nine rounds. Four of the locals dropped under the bump stock's rapid firing. There were screams, and another kid with a big, ugly knife rushed forward. I shot him in the chest. Every movement was instinctual. I wasn't thinking anything through, just reacting to what I saw. Five dead locals, four left standing, two on either side of the van. They smashed out the driver's side window and battered the old van's body with their weapons. I jumped out the rear of the van, turning so that I was moving backward away from our vehicle.

"Get away from there!" I snarled.

There were only two girls left. One shrieked with rage as she ran toward me. I wasn't sure what she was holding as a weapon, maybe the butt end of a pool cue. I shot her, watched the blood spray from her back as her feet flipped up and she fell hard onto the dirty concrete of the parking lot. The sound of her head hitting the ground was sickening, and I felt a matching jolt of shame.

The last boy, the same one who had broken the driver's window, got the door unlocked and pulled open. I shot him. The bullets hit his hip, probably shattering it. He fell to the ground screaming in pain. The last two locals ran away. My heart was pounding hard and fast.

"Hank!" Cat shouted.

"I'm here."

"Are you hurt?"

"No," I said, walking toward the wounded guy who had broken the van window.

"Who's screaming? What's happening?"

"It's over," I said, kicking the hammer that the local boy had used to shatter my window.

The hammer skittered across the ground. The boy, maybe nineteen if he was lucky, was writhing on the ground as blood pumped from the bullet wound in his hip. I knelt down beside him.

"Hey, kid, I'm sorry," I said.

"Help me! Help me!" he shouted.

"I can't," I told him honestly. "There's nothing I can do for you now. It's too late."

"N-n-no!" he whined, tears cutting trails across his dirty face. "You have to help me."

"All I can do is help you find forgiveness in Jesus," I said. "He loves you. It doesn't matter what you've done. He'll forgive you if you call out to him. Would you like that?"

That's when the local with a slug of hot lead inside his body, and a shattered hip, opened his eyes wide, staring right at me, and spit in my face.

"Go to hell!" he screamed. "You just killed me. You just killed my friends."

"Jesus still loves you," I said, wiping the spit from my face.

"He can..." the kid was panting for air, his voice growing weaker with each word he uttered, "go...to hell...too."

"You don't mean that," I said.

"...all...your...fault," he said. They were his last words.

I felt sick and had to turn away. My stomach heaved, and I hunched over my knees, nearly dropping the rifle. I spit the foulness away and stood up straight, stretching my aching back. The girl came at me from behind. Her weapon was an aluminum softball bat. It hit me on the shoulder, and I dropped to the ground.

She bellowed in victory, raising the bat high with the intent of bashing in my skull. I had just enough time to roll onto my back. Every cell in my body was screaming with pain, and there were sparks in my vision, as if the stars above were dancing around the wild-eyed girl with the bat. She chopped down with her weapon, and I instinctively rolled to the side. The metal bat made a pinging sound as it hit the concrete. Unfazed by her miss, she raised the bat again. I still had the rifle in my hands, but didn't want to kill her. I never wanted to hurt anyone, much less kill them. Instead of shooting I kicked her. My hiking boot slammed into her knee. It bent inward at a sideways angle it wasn't meant to move. She screamed, the bat fell out of her hands, and she toppled sideways. I rolled to my knees, tried to get up by putting my hand on the ground, but before I could do more the pain in my shoulder flared so hot that I nearly passed out.

"Hank!" Cat was shouting.

"Stay in the van!" I bellowed.

It felt good to yell and release some of the pain I was feeling. I didn't know if a bone was broken, or if something was out of its joint, but my shoulder really, really hurt. I had to lean toward the opposite side and slowly got to my feet. Holding the rifle with my left hand hurt, and I couldn't lift it, but I didn't drop it either. With my right hand I steadied myself, then took control of the rifle. It was light enough to shoot with one hand, but the bump stock wouldn't work right. I didn't want to shoot anyone or anything ever again, but I feared I might have to.

The girl with the bat had crawled over and had the weapon in hand again. There was little I could do for her. Instead, I staggered past her and leaned against the van.

"You okay?" I asked Cat.

She was up, squatting on her good leg, the other stretched

out in front of her, with her back against the driver's seat. She held the pistol in both hands, her arms extended away from her body, the weapon pointing out the back side of the van. I could see it trembling.

"I'm not hurt," she said, "but there's glass everywhere."

"Yeah, I know," I said, setting the rifle down on the console and passenger seat while I swept the glass out of the driver's seat.

The shards bit into my hand, but I didn't care. I needed to get away from the carnage before someone else came along and finished the job.

"We've got to go," I told Cat. "Get the keys."

"Okay," she replied.

I stepped over the body of the dead kid who cursed me and got the van doors closed. They would never lock again, but they were secure enough for driving, which in that moment seemed like a miracle. I looked at the bodies. I had killed six people. The knowledge of that fact seemed to burn into my soul like a cattle brand. I was a murderer. You may think differently, but that's how I felt. Our enemy isn't called the accuser for nothing. And at that moment I couldn't help but believe that I was a murderer. Sure, it could be argued that I was acting in self defense, but let's not kid ourselves. There had been six living people, and in a matter of seconds I had slaughtered them. They were gone, and no one could ever bring them back.

Those were the thoughts that settled in that night as I lumbered back to the driver's side of the van, dropped into the seat and got the vehicle started. The cold night air was bitter, the gloom around us seemed vastly deep, and yet I felt the presence of something sinister lurking on my shoulder. I couldn't escape it.

Cat, fully awake, took our atlas and ripped the cardboard covers off it. She taped it together with a roll of duct tape, and after forcing me to pull over, taped it to the outside of the driver's door window. She used more tape to fill in the gaps. It wasn't perfect, but it kept the cold air out. We cranked the heat and drove until dawn, but I couldn't stop shaking. Nor could I stop reliving the events of that night. They would haunt me for a long, long time.

CHAPTER 21

BY DAWN I WAS SPENT. And not just physically, but emotionally. We stopped at Carlsbad National Park, which is due south of Roswell. I hadn't even known what direction we were driving in. The nights were cold, and the weak sunlight filtering through the dust and ash kicked up into the atmosphere from the war didn't warm things much.

We pulled into a parking lot for the park and tried to rest, but my guilt weighed heavily on my mind. Cat checked my shoulder, her strong fingers working carefully over the bones in it. It hurt, but not so much that I cried out or felt faint.

"I don't think anything's broken," she said.

"It was a hollow core bat," I confessed. "It probably didn't break anything. Hurts though."

"I'm just glad it isn't dislocated," Cat said. "That would have been really bad."

"If something like that happens you need to drop me off

and keep going," I told her. "Don't saddle yourself with me if I can't pull my own weight."

"Sure, whatever. I'll just dump you on the side of the road and ride off into the sunset."

"I'm serious."

"So am I, you dope. We're in this together."

I can't say what changed for Cat. She had been on her own for a long time, living off-grid, just wandering in the mountains. Maybe it was the war or getting shot, but she seemed pretty committed to me. At that moment in time I couldn't think of a good reason why. I won't bore you with my self pity, but I was at the lowest of lows after the attack in Roswell. Knowing that I had killed to defend us had driven a toxic thorn deep into my soul.

In my mind I did my best to defend my actions, yet there was a part of me that thought it would have been better to let the gang in Roswell live. After all, I knew where I was headed when I died. I can't be as sure about Cat, she hasn't settled things in her heart yet, but I didn't feel like my life was worth more than those six young people in the diner parking lot. Of course I thought of Lorenzo's work, of the people he could still reach as long as I kept his videos online. Maybe that work was worth more than six lives. And from the response of the one guy I tried to help, their eternal fate was already settled. That guy had wanted nothing to do with Jesus or forgiveness. I knew there were a lot of people in the world who felt the same way. They saw Christianity as simply an oppressive religion, not a genuine connection to Almighty God. So, maybe it was their time to die, who was I to say? Only none of those rationalizations alleviated the guilt and shame that were threatening to smother me.

At noon we went looking for fuel, but found none. I was forced to finally use the ten gallons of gas we had been carrying from Spokane. We drove for a couple of hours after that and caught up to a caravan of people heading east at Pecos, Texas. The government aid camp was being set up just outside Abilene, which would be a half-day's drive, if we could find enough fuel along the way.

The caravan was mostly people on foot, although there were a few vehicles too. People in tents, with wagons and wheelbarrows full of supplies. There was no one person in charge of the caravan. They were all regular people headed for the same place, who were sticking together for safety.

"Looks like you've had some trouble," a man named Rob Kiner said as he looked at our van.

"A little," I admitted, hoping he couldn't tell that I was a killer just by looking at me.

"Where you from?"

"Spokane," I replied.

"Washington?" he asked. "Man, that's a hell of a trek."

"We got lucky," I admitted. "Found a few places still willing to trade for fuel."

"Well, hopefully we'll be in the Abilene camp tomorrow. At least we'll have food and safety."

"That sounds pretty good," I said.

There wasn't a lot of fuel for fires. Someone made a run to a nearby ranch house that was abandoned and brought back enough furniture and wood that could be burned. Not everyone in the caravan had food. We shared a little of our supplies, mostly the canned goods. People were happy for whatever they could get: beans, soup, peas and carrots.

As the group hung out by the fire, a few people told stories, and others crowded around computer and tablet screens for news. Our laptop was fully charged. That was one of the good things about the van. We were able to keep the electronics juiced up, and Starlink satellites bathed the planet in free Wi-Fi. It was one of those strange circumstances that made me feel like God was at work. Under different conditions we wouldn't know what was happening a few blocks away, much less in other states and other countries.

The evening newscast by the various agencies had become the most highly watched programming. People still needed stories and an escape from the horror and stress of the tribulation, but it was the news they craved. We watched as the death toll ticked up. And there were stories of wild animals attacking people, some of it caught on video. Packs of wild dogs had become commonplace in the larger towns. And most predators were getting a taste for human flesh. We had become the easiest food source as bodies were left to rot by military battles and fighting between people all over the US.

There were scenes from the celebrations in Babylon. The week-long Peace Festival was in full swing, and there were videos of people partying in the streets. It made Mardi Gras look like a preschool party.

"Bastards," an old man with a gash on his forehead that had been covered with a piece of dirty duct tape said. "We're starving, and they're living like they haven't got a care in the world."

"Now we see how the rest of the world felt about America," a younger woman said. She had on tattered sandals and a dirty sweatshirt that said *UNLV* across the front.

"Connie, we don't need your woke diatribe," the old man said. "Not again."

"I'm just saying the shoe's on the other foot now," she grumbled.

I didn't say anything. It was hard not to see the wild celebration for what it was–a complete embrace of carnality. The world had cast off all restraint.

"Have you heard the theory that the Bible predicted all of this?" Cat ventured.

I felt a shiver of fear run down my spine. We hadn't talked about sharing the hope of Jesus with the people of the caravan. And frankly, I was surprised that Cat would bring it up. She wasn't a fearful person, but she was usually pretty cautious about anything that might be dangerous.

"That's a load of crap," the woman named Connie said. "If there's one good outcome to this wretched disaster, it's that we're finally free of religion."

"Speak for yourself," an older woman in a long dress said. She had gray hair and wore glasses. "We could use a little charity and brotherly love right about now."

"I can't say I believe in that Bible thumping," the old man with the cut on his forehead said. "I've heard stuff like that all my life. The Bible says this, and the Bible says that. It's like every preacher had a different interpretation."

"More like they all had a different agenda," Connie complained. "The only thing they all agreed on was the need for your money."

I looked at Cat. Her eyes had gone back to the video on

the computer screen. The image had changed from close-ups of the celebration in the streets, to a view of the dazzling city at twilight. It glittered and gleamed in the last rays of the sun. Above it floated the circular ship that had once hovered over the EU building. I remembered seeing it on television in Lorenzo's house just after the Rapture.

That night as we settled into the van, I brought up the Bible app on my phone and read a passage to Cat:

"The coming of the lawless one is by the activity of Satan with all power and false signs and wonders, and with all wicked deception for those who are perishing, because they refused to love the truth and so be saved. Therefore God sends them a strong delusion, so that they may believe what is false, in order that all may be condemned who did not believe the truth but had pleasure in unrighteousness."

"Is that what you really believe?" Cat asked me.

"I do," I said. "I'm no expert, but I believe that the Vanishing was God taking the church, the true believers out of the world, before the judgment."

"And we're living through the judgment because we didn't believe in Jesus."

"That's right."

"So we're being punished."

"I think it's actually that we're suffering the consequences of our actions," I said. "Evil has been taken off the leash and is running rampant in the world."

"I don't know, Hank. I just want to feel safe again. I just want..."

She couldn't finish. I was holding her close and felt her body shaking with sobs. Soon I was crying too. We both cried ourselves to sleep that night. The world seemed out of sorts, and we felt ourselves getting lost in the reshuffling that was taking place. Not just the fall of the United States, but the new way of living on our ailing planet.

My mind kept going back to that passage in 2 Thessalonians, chapter two, specifically verse eleven: *"Therefore, God sends them a strong delusion..."* I had no doubt that the world was currently under that delusion. They believed the lies being fed to them by Paul Eon, by his Prophet, and the new world government. People didn't want to hear the truth. And it made me wonder about my own life up until that fateful day when I had found the body of a giant stuffed into an Air Force crate at Fairchild Air Base. Had I wanted to hear the truth? Probably not.

In the back of my mind a voice told me to look at my life. Has believing in God really made things any better? I hadn't been saved. I was worse off than ever before. And I wasn't a better person either. I was a killer, a murderer, no better than a convicted felon. It didn't matter that those locals in Roswell were going to steal from us, and probably worse. Maybe they would have killed us, but I didn't give them the chance. Maybe all they wanted was something to eat. How could God use me when I didn't feed the needy...instead I murdered the innocent.

Like I said, it was a dark time for me. The only spark of hope left was knowing that Lorenzo had told me many times that God can and will forgive us, no matter what. I clung to that hope with every ounce of my strength and prayed that I wasn't wrong about everything.

CHAPTER 22

THE NEXT MORNING Cat and I loaded the top of the van with belongings from several people. It wasn't required of us to help, but we were glad to be able to do something. We rearranged our gear in the back, including the inflatable sleeping pad, so that there was room for four more people to squeeze in. Interstate 20 was the best route to Abilene, although we had to go slow to let the people on foot keep pace. If fuel had been more plentiful we might have gone back and forth, ferrying people. As it was, we had to drive around potholes, craters, and abandoned cars. We spent as much time driving on the shoulder and even on the weedy median between the lanes of the interstate as we did on the road.

What should have taken a few hours, took all day, from dawn until after dark. We didn't actually reach the aid camp that evening, but Abilene was in sight. Like most large towns, it had come under fire. But, if the rumors were true, there were still city services available, which meant clean water and electricity. It had been nearly a week since my last bath, and I was past due.

The wind kicked up that night. People didn't congregate outside. Our van was used as a windbreak by several people as the temperatures dropped pretty low. It was miserable and I felt guilty inside the van when there were so many needy people with little more than a dirty blanket or a bit of old tarp to shelter them from the elements. Sleep was hard to come by. I just couldn't let go of my guilt. It felt like it was physically bumping my shoulder. My eyes burned with fatigue, but when I dozed I dreamed of the fight in Roswell. I saw the blood, heard the screaming, and felt something prod me back to consciousness. I was so tired that I felt like I was getting sick, but I wasn't asleep when the shooting started.

"What's that?" Cat said, sitting upright.

"Gunfire," I said. "Pretty close too."

Scrambling from the sleeping bag I pulled out the AR-15 and checked the magazine. Reloading it had seemed obscene to me, but I had forced myself to do it. Maybe it was the Air Force training–although I hadn't been in a combat career track and couldn't remember a lot from basic training, I still understood the importance of being prepared. The only thing worse in my mind than reliving the fight was thinking of what could have happened had I not been prepared.

Cat unzipped her side of the sleeping bag and picked up the pistol.

"What should we do?" she asked.

"Don't know," I said. "But I don't want to stay here."

We both got out the back of the van and joined a crew of other people from the caravan. Rob was there. He didn't have a firearm, but he had a walking stick and a pretty big bowie knife in his belt.

"Can anyone see them?" Rob asked.

"There were flashes out that way," a man with a scraggly beard said, pointing.

I wasn't sure if the caravan was filled with older people, or if the hardships of the Tribulation had simply aged us all. I was only twenty-seven years old, yet I felt much older. Maybe it was the lack of sleep or the constant worry, but my nerves were on edge and my body was stiff.

"Have you got ammo in that thing?" Rob asked me.

"Yeah, thirty rounds in this mag. Another in my belt," I told him.

"That's music to my ears, bro. All we've got are a few hunting rifles between the rest of us. Have you had to use it?"

I felt shame flood my mind. I nodded, not sure if he would see me in the darkness.

"Sorry to hear that," Rob continued. "It's a bitch out there. At least you were able to defend yourself. I've heard horror stories about those that couldn't. Seen the evidence of it too."

I didn't want to think about it. And fortunately, a group of men came rushing into our camp, so I didn't have time to dwell more on the past.

"Who's in charge here!" one of the men asked. They were all armed with weapons. There wasn't much light in the caravan camp, but the newcomers had fluorescent emergency lights and flashlights mounted on their weapons.

"Cover me," Rob whispered to me, and then he stepped out from behind the Ford Explorer we were crouched behind. "That'd be me."

"Tell me you've got some people here with guns," the newcomer barked.

"A few," Rob admitted. "Who are you?"

"Security, from the NAR Camp at Abilene. My name's Smith. We're here to help, but you're too damn close to the city. There's a group of outlaws on their way here right now."

"What should we do?" Rob asked.

"Can you get everyone into these vehicles?"

"No," Rob admitted.

"Well then, it's best if you take cover and get ready for a fight. My guys are marked with green. Don't shoot us. We'll help you."

Rob turned around. "Get everyone who doesn't have a firearm back," he ordered.

To my surprise, Cat spoke up. "Join me on the other side of our van," she called out.

People didn't have to be told twice. We were parked near an old pickup truck, and there was an abandoned car just a few yards away too. People hunched down behind the vehicles, hoping that the rest of the caravan could hold off whoever was coming. I strained my eyes, but the wind was blowing sand into our faces, and it was too dark to see.

Rob returned to my side. I could tell he was scared. It was a terrible thing to be in a fight without a decent weapon. I silently thanked God for my rifle and asked for His help against whatever was coming our way. A few minutes went by. I was kneeling by the rear of the Explorer, the rifle against my shoulder and the barrel held against the SUV's back fender panel for support. The security man named Smith fired a flare into the night sky. It shot up in a streak of red sparks, then flared bright, throwing light down onto the caravan and beyond. The outlaws from Abilene were caught out in the open, but it wasn't their first battle. They immediately dropped onto the ground and started shooting.

I pulled back as bullets cracked around me. Some hit the ground, others punching into the vehicles. The loudest were those that flew past me, the tiny sonic booms sounding like little claps of thunder. The security forces shot back. I took a chance, leaned out, and fired at a person on the ground. I saw the muzzle flash from the attacker's weapon, honed in, and put a round as close to it as possible. It was impossible to see if I had hit my target, and after firing I immediately pulled back. Several shots pinged into the Explorer in retaliation, but when I leaned back out the figure I had aimed at wasn't shooting any more. I found another target and fired. The AR-15 was a semi-automatic weapon. The bump stock worked only when the shooter kept the trigger pressed down, so I was able to fire individual shots and conserve my ammo. I had fired on three different figures when a whistle sounded. It was an umpire's whistle that clearly signaled the outlaws to charge. They came rushing into our camp, firing their weapons. All I could do was hold my position behind the SUV's rear tire. Rob was right behind me, crowding close. It felt good not to be alone, but I was silently praying no one got close enough to us that we had to use his stick to fight them off.

There was a lot of shouting. I stuck the rifle out and fired off a few rounds completely blind. Someone ran into the Ford Explorer we were using for cover. The outlaw had the same idea. I dropped down low, brought my rifle toward the feet that were nothing but darker shadows amid the unsteady light from the flare above, and fired. The person on the other side of the SUV screamed. It was a woman, and I felt a stab of shame as she dropped to the ground.

I can't say what drove me out from behind the SUV after that. Hearing a woman screaming in pain may have hit on some primal instinct, or maybe it was the shame. Part of me hoped that I would die. It just felt so wrong. Why were we fighting? I couldn't make sense of anything, yet I wanted it to end, one way or another. So I ran out.

"Hank!" Rob yelled from behind me. I ignored him.

A big man in hunting camo was running toward our SUV. We raised our weapons at the same time. I was moving side-ways when the shooting started. How I hit my target when he missed is another mystery. Perhaps God was protecting me–I can't say. But he went down, only to be replaced by three more intruders in dark clothing. I didn't see the fluorescent light from the glow sticks, so I let go of a ten-round burst from the AR-15. The bump stock did its job and I took down all three men before they could return fire.

I was moving to my right and shooting toward my left. Out of the shadows a woman in some type of armor leaped up at me. She had a pistol and fired but missed. The bullet flew past my ear as I swiveled toward her and returned fire. Two shots took her down. She didn't cry out like the woman whose foot I had wounded. But I saw her face implode from the gunshot that hit her. The second bullet hit her neck and nearly decapi-tated her.

"Fall back! Fall back!" someone screamed.

I saw figures running away as I dropped to my knees. There was more shooting, probably from the security force. I bent over and threw up. The urge to put the rifle under my own chin and fire it was incredibly strong. I was crying and spitting bile from my mouth when I felt Rob's hand on my shoulder.

"It's over!" he said. "It's over, Hank. You did good, man. Outstanding."

I wanted to tell him how wrong he was, but I couldn't speak.

"You okay, man?" Rob asked.

I nodded. He squeezed my shoulder and went off to help the others. When I turned around someone from the security team was hunched over the wailing woman I had wounded. The flare above us was fluttering out.

"Alright, excellent work," Smith called out. "Bravo team, do a sweep. Alpha and Charlie teams, stay on alert status. This might not be over people. Carnes, tell me you've got eyes on those bastards."

"Running scared, LT," someone replied. "Looks like we got about half of 'em."

I didn't move from where I was kneeling. The security team began to move. Bodies were checked. Only two of the attackers had survived. I tried telling myself that I was defending the innocent, but deep down the voice of the accuser continued to torment me.

"Looks like your van is out of commission," Ron said. "All the vehicles took fire. We're walking the rest of the way to the camp."

"How far is that?" I asked, wearily getting to my feet and automatically swapping out the half-empty magazine for the fresh one in the back pocket of my jeans.

"The security guy, Smith, said it's about four miles. So probably two hours, maybe more. They're going to escort us if we can get moving quick enough."

He hurried off to tell someone else what was happening while I went to the van. Cat was waiting for me there, still holding the Beretta 9 mm.

"What is it?" she asked. "Is it over?"

"Yeah," I told her. "We beat them off, but we can't stay here. Gotta head to the government camp tonight."

"That's okay," Cat said. "None of us would be able to sleep after that."

We looked at the van. The passenger window was shattered, and there were four bullet holes in the windshield. Worst of all, liquid was dripping from the engine, and I could just make out a puddle underneath. The old, reliable cargo van had gotten us as far as it could. We opened the back. One of the cans of coffee had been hit. The precious coffee was scattered over everything else.

We salvaged what we could. There wasn't much food left, but it fit into my duffle. We got all the bullets for our weapons and one coffee pot that had avoided damage in the fight. We stuffed the extra coats and blankets into my old rucksack, along with two wool blankets and our sleeping bag. The inflatable pad had been hit with some shrapnel and ruined, so we left it behind. From Lorenzo's expeditions we took the old coins and the ancient sacrificial knives. Then we joined the rest of the caravan on the long walk to the NAR aid camp, hoping to find relief, but there was none to be found.

CHAPTER 23

WE MANAGED to reach the camp before dawn. Our entire group was told to sit down on the ground and wait while the aid workers checked us in. A man with a clipboard or pad of some sort came along and took our names.

"I'm Henry Downes," I said, handing over my driver's license.

"And you?" the man asked Cat.

"Mira Jones," she replied.

"ID?"

"Don't have it," she said.

"Great! Another one," the man said. He was clearly annoyed. We didn't say anything until he was out of earshot.

"What do you think that's about?" Cat asked.

"He's a bureaucrat," I said. "They're supposed to be rude. It's in the job description."

By the time the sun was up they had taken everyone's

name and ID. A group of workers had even begun calling out names. Mine was the first.

"Airman, Downes," a heavy-set man with a thick mustache called. "Henry, AKA Hank."

"That's me," I said, waving a hand and getting slowly to my feet.

The big man waved me over.

"Let's go," I told Cat.

"They didn't call my name," she replied.

"But we're together," I said. "We're staying together."

Cat nodded and got to her feet. Our gear was heavy, and I was tired. I couldn't imagine how the people in the caravan without vehicles had made it so far. There were people from all over the southwest, although we were from the farthest away. Cat followed me to the group.

"You Downes?" the mustached man asked.

"Yes, sir," I said.

"You did eight years in the Air Force?" he asked, looking at my rifle. "That right?"

"Yes, sir," I replied. "Logistics."

"We don't need that. We need security. You're being recalled to active duty by the North American Regional Defense Force."

I must have looked dumbfounded. My entire body went numb. Maybe I should have expected to get roped into the military–there was a war on for crying out loud–but I was still completely shocked.

"Don't look so surprised, Airman," the mustached man said. "You know you're eligible for recall to active service in the case of a national emergency. Well, this is it. We need every able-bodied man and woman to help us. This camp already has over two thousand refugees. We're expecting that number to quadruple in the next few weeks, and when spring hits, we'll probably triple that number again."

"Sir, yes, sir," I managed to say.

"At least your service earns you a tier two pass in the camp. That's a heated tent and three squares a day, Airman. Tell me it was better for you before you arrived."

I couldn't. I had spent the last two months either scraping and clawing for anything of value in Spokane or slowly freezing in the old van. My mouth watered at the idea of three hot meals a day—I couldn't deny it.

"Leave your weapons here. They'll be logged into the armory," the mustached man said. "Do you have anything that might be used as a weapon in that gear you're carrying?"

"I've got some trade goods," I said. "Antique knives."

"That's a weapon. Leave them. We'll log it and hold it in the armory until this mess is all over. Follow me, Airman. We've got a lot to do this morning."

"Sir, my..." I wasn't sure what to call Cat, so I just blurted the only thing I could think that might get her into the camp with me. "Wife."

The big man turned back around and looked at Cat.

"Do you have proof of nuptials prior to the Vanishing, Airman Downes?"

"No sir, just my word," I said.

He looked at Cat. "Where were you married?"

"In Washington state, sir," I began, but he waved me off.

"I'm asking her," he demanded.

"He's right. We had a Native American binding ceremony," she said without missing a beat. "We walked the path and got a blessing from the tribal elders."

To my knowledge Cat wasn't Native American, although I knew she had spent time with people from various tribes who taught primitive subsistence skills.

The fat man's eyes narrowed. "You're tribal?"

"Kalispell," she replied. "People of the Oreille."

She pronounced the last word like "O'Ray," referring to the Pend Oreille river and lake that flows through Washington, Idaho, and Montana.

"A native marriage," the fat man said, "will be hard to authenticate."

"I have no idea what the tribal records are like now," Cat said. "But he's my husband, in body and spirit."

"Fine, whatever," the fat man said. "You can share quarters, but don't expect any real privacy. And you'll both need to work."

"We can do that," I said quickly. "Thank you, sir."

"Don't thank me yet, Airman. Follow me."

I was never a good poker player and had trouble containing my smile as we followed the big man. He was clearly a high-ranking part of the camp's administration, and he certainly didn't believe that we were married. I didn't want to give it away by giggling like a child, so I forced myself not to look at Cat. The woman was full of surprises.

We were taken to an official intake area. We signed forms, got camp IDs made, and were shown to a prefab building that was half open barracks and half tiny rooms for couples. The walls were thin plastic and only rose up six feet. A person could peek over the wall from one room to the next. It wasn't private, but it wasn't just an open barracks either. There was a lock on the door with a key code. Of course, a hard shove would break the little locking mechanism. The room wasn't safe, but it was ours.

Cat stayed there, getting our gear stowed away. I was issued combat fatigues and new boots, which I changed into, and the rest were hung in a storage locker that was the only real furniture in our room, other than the two camp beds which were pushed together. The best part of the housing unit was the heat. It blew from overhead vents, and while not very efficient, it did keep the temperature in the prefabricated building at around sixty-five degrees. The downside was sharing the latrines. Tier two personnel had access to our own shower house, which was a combination of open bathing areas and stalls, but there was usually a waiting line for privacy.

I was taken past a mess hall that served hot meals for tier one and two personnel. The people who worked at the camp got food served three times a day, while the refugees would get one cooked meal and dry rations. It was a relief to know that we wouldn't starve, but I had my misgivings about being part of the camp personnel. The war was still being fought, and if I had really been recalled to active duty, there was a better than even chance that I might get sent to fight the Chinese.

The first stop after the dormitory building was the security area. It was surrounded by a high fence with loops of razor wire around the top. There was a main entrance on one side, with a lobby for the refugees to speak to someone should a crime occur. There were four people already seated inside, waiting to speak to someone. The mustached man's name was Miller, and he was apparently an assistant to the camp's Special Administrator In Charge.

"Yo, Miller," a big black man said as we entered the admin section of the security building. "What 'cha got for us this morning?"

"Airman Henry Downes," the mustached man said. "Recalled to active status."

"Air-man, eh? We don't have too many planes around here. What'd you do, Downes? Wrench spinner? Desk jockey?"

"Logistics," I said. "I was an expert bean counter and cargo loader."

The big man barked out a loud, contagious laugh. I have to admit I liked him immediately. He stuck out a big hand, and I shook it.

"Welcome to the team, Downes. I like a man who knows what he's good at. How'd you get here?"

"This is where I leave you two," Miller said with a frown. "Try not to have too much fun."

"We are living in extraordinary times, my man. Better have fun while we can," the big black man said.

He had officer bars on his collar, and the name Barski was stenciled over his left shirt pocket. His sleeves were expertly rolled and ironed. But there was gray at his temples and a full belly pressed against the buttons of his fatigue shirt. I guessed he was former military, probably recalled just like me.

"I'm Major Lester Barski, but everyone calls me LB. We run a pretty loose ship 'round here, if you catch my drift. We're all military, but we've been around the block. Some of us more than once. You do your job, and we're good. You slack or take advantage of your rank, and I'll stick you with the maintenance crew scrubbing the shithouse. You get me, Downes?"

"Yes, sir," I said.

"Good. So you're a logistics man, which means you know military invoicing. That's good. We're in charge of protecting the incoming shipments of necessary materials. Food, meds, you name it we're supposed to get it, but the convoys are plumb targets. We need to get them in, unloaded, and out as quickly as possible. My security teams will watch the perimeter, and you can check in whatever we get."

"What system are you using?"

"Ain't using nothing," LB said. "The new government is still taking bids. I mean, what the hell is the world coming to? People can't eat. But the government is taking its own sweet time to give us what we need to do our job. I'm just glad I'm not regular duty any more. I can't imagine fighting the Chinese with combat knives and hunting rifles."

"Why would you do that?" I asked.

"Cause damn Congress sent everything to Ukraine," he said. "I know guys on the front lines don't even have bullets. They been told to get weapons from the Chinese they kill. Can you imagine that?"

I couldn't, although I remembered reading that Confederate soldiers would pick ammunition and gunpowder from the dead Union troops after their battles. I suppose it was a part of war, but like the major, I was glad not to be sent to the front and told to get my weapons from the dead Chinese fighters.

"Well, we shouldn't have to worry too much about that here. The civil defense force–that's us–got hold of some surplus military gear, including M-16 carbines. So we've got guns, just not a lot of ammunition. You'll be issued a sidearm, but only allowed to carry it when on duty. And I want you armed, Downes. Tell me you're not a pansy-ass pacifist."

"No, sir," I replied. "I came in with a Beretta 9 mm, and a custom AR-15."

"Well, now, you are a renaissance man, Downes. I'm starting to like you. All we got for logistics are yellow notepads. You can set up a database however you like. We're lousy with computers, but I never had much use for one. Let me show you to your kingdom."

There were two main buildings behind the security fence. One was part holding cells for criminals and part armory. All weapons had to be checked out, which meant writing your name on a clipboard. There was even a pencil hanging from a string that was taped to the back of the board. An old man was in the armory. He already had my custom rifle and pistol, along with the cans of ammunition. The .223 rounds were nearly used up, but there were still plenty of 9 mm bullets in the can.

"Arnie, this is Downes," LB said. "He's our new bean counter."

"Pleased to meet you," he said. "You the one who brought in these weapons?"

"Yes, sir," I said.

Arnie was wearing camouflage, but no one had stripes, so it was impossible to tell what their rank was.

"I'm Staff Sergeant O'Neal. Don't call me sir," the old man grumbled. "You take care of your weapons. That's good."

"The rifle was used last night," I said. "I haven't had a chance to clean it."

"Last night? You's with that outfit that got hit by the local mob?" LB asked.

"Yes, sir," I said.

"Alright then, you know the lay of the land. There's plenty of locals who don't like us. Plenty that want what we got. They haven't hit the camp yet, but it's only a matter of time."

"There weren't enough in the group that hit us to raid the camp," I said.

"No, Smith told me that. His report was thorough. But like I say, it's only a matter of time before these criminal groups band together and come at us hard. That's why I want you armed at all times when on duty."

"Yes, sir."

"Your Beretta's fine, but standard issue is the Colt .45," Arnie O'Neal said. "You can check out your own piece once I ensure it's kosher."

"Got it," I said.

"Sign the form."

The form had a list of names. Beside each entry was at least one weapon. I wrote down my name, then .45. Arnie gave me a pistol, a thigh holster that slid onto my belt and was secured around my leg, and two extra clips of ammunition that went into a holder that clipped onto the belt on my left side.

"She's locked and loaded, Downes," O'Neal said. "Keep your firearm safety in mind at all times."

I pulled the slide back on the .45 automatic. It wasn't as smooth as the Beretta, and the oil looked a little gummy. But I caught sight of the brass in the chamber and moved the slide back into place. The hammer was back, but the safety was on, so I pushed it into the holster and flipped the safety strap over the rear of the weapon.

"You're good to go," LB said. "Let me show you the warehouse."

That was the other building inside the secured area, with pallets scattered haphazardly around. Some were still wrapped up in plastic; others had been cut open.

"I don't have the manpower to police all this," LB said. "We don't let nobody in at night, but during the day the kitchen staff come and take what they need."

"No inventory?" I asked.

"Not yet," LB said. "That's going to be your job. I'm promoting you, Airman. How's Lieutenant Downes sound? Kind of rolls off the tongue. You're in charge out here. Get it all organized and let's keep tabs on everything. That something you can handle?"

"Yes, sir," I said. "It's what I do."

"I like a man who knows his business. You answer to me, and only me. We'll use whatever system you can put together on the fly. Try not to piss off the kitchen staff. I don't want 'em spitting in my chili, but at the same time, don't let them take more than they need. We can't afford for this to turn into a black market swap meet. You feel me?"

"Yes, sir," I said.

"Good man. Glad to have you on board."

"Good to be on board, sir."

"Great, let's get some chow. Then I'll introduce you around town."

CHAPTER 24

YOU MIGHT BE EXPECTING me to say how terrible
things were at Camp Abilene as we came to know the place.
But that all depended on which side you were on. The camp
was divided between the facilitators of the camp, and the
people they were tasked with helping. Cat saw the division
and the camp conditions close up. She was recruited by the
medical staff to help in the infirmary, which quickly came to
be the busiest section of Camp Abilene as a new virus swept
through, but I'll get to that in time.

First, you need to understand that while Cat and I
enjoyed a relatively warm room in a rigid structure, the
refugees–that's what we called the displaced people who
sought shelter at the camp–were in canvas tents. They were
wide, common areas with simple folding cots for bedding. The
whole facility was put together with century-old equipment.
Each of the refugee tents had a kerosene heater for the cold
nights. North Texas in winter was a cold place–we even got

some snow—and the wind never stopped blowing. At nights people huddled around the heaters in their tents, which were supposed to house up to twenty people, but in reality there were more than twice that number crammed into the tight spaces.

Where we on the facilitators' side of the camp had decent hygiene and ample food, the refugees fought a constant battle with hunger, unsanitary conditions, and unchecked aggression. There simply weren't enough people in Major Barski's security force to police the refugees. I was relieved to be given a logistical role instead of being forced to join one of the bands of armed soldiers who kept the gangs away from the camp. I saw those desperate people firsthand. The supply trucks rolled in on no given schedule, and anything that arrived after dark was especially vulnerable. The warehouse wasn't built for secure unloading of goods. Therefore, when the supplies were taken off the truck and before they were moved into the warehouse, it was a prime target for the hungry people of Abilene who resented that they were required to leave their homes if they wanted a share of the food, medicines, and clothing being handed out freely to the refugees. More than once I was driven down to my knees and forced to hide just inside the warehouse when shooting started at the loading platform.

As per my assignment, I had taken stock of everything in the warehouse. I don't brag about my ability to count things and keep tabs on them. The real skill is being able to do that work without succumbing to the mind-numbing boredom. I set up a database, regulated the goods, eliminated waste, and stopped the black market of illicit goods being stolen from the government. And it wasn't because I was patriotic toward the new North American Regional Administration, or NARA as we called it. My loyalty was to God and to Cat, but I was good at my job and did my best. In the evenings, when we weren't disturbed by an unexpected supply delivery, Cat would tell me what she was seeing in the camp.

"It's filthy," she often complained. "Too many people and no real way to deal with everything."

"They moved the latrines back, didn't they?"

"Yeah, but if you move them too far people won't use them. No one wants to walk five hundred yards in the freezing cold at night just to use the bathroom."

"Yeah," I said. "Makes sense."

"It's making people sick," Cat continued. "On top of everything else, there's just no way to stop the spread of germs. The infirmary is bursting at the seams."

I knew what she meant. The virus hit not long after we arrived. There was no real name for it. The doctor's called it Torvis IV, but most people called it Death Flu. There were a lot of rumors about it. Some people claimed it was from a biotech lab, others said it was biological warfare from the Chinese, but in all likelihood it was brought on by the unsanitary conditions in the west and exposure to the dead. I knew exactly what it was: the fourth seal judgment. The Bible says: "And I looked, and behold, a pale horse! And its rider's name was Death, and Hades followed him. And they were given authority over a fourth of the earth, to kill with sword and with famine and with pestilence and by wild beasts of the earth."

A fourth of the earth–that was nearly two billion people.

In what was left of the United States we saw a much higher death rate. After millions were killed in the nuclear bombardment that had wiped out the east and west coast, along with Denver, Phoenix, St. Louis, Chicago, and Atlanta, we were down to half the population. Then the radiation poisoning and ground fighting killed even more. There were bodies left out on the streets and in the fields. Birds, rats, coyotes, wild dogs, and feral cats feasted on the dead. They also spread disease. Camp Abilene was one of six government aid facilities in the former United States. There were more in Canada, which was being ravaged by the extreme winter brought on by the nuclear explosions kicking up dust and ash into the atmosphere that blocked the sunlight. And some facilities also in Mexico, which wasn't officially at war, but was a battleground for the cartels. They had no money and little in the way of drugs, but they had plenty of guns, so they fought one another and killed the innocent.

Death was everywhere and only growing worse with the Death Flu. The infirmary had medicines, but not a real cure. It started with flu symptoms but quickly morphed into a multi-phase attack on the human body. The lungs filled with fluid, the digestive system's overproduction of enzymes in essence destroyed itself, and finally the body began to hemorrhage, making it difficult if not impossible to stop the spread of the infected body fluids. Every day pits were dug outside the camp and bodies were burned, but there were rumors that the Death Flu spread in the smoke clouds. Everyone was afraid, even me. Yeah, I knew where I was going when I died, but the Death Flu seemed like a terrible way to die. And Cat was in the thick of it.

She didn't have medical training and was essentially a janitor in the infirmary. She wore a hazmat suit and helped remove the bodies of the dead. It was a soul-crushing job, but a necessary one. She understood her role, but hated it just the same. I could see her yearning for the wilderness, but we both knew that it wasn't safe outside of human settlements anymore. The wildlife had been pushed inland from the bombardment on the coasts and the destruction of their habitat. Bears, cougars, wolves, and even big cats from wildlife refuges and zoos roamed free and killed people on a regular basis. We had moved way down on the food chain, into the most preferred meal section.

The biggest issue near Camp Abilene was the dogs. Once domesticated pets, they had been turned out and forced to forage for whatever food they could find. And there was plenty of meat if one didn't mind feeding on human flesh. It didn't take the dogs long to get the lay of the land. They formed packs and not only devoured the dead, but they attacked the living. Snipers on towers at either end of the camp killed dogs on a regular basis. The sudden report of a rifle from the towers was so frequent it didn't even register to us most of the time. That was life at Camp Abilene.

No surprise, I didn't have a lot of time to put up videos during that winter. My laptop stayed in our little room, charged but unused. I had a work computer that I carried in a satchel with the camp's supply data. Every day I stopped at the armory and updated our ammunition supply. The kitchen workers quickly adapted to my logistics procedures for the victuals, and we couldn't keep a surplus of medical supplies. As soon as they arrived all medical supplies were delivered to the infirmary. We had an overflow of biomedical waste, which was also burned outside of camp. I'm sure you can imagine the scene. It was a bleak winter to begin with, the sky hazy with debris from the war even when there were no clouds. But more often than not a thick cloud cover hung over us, and the smoke from the fires that were kept burning to dispose of the biowaste and dead bodies billowed black. Worst of all, it was constantly damp, which meant the ground was muddy, and the stench from the latrines permeated the entire facility.

"Butts and guts," LB often said with a shake of his head. "That's all I know anymore."

I knew the feeling. My days were filled with numbers and invoices. The head administrator praised my efforts, but we all felt a sense of futility. We were keeping people alive with food and shelter, only to see them die from disease. Occasionally military troops came through the camp too. When they did, the staff worked hard to make sure they were all fed and had whatever they needed from our meager supplies. The stories they told made it abundantly clear that the United States of America, the country we had known and loved and perhaps taken for granted, was gone. Estimates of our population were down in the low tens of millions, a drop of almost ninety percent. Worse still, the radiated areas were growing. Water contamination was a major issue. And outside the NARA camps the survivors were few.

"Abilene, Hattiesburg in Mississippi, and Camp Le Grange between Houston and Austin are all that's left," a grizzled infantry sergeant told me.

He had come through with the remnants of an armored brigade that was down to two tanks and three armored personnel carriers. They were on their way north after a nasty battle with the cartels who were pushing north in search of supplies.

"It's a wasteland to the north, and there are wolves at the door," he continued. "Mexico wasn't hit with the nukes, but the famine was devastating. They're armed and desperate, if you know what I mean."

I was no soldier used to fighting, but I could imagine.

"So that's it then," I said. "What about the Chinese?"

"We mopped up most of them," he replied, talking with a mouth full of rice and beans that the kitchen staff had whipped up when the ragtag brigade was spotted heading north. "They just left their people here. After they wiped out most of the big cities, things got bad for them. You can't fight without supplies, and even though they set up camps around airfields, the planes stopped coming. I hear it's just as bad if not worse in Asia. But who the hell knows for sure."

That was Camp Abilene for the entire winter: a nasty, deadly, hopeless place on the edge of the American desert. Hope was fading fast, and I knew that things weren't going to get better, yet somehow we endured. I even made friends. The security forces were all former military or law enforcement. It wasn't so much a brotherhood in arms as it was a feeling that despite everything that was going on, we didn't have it all that bad. The administrators hid in their offices, and the medical personnel were overwhelmed, but our tasks were clear-cut and within our abilities to accomplish them. Added to that was the feeling that what we were doing was making a difference. Protection and provision work were things you could be proud of.

And while I wasn't posting many of Lorenzo's videos to the internet, I was heavily involved in an underground church. We met in the dormitory, usually at night. It wasn't unusual for people to congregate in groups. Ours was about fifteen strong, and while we didn't parade our Bibles around, we did find ways to study scripture and plan for what was coming. The fifth seal judgment was, without any doubt, persecution of believers. Some people called us Tribulation Saints, but that's a bit of a misnomer. We were more like Jesus Freaks, and it was abundantly clear from the global government, down to the camp administrators, that only one religion was sanctioned–Pax Divino. All others were forbidden...officially. But it wasn't yet a problem. In fact, the camp was a place where nothing was off-limits. Stealing was frowned upon, but no one could stop the strong from taking whatever they wanted from the weak. Sex was practiced openly despite the unsanitary conditions. And with so much death around us, people simply didn't want to do anything that would make people sadder, which included enforcement of the religious mandate handed down from the North American Regional Administration.

So we kept our activities on the down low and made plans for the day we knew was coming. Only, despite all that we had endured, no one was really ready for the fifth seal judgment, what became known as the Great Purge.

CHAPTER 25

"DR. PADMAL IS SICK," Cat told me one evening.

I was sitting down on my cot, scribbling out a passage of scripture from Lorenzo's Bible which I usually kept hidden, but her words got my attention. I looked up as she hung her coat in the storage locker.

"What?" I asked.

"He's the last one," she said. "But he got the fever spike today. That's all the doctors, Hank. They're all dying."

It was a difficult fact to accept. I admit I had gotten used to being a level two member of Camp Abilene's staff. We weren't living like kings, but compared to the refugees we had it easy. Even the work I was doing felt important, and I had begun to believe that what affected the refugees wouldn't touch us. But Cat's announcement shattered that myth.

"And it's only a matter of time," she said, sitting down next to me.

"Before they die?"

"Before we all die," she said, looking me right in the eyes. "Hank, I can't keep working in the infirmary and not get sick."

"You have so far," I pointed out.

"Yes, so far."

"You've got hazmat gear."

"So did the doctors."

"Well...I guess they were careless, but you aren't," I said.

You may think I'm crazy. How can I face an armed gunman and the virtual end of the world with calm, but then freak out over the possibility of Cat getting sick? The simple truth was that I loved her. And no one who got sick ever got better. Some lingered longer than others, but the Death Flu had a one hundred percent kill rate at Camp Abilene.

"Everyone is careful," she said. "We're too afraid not to be. But the equipment is wearing out. It wasn't meant to be used so much for so long."

"Then I'll get you more," I said. "I'll get you a new suit."

"How exactly are you going to do that?" she asked. "You complain all the time about how little is available and how irregular the deliveries of goods are. Do you have new hazmat suits?"

"No," I said.

There were a lot of things in my warehouse. That's how I thought of it, as my little kingdom. The other security personnel were glad to have someone in charge. I was the nerd who liked keeping up with supplies and materials. Since coming on board I had stopped the theft and gotten every-thing organized. Maybe it was just the way my mind worked, but I could usually remember everything we had, and how much. Medical supplies were hard to come by, and everything we got in went immediately to the infirmary that was filled with patients of the Death Flu.

"Okay then," she said calmly. "I'm going to tell you something and I don't want you to freak out."

"You're sick?" I asked, on the verge of doing exactly what she asked me not to do.

Cat shook her head. "No, I'm not sick. I feel fine. But I don't want to stay here, Hank. We can't stay. It's filthy. The refugee section is like a concentration camp."

"We're providing all we can," I argued.

At some point I had come to feel like I belonged there. Maybe it was the three warm meals a day, or the sense of camaraderie I felt with the other members of the security team. In the Air Force I had always been a loner, friendly but content to keep to myself. At Camp Abilene I had made friends. We were part of a group of Christians who depended on one another. And I had a rank of importance. Without even knowing it, I had started to identify with the staff of the facility. And, truth be told, the idea of leaving seemed absurd. Why on earth would I give up a warm, secure place to live and regular meals? I didn't want to go back out into the crumbling ruins of what had once been the greatest country in the world. I didn't want to see the dead bodies lying in the streets, or have to kill to keep what little I had managed to scrape together, never knowing what might come in the dark days ahead.

"There's some debate about that, but it doesn't matter," she said.

"It does matter," I said. "I know. I'm in charge of logistics, Cat. I know exactly how much we have."

"Do you know how many refugees we have?" she asked. "Do you know how many bodies were burned today?"

"No, look, I'm not saying that conditions are perfect, but it's better here than it was out on our own. You remember how that was. We were nearly killed, *you* were nearly killed. Remember?"

"Of course I remember," she said. "I'm just telling you how it is. Maybe you don't care, but I see people dying every day. I know what's coming. And I'd rather take my chances, Hank. It's been nice having food and a warm place to sleep, I won't deny that. But we can't hide from death here. Death is coming for everyone in the camp. Soon it'll be worse here than out there."

It was hard to believe, but I had to admit that I hadn't walked the camp in weeks. I didn't like going to the tent city. It was smelly and crowded. Spring was coming. And while no one would say it was getting warm, it was getting warmer. There were a couple of days when the temperature rose above freezing. That's when the sewage started to thaw and seep into the camp. I preferred the administrative section. It wasn't pristine, but it was a whole lot cleaner than the refugee section of the camp.

"We can't just leave," I said.

"Yes, we can," Cat said. "We don't owe these people anything."

"Yeah, okay, but we'll need supplies."

"I'm sure we can find what we need."

"Trust me, we can't," I told her.

"So we'll gather what we can here and take it with us."

"I'm not stealing," I said, knowing instantly how sanctimonious I sounded.

"I'm not telling you to," she replied, starting to get angry. "Look, I'm going. You can come with me, or stay. I won't force you to do anything you don't want to do."

"Of course I'm going with you," I said. "You're my wife after all."

It was a joke. We weren't really married. There had never been a ceremony on the Kalispell Indian Reservation. But we were living like a married couple. In fact, we were living more like normal people had before the Vanishing than at any point since I had known Cat. We got up in the morning, went to our jobs, worked all day, had dinner, hung out with friends, and went to bed. In truth we were more like roommates than lovers. Life had become routine, and I hadn't guarded the romance we once shared. Maybe it was because I saw people flaunting sex everywhere. The videos from Babylon were pornographic. Even among the staff at Camp Abilene there were affairs and illicit relationships. Many members of the administrative staff had wives or had bribed people into living with them. They had all begun to trade partners, like some perverted game of musical chairs. I had been propositioned a few times myself, from desperate refugees hoping that I would look the other way while they helped themselves to goods from the warehouse, to the man in charge of camp cleanup who had asked if Cat would be available. Sex had become not just commonplace and public; it had become like a commodity. When people had nothing to barter with, they traded their bodies. For some, it was the only pleasure left.

So far I have managed to avoid sexual promiscuity. And as

far as I knew Cat had as well. We really were a couple and enjoyed intimacy, but I couldn't deny that part of our relationship had grown cold. I chalked it up to overexposure and fatigue, but the truth was I had found satisfaction in my position in the camp and neglected the woman I loved.

"You don't have to," she said. "I've been fine on my own for a long time."

That was true. Cat was older than I was by maybe four or five years. While I was in the Air Force, she was living a primitive lifestyle in the Rocky Mountains, slowly moving north. Most of that time she had lived alone, not just single, but completely alone. The world had changed, and there was no way I would leave her alone, but she certainly had the experience that led her to believe she would be alright.

"I'm not doing that," I said. "We're a..."

I wasn't sure how to finish the sentence. What were we for real? I started to say team, but that sounded ridiculous. And saying partners wasn't any better. Perhaps things between us had devolved into a give-and-take based on need, but the truth was I loved Cat.

"I love you," I blurted, giving up on my failed attempt to define what we really were to each other. "I want to be with you."

"And I want to be with you," she replied. "But I can't stay. I don't want to die."

"Alright, I get that," I said, my mind kicking into gear. "We need to start preparing."

"How?"

"Well...food for one thing. Let's start saving the protein

bars and powdered drink mixes every time we go to the mess hall."

In addition to the meals prepared by the kitchen staff at Camp Abilene, we also had access to snacks. They were mostly military grade protein bars, the occasional piece of fruit, and a few confectionary treats that the staff managed to prepare. Most people took something to keep on them, just in case something came up and they weren't able to get to the mess hall in time for a meal.

"Alright, that's smart," Cat said.

"It won't be enough, but at least we'll have food for a few days," I told her. "We've still got our sleeping bags and winter gear."

"It's spring," Cat said. "Things will warm up soon."

"Maybe," I said. "But I wouldn't count on it."

She nodded, but didn't argue. The atmosphere wasn't clear, and reports from government sources aside, there wasn't much hope that it would clear. It was cold and probably going to stay cold. If enough debris had been kicked up by the bombings, it was possible the earth could slide into a new Ice Age. I wasn't sure how much of all that I believed. Science was not my wheelhouse. The Sotos, my foster parents, had been strong defenders of climate change. They believed that the world was getting hotter at a catastrophic pace. I wondered what Peter Soto thought of things now, or if he had even survived the war, famine, and pestilence that had swept through Japan just as it had swept through the United States. Part of me was glad that Nora Soto hadn't lived long enough to struggle with life in the tribulation. Of course, thinking of her also made me sad because I was pretty sure she wasn't a believer in Jesus. They weren't religious people, despite living in the Bible Belt.

Lorenzo had a completely different take on the supposed Ice Age. He believed that the Earth was only about six thousand years old, and that what people thought of as the Ice Age was actually a result of the flood from Genesis. He had taught that the Earth had been slowly warming ever since that cataclysmic event. And while he supported the idea of Earth stewardship, he didn't buy into the fearmongering, as he called it, over climate change.

The truth was I didn't know much about it, except that I had read a news article at some point in my life that said detonation of a limited number of nuclear weapons could slow down, halt, or even reverse the global warming being recorded by climate scientists. I wasn't sure if that was what had made the cold so widespread over the past five months, or if it was a true nuclear winter that was going to impact the globe for decades. All I knew for sure was that it was cold outside and not getting warmer any time soon.

"We have good gear," she said. "We'll be alright."

"Okay, but we need a plan," I proposed. "I think going north is a mistake."

"You want to go south, into Mexico?"

"No way," I said. "Too dangerous."

"So where?"

"I don't know. East has to be our best option. Let's just think about it while we gather what supplies we can."

"So, you're really coming with me?" she asked, a glimmer of hope in her voice.

"Yes," I replied. "Where you go, I go."

She scooted closer and kissed me. Our arms wrapped around each other, and it felt good to hold her close. It reminded me of being in the fire watch cabin when the war first broke out. We had needed each other then. And it felt good to know that we still needed one another.

"Thank you, Hank," Cat whispered.

"I love you," I told her.

"I love you too," she said.

There's no denying that I was scared. Leaving the camp was hard to wrap my mind around. But it was inevitable. I just wish we had left sooner.

CHAPTER 26

"MY MAN!" LB declared when he saw me at dinner. "We got a poker game going tonight, Downes. You in?"

He dropped into a seat next to me in the mess hall. The menu was either spaghetti with meatballs–beef but vat-grown, not natural meat–or chicken-flavored fried rice with tofu and egg substitute. I know it sounds less than savory, but compared to eating canned soup or rehydrated military rations, it was excellent.

"Nice to see you, Mrs. Downes," LB continued in his jovial tone. "You are looking mighty fine tonight. I guess you heard about Dr. Padmal? Hell of a thing. Hell of a thing. The man devotes his life to helping people and now he's struck down with the Death Flu. I sure hope they come through with that vaccine."

"Thank goodness there are still places where it can be created," Cat replied. "But I'm sorry to tell you that Hank isn't available tonight."

"He's not?" LB asked in surprise.

"No," she said with a big smile. "He's spending it with me."

"Well, now, I can't say that I blame him for that. Shoot, he would just lose his money anyhow."

We were being paid. I don't think I mentioned that, but it's true. Not physical money of course, but digital dollars in NARA accounts that we were told were secure. But at Camp Abilene a barter system had arisen. There were things that were needed that weren't widely available, such as razors, socks, tobacco products, alcohol, combs, and candy. Everyone had their little hordes of what were thought of as luxury items. Cat and I had spices, sugar, and a sewing kit. I know that sounds mundane to those of you in the civilized world, but they were very tradable goods in Camp Abilene. We had food, and there was access to some basic spices, like salt and black pepper, but if a person wanted garlic, dill, chili powder, or cumin, they had to come to us. And while instant coffee was available, sugar to sweeten the bitter brew was not.

"You can't run forever, Downes," LB joked. "I'm getting low on sugar, and you know how testy I get when I'm forced to drink my coffee black."

That was the way of things. Life for those who ran Camp Abilene was comfortable and even jovial at times. As long as we didn't think about what was going on in the tent city, where the refugees were struggling to survive in the squalid conditions.

While life had come to a screeching halt in the U.S. and most of the western world, the Near East was enjoying a revival that no one had seen coming. With the shift in global temperatures and changing weather patterns, the arid lands from Israel to Iran became cooler and wetter. The desert bloomed in a way that no one had ever seen. Rivers flowed through the Arabian Desert. Fields were cultivated to grow food. Breakthroughs in medicine and technology were driven by the tech industry centered in Israel. Artificial intelligence was being hailed as the cure for the world's woes. There was plenty to talk about that had nothing to do with our day-to-day struggles. The internet still worked, and video from around the world was available. The new world capital of Babylon was nothing short of spectacular. In less than a year the ruins in the desert had become a startling wonder. The city was a combination of massive stone blocks carried in and set in place by teams of actual giants. They were much bigger than the one I had seen. Some were forty or fifty feet all. They all had red hair, huge muscles, and six fingers on each hand. A few even had two rows of teeth. Watching them work was a marvel, as they laid the foundations for towering skyscrapers of glass and steel.

Then there were the two old men in Jerusalem who continued to preach day and night. They called on people to turn from their sin and call out to God for mercy. Unfortunately, they had become a sideshow. New videos from tourists visiting Jerusalem hit the internet daily. While most of the world was at war or struggling with poverty from the financial collapse, there remained a wealthy elite who flocked to the countries of the Near East, which were part of the Southern Asia region. I wasn't the type of person to envy others, but it was hard not to feel as if the rug had been pulled out from under us. What had once been the cultural and economic center of the world had fallen in a morass of war and poverty. The videos from the other side of the world seemed exotic, colorful, and free. Everyone seemed happy, sometimes ridiculously so. Case in point were the two witnesses in Jerusalem. They stayed near the temple mount. On many of the videos the gleaming new temple was visible behind them. And while they cautioned people not to make sacrifices and burnt offerings at the new temple, the onlookers ridiculed and mocked them.

"They say Abdul bin Salman is making a big announcement soon," LB said around a mouthful of spaghetti. "What do you think that's all about?"

"Can't say," I replied.

"Come on, Downes, don't hold out on us, man," LB said.

He was my boss as the man in charge of the security personnel, but he was a very informal manager and remained friendly with everyone, from those patrolling the camp itself, to the teams in charge of helping people get to the camp.

Our table was filled with mostly security team members. They all leaned in close, some curious, others amused. I didn't make a big deal of knowing what was coming, but I had mentioned it. Most of the people knew I was a Christian, but I didn't push my beliefs on anyone, not even Cat, who was still on the fence when it came to her faith.

"Yeah, Lieutenant," one of the camp security personnel added. "Tell us what you know."

"I don't know anything," I said.

That was the truth. What I knew were the big, overarching details explained in the Bible. For instance, I knew that Paul Eon was going to make a big political move at some point.

He was what the book of Daniel called the little horn. He would supplant three of the ten regional administrators and the remaining leaders would follow him, in essence making Eon king of the world.

"You know," LB said with a chuckle. "What's the good book tell you is coming down the pike?"

"A vaccine," another of the security workers said. "Has to be."

"Could be months before we see it," a woman who had been a diesel mechanic in the army said. "We might all be dead by then."

"Dang, Gloria, that's dark, girl," LB said.

"Just calling 'em like I see 'em," she replied. "You heard about Padmal, right?"

"Yeah, that's a shame," LB said. "Don't ya wear hazmat suits in the infirmary, Cat?"

She nodded. "We do, but they're getting old."

"Discomfort is a small price to pay for staying alive," someone said.

"She didn't mean it that way," I said.

"Nah, everything is wearing out," LB added. "That's for sure. We need new hazmat suits. We've put in multiple requests to the RA, but so far..."

"Bupkis," another security worker said.

It was a common complaint. The Regional Administration was slow to respond and rarely provided what was actually needed. I had been in the Air Force long enough to understand how a government bureaucracy worked. Slow was the norm. And I do mean glacially slow. Usually you didn't get what you needed until you didn't need it anymore.

Cat and I finished our meal, then headed back to the barracks and our small room. There was still a lot of planning to do. We were huddled together, speaking in quiet tones when someone knocked on our door. I answered and found the heavyset man with the mustache, Greg Miller, Assistant Administrator in Charge, the same man who had checked us into Camp Abilene weeks ago.

"Sir?" I said when I saw him.

"Camp-wide announcement," he said. "Tomorrow at noon. All security personnel are required to be on-site."

"Copy that, sir," I replied. "I'll be there."

Miller grunted and moved off to the next door.

"What do you think that's about?" Cat asked.

"I don't know," I replied. "I doubt it's good news though."

"Should we try to leave before that?"

"No," I said. "We still have several things to round up, and I don't want to go before we're ready."

"But you aren't going to tell LB, are you?"

"No," I said, wishing I could tell the jovial major. "Officially I'll be a deserter. I have no idea how or even if they would punish me for that, but I don't want to give them the chance. When we go, we'll need to slip away when we won't be noticed and get as far away as we can before they do. If we sneak out tonight they'll know we're gone in the morning when people are gathering for the announcement."

"Yeah, that makes sense," she said, looking at the list of supplies we had, and ones we still needed to get our hands on. "We just shouldn't wait too long."

"Agreed," I said. "Maybe the day after tomorrow. Let's just see how things go."

She leaned against me and smiled. "I can't wait to get out of this place."

I felt the exact opposite, but I didn't want to tell her that. I knew that sooner or later we would have to leave. I didn't want to see Cat catch the virus. And while I felt pretty safe in my position, I knew we were living on borrowed time. The camp felt like a bad imitation of normal life, and I had succumbed to the illusion for too long. There was no safety in the camp—it was a gathering place for the dead and dying. Yes, I had friends there, people that I genuinely cared about, but Cat was spending eight to ten hours a day in the infirmary. She was on the front lines, and I couldn't blame her for wanting out. Nor did I want her to leave alone. I had lost all the people that I loved in my life. I didn't want to lose her either.

"It won't be long," I promised.

But the following day, everything changed.

CHAPTER 27

I WAS WALKING to my assigned post when she saw me. I hadn't realized she was at Camp Abilene, not that I rubbed elbows with the refugees very often. My duties kept me in my neat, well-organized warehouse most of the time, and I was just fine with that.

"Hank?" a familiar voice said.

I looked up and didn't recognize Ruth at first. She had lost weight, a lot of it. Her face was thin, the skin seemed to stretch too tight around her eyes and across her forehead. She was bundled up in a big coat that was several sizes too big and dirty.

"Ruth?" I asked.

"Yeah, it's me," she said. "I can't believe it. Where have you been?"

She was looking at the M-16 rifle slung over my shoulder and the body armor strapped around my chest. I had the Beretta her father had given to me on my right thigh. It was normally the only weapon I carried when on duty, but we were all expected in the muddy field that separated the administration side of camp from the refugee space. A big screen had been set up with an enclosed rear projector and a set of PA speakers. News was coming down from the Regional Administrator, and we were all required to be there. Security personnel, of which I was one, were supposed to be making a show of force. No one knew what the announcement would be, but Camp Abilene's Administrator in Charge felt it was better to have people in place in case the news was bad. I think he just wanted to make sure the refugees didn't turn against him, but I couldn't really blame him for that.

"All over, really," I said.

"Are you a guard here?" she asked.

"I'm on the security team," I said. "All former military were recalled to active duty. But I'm not really a security guy. I'm in charge of logistics."

She stepped close to me and put a hand on my arm. There was a strange look in her eyes, like she was pleading with me, or offering herself to me. I couldn't really tell.

"This is so good," she said. "I felt like it was the right thing for me to come here. Daddy died. Some people came around after the war started. They wanted his guns."

Tears filled her eyes. I didn't have to ask what happened. Leon wasn't the type to let anyone steal from him. Perhaps if I had been there Leon might still be alive. Of course, they hadn't wanted me around once the peace accord had been made and everyone thought the world was back on track. Ruth was out partying hard almost every night, and Leon had never really trusted me all that much.

"He was a good man," I said, even though I didn't really think that. Leon was stubborn, crass, and mostly a very hard person to spend much time with. But it seemed like the right thing to say.

"Thank you," Ruth replied, shifting her weight and leaning her body against me.

I felt awkward and uncertain. Her behavior wasn't exactly flirtatious, and there had never been any romance between the two of us, but the way she was leaning against me didn't feel appropriate either. I wanted to step back, to get away from her, but I was afraid she would topple over if I moved.

"You've got it good here," she said, looking up at me. "You don't know how hard it is in the tents."

"I've heard," I said.

"We took you in, Daddy and I. We took you into our home when you had nowhere else to go. We fed you, shared our lives with you."

"Okay..."

"I'm not asking for a lot here, Hank," Ruth said.

"What exactly are you asking for?"

"I can make you happy," she said. "Whatever you like, I'll do it. Just get me out of the tents, Hank. You owe me that much. You owe it to me."

"I can't do that," I said.

"Why not? Tell them I'm your lover."

"Ruth, I'm married," I said.

She laughed. It was a high-pitched cackle that made the hair on the back of my neck stand up.

"Married? Who's married anymore? Why does it even

matter?" she said, although she didn't sound like herself. "You can have two wives."

Her hands were clutching my arm. I was at a complete loss of what to say or do. It was embarrassing, and even a little frightening. Ruth was propositioning me, that was clear, but I wasn't even sure I was still talking to the woman I had spent time with on her family farm. That Ruth had been desperate and scared, but she knew what was happening in the world, and she still had dignity. In all the time I spent with her she never flirted with me, never seemed to be attracted to me or interested in any sort of relationship. When she started going out to join in the celebrations in Missoula, I knew she was drinking and I assumed she was having sex. She was sometimes gone for days at a time. That was a sad state of affairs, but she had really gone downhill since then.

"Look Ruth, I'm sorry, but I can't help you," I said, pushing her gently away.

"What's going on here?" LB asked as he strode up beside, his big voice booming. "You got trouble, Downs?"

"No, sir," I said, still looking at Ruth. "Just an old acquaintance from up north."

"Well, you better get into position. We'll be kicking things off any time now."

My position was near the front, not far from the screen. I took a step in that direction, but Ruth moved in front of me.

"You owe me, Hank," she insisted.

"I'm sorry, Ruth, but I'm not in a position to do anything for you."

She spat in my face. I won't relay the curses she shouted at me. Needless to say she could hold her own with the drill instructors I went through basic training with. It was an ugly scene. Cat was with the other healthcare workers, and I caught her eye as I made my way across the muddy field. The clouds were thick, the light filtered through dull gray. I felt awkward and ashamed as Ruth followed behind me, cursing my name.

But that's the way things were. There was an us versus them mentality on the part of the facility workers and the refugees. In the sad little economy of the camp, we were the haves, and they were the have-nots. I wasn't sure how I had become the center of attention, but soon there were people laughing and jeering at us. Ruth was undeterred by my lack of attention or care. She stayed right on my heels, shouting vile insults and demeaning my manhood. Even though we had never been intimate, she made false claims about my love-making ability.

Finally, just before reaching my position, I caught sight of the Administrator in Charge, Evelyn McComber. She was twice my age and slightly overweight. Her cheeks and nose were perpetually red from the alcohol she consumed from the time she woke up until she passed out each night. I knew of her habits because early on in my work as the logistics officer at Camp Abilene she had let me know that she expected to get the best liquor that was sent in from the NARA supply runs. She was my boss, and despite her own struggles, she was clearly not pleased with the scene Ruth was causing.

I turned around suddenly and pointed at Ruth. "You're out of line," I snarled. "You need to be quiet and leave me alone."

"I will not," she shrieked.

"All I've got to do is say the word and you'll get thrown out of camp," I threatened.

I had never wielded my favor or position within the security ranks, but I was desperate to get her to stop making a scene.

"Is that what you want?" I hissed.

"No," she said, fear and desperation finally getting through to her.

"Then shut up, and leave me alone," I hissed.

"You are such an ungrat—"

"Now!" I snapped.

She backed away. I felt terrible. Sure, I had done things growing up that I wasn't proud of, but I wasn't a bully. In the Air Force there were times when I could have spoken up on behalf of the less fortunate, but I was too busy being invisible. Helping others was a surefire way to make yourself a target. But never before had I been the one to dash another person's hopes. And it felt terrible.

Ruth stumbled backward, her feet got caught in the mud and she fell into the muck. People were laughing, and Ruth was crying. I turned back toward my assigned post and saw AIC McComber nodding approvingly. Even LB, who was with the other bigwigs of Camp Abilene, gave me an encouraging nod. It wasn't until that moment that I realized how much I had changed. My eyes found Cat, but she was looking away, probably too embarrassed to watch me be so cruel to someone.

I made it to my position near the screen and turned to face the growing crowd of refugees. They were coming from the tents. I understood that conditions on that side of the camp weren't ideal, but I really had no concept of how bad it was. Filth was the unifying descriptor of all the people from every walk of life. I saw people in gym clothes and people in tattered business suits. Some had long coats that had probably been expensive, and others wore parkas that were ripped so badly they were barely held together by loose stitches made from old shoelaces. And despite the cold there were some people in the nude. It had become commonplace to see people in various states of undress or doing lewd acts out in the open.

"Welcome," Evelyn's voice boomed through the speakers. "My name is McComber, Administrator In Charge. And today we have a special announcement from the GCP Ten Regions Administrative Governments. Please give them your full attention."

A pre-recorded video of the North American Region Administrator, Ian Jesper, came on. He said essentially the same thing as Evelyn had. And then the video changed to a live feed from Babylon.

I still have trouble saying the name of the new global capital with a straight face. Babylon seems more like a cliche than an actual place. But the news feed showed the magnificent new city. It was unlike any place on earth. Wide streets lined with bright white sidewalks that were dotted with colorful flora. The buildings were sleek, yet architecturally unique, and not just from one another, but from anything that had ever been built before. A wide plaza in front of a wide ziggurat was the setting for the feed. In the plaza were thousands of people. In stark contrast to the refugees before me, the people in Babylon were clean and well-dressed. They looked well-fed too, and some were even eating and drinking from fare that was being served in booths along the edges of the plaza.

There were large statues in the plaza as well. Some of mythical beasts, others of alien-looking figures that would have been at home in a horror film. There were people climbing onto the statues, all trying to get a good look at what was happening near the top of the ziggurat where a group of people were coming out of the odd building.

Above it all hovered the strange alien ship. It was a classic flying saucer, only much larger. It should have cast a shadow on the scene, but somehow the light seemed to bend around the ship. I was hit with the sudden realization that perhaps the ship wasn't there at all. Perhaps the city wasn't as grand as it appeared. Maybe it was all an illusion. But when I looked across the crowd toward the infirmary where the medical personnel, as well as Cat, were watching, I saw them transfixed by the images on the big screen.

"It looks like the world leaders are going to make an announcement soon," a warm, almost comforting voice from the video feed said. "This looks to be an historic day here on our little blue planet."

A hush fell over the camp. We were on the verge of something, and everyone could feel it. I should have been more prepared, but I was caught completely off guard. My place in the camp had lulled me into a false sense of security. That all shattered with what happened next.

CHAPTER 28

ABDUL BIN SALMAN was clearly the leader of the pack. The ten world leaders, not elected but appointed by the Global Council for Peace, which I had never heard of before the vanishings, came out of the ziggurat. There was a balcony near the summit. The Region Administrators lined up, and bin Salman stepped forward. I didn't see a microphone, but his voice carried across the plaza full of people and onto the video feed.

As the camera zoomed in on the Arab leader's face, he began to address the world in his native language. The volume of his voice was quickly dialed back, and a translator gave the address in English.

"Citizens of the world, it is our privilege today to announce a global ceasefire," bin Salman said. He paused while the people in the plaza cheered. The refugees in Camp Abilene joined in, shouting and whistling their enthusiastic agreement with the global government's decree. "Our planet has gone through the birth pangs of revolution as we adapt to a new, higher plane of living. We are no longer divided, nation-alistic, self-serving tribes, but one race. Our call is to rebuild what was lost in this transition. With the help of the Apkallu, we shall rebuild our world better than before."

Another pause, more overwhelming applause.

"This is not the time for war. Nor will war ever be the norm again on planet Earth. She who birthed us is raising us to a new level of consciousness. No longer are we deceived by the traditions and mythologies of the past." Abdul bin Salman raised an arm toward the floating spaceship over his head. "Our guests have shown us the truth. We are their offspring, and we can embrace their legacy of peace as we restore the natural balance of our world. We shall stabilize the global climate, clean up the oceans and landfills, and restore the natural wonders we have stewardship of. In the process, we shall heal what divides us, and overcome every obstacle.

"To this end, we shall not tolerate the divisive mythologies that have held us in bonds of hatred for thousands of years. We shall cast off those bonds and become the divine heirs to this celestial world that it deserves."

The applause was at a fever pitch, both on the screen and in the camp. I felt nervous. The M-16 automatic rifle that I carried was slung over my shoulder, and I had to fight the instinct to rotate it around into my hands. Ruth was in the throng of onlookers, and like the rest she was cheering the news from Babylon. With hands raised high, and her face turned upward, she screamed her acceptance of what the world leaders were proclaiming on the big screen. Behind me,

AIC McComber and Major Barski were both clapping, although with much more reserve than the refugees.

I looked across the crowd, trying to find Cat, but it was difficult to see past the refugees who were jumping up and down and waving their arms. On the screen, on a level below the world leaders, two huge men came out. They wore skin-tight pants, tall boots, and compression shirts with rainbow badges. Each one carried what looked like a machete. Behind them appeared a group of people. They were bound together with chains around their waists and their hands in cuffs that were linked to the larger chain. The big men with machetes moved behind them and pushed them down onto their knees.

I didn't see Paul Eon appear on the upper level. My focus was completely on the prisoners, and my chest felt tight. I didn't need an interpreter to know what their crime was. Paul Eon spoke in Arabic, but was translated into English, just like bin Salman's words had been.

"These ten people before you now are guilty of the crime of profaning peace by preaching their so-called gospel."

I was listening to the translator, but it was impossible to miss the disdain in the diplomat's voice. And the translator sounded angry too.

"They have chosen to spread lies about who we are and where we come from. With the proof right before their eyes, they revert to the pagan beliefs of the past. From this day forward, let it be known that anyone who claims the title of Christian, shall be guilty of treason against the global citizens of earth. And that guilt comes with a heavy penalty."

Paul Eon walked up to the first of the prisoners. He was jerked upright by the muscular guards. The camera zoomed in on the man's face. I was shocked to see he was in what appeared to be a Catholic priest's clothing, although it was dirty and torn. He was shaking with fear, his eyes bulging. Eon stood by him, tall and stately in comparison, completely without fear.

"Name!" Paul Eon demanded.

"F-f-fath-father Gorsetti," he stammered.

"You have been found guilty of preaching division and dissent. How do you plea?"

"I-I-I have shared the love and m-m-mercy of J-J-Jes—"

Paul Eon slapped him so hard the man nearly swooned. Only the muscle-bound guards held him upright.

"That name is outlawed across every region. To speak it is death. Now, renounce your divisive faith and swear allegiance to the Global Council for Peace."

"I-I-I ca-cannot," the priest said.

"Then you will die," Paul Eon declared. "The world finds you guilty of seditious beliefs and the spreading of divisive lies. Your punishment is death."

He stepped back, and one of the guards yanked the priest to his knees. The other raised his machete and chopped it down onto the priest's neck. The blade was razor sharp and cut straight through, decapitating the man with one savage blow. His head seemed to shoot forward, as if propelled by the thick blade, or maybe by some internal pressure. It bounced on the platform where the prisoners stood, then toppled down the sloped side of the ziggurat. I felt like I was going to be sick. The priest's body collapsed as blood gushed from the wound.

The crowd in the plaza went crazy. The refugees weren't as quick to join the frenzy, but they cheered the public execution. I felt weak in the knees, and my hands were trembling. The fifth seal had been broken. The martyrdom of the tribulation believers had begun.

The second man on the platform was even more terrified than the first. He was also beheaded. The third renounced his faith and was spared. I think that was more shocking than the executions. I felt the loss of the man's convictions on a deep, personal level. And the spiritual assault in my soul intensified. What would I do if I were on that platform? I didn't want to know.

The fourth and fifth prisoners renounced their belief in Jesus. But the sixth stood up boldly. He was a black man in brightly colored robes and a smile on his face. I couldn't believe what I was seeing. Paul Eon ordered him to renounce his faith, but the prisoner shouted out instead.

"Jesus saves! Jesus is the Lord of all!"

One guard kicked the back of the man's knee. He dropped hard, unable to catch himself because his hands were shackled to the chain around his waist. He fell forward, his face smacking the stones of the platform. The second guard yanked him back upright. Blood streamed from his nose and lips. His white teeth were stained pink, yet he continued smiling.

"Trust in Jesus. He is the way, the truth, and the li—"

He was cut off as the guard lopped his head from his shoulders. The smiling face remained on the severed head as it flew upward, and then bounced down the side of the ziggurat into the hands of the frenzied crowd below.

It was all I could stand. I had to turn away from the screen. Death was close to all of us since the Vanishing. I had seen it, been threatened with it, and narrowly avoided it. Worst of all, I had dealt it out. The faces of the locals in Roswell, New Mexico that I had gunned down came back to me at that moment, along with the men and women I had killed when they attacked the caravan. It was horrible to accept that I was a murderer, and worse to be reminded of what I had committed. The truth was, I was afraid. Yes, I knew that I was loved and accepted by God. I knew nothing could separate me from his love, not even killing people, which I had done to protect myself and Cat. Yet I felt a coldness deep inside, and a sense of loneliness that I hadn't felt since my parents had died when I was just eight years old.

I heard the cheers as the seventh and eighth prisoners were executed. The last two renounced their faith, which in many ways was worse. The crowd at the plaza in Babylon sounded like a horde of demons. They laughed and cheered and called for more carnage. Their high-pitched voices made my blood run cold. And then Paul Eon spoke again.

"This is not just a show of force here, in the global capital city of Babylon," the diplomat declared. "This how we deal with anyone who would disrupt our peace with their lies of judgment and damnation."

Bin Salman, on the platform above where the prisoners had been executed, stepped forward and spoke. "From this day forward, anyone who does not embrace Pax Divino is guilty of treason. This is the global law, applicable in every region. They shall be detained and publicly executed unless they renounce their beliefs publicly and turn from the mythologies of the past. We ten here, have spoken. So shall it be."

"And it begins with the two fools in Jerusalem," Paul Eon shouted.

I turned back to the screen in time to see a look of annoyance cross the face of Abdul bin Salman. He obviously didn't like Paul Eon trying to upstage him. But the video feed shifted from Babylon to a group of armed police in Jerusalem. They were marching toward the two witnesses and scattering the crowds around them.

"Cease and surrender," one of the policemen shouted at the witnesses, who were standing side by side in a clearing beside the remnants of the old city walls below the temple mount. The Hebrew words meant nothing to me, but once again an interpreter translated what was being said. "You are under arrest. Get on our knees!"

"Hear what the Lord of Heaven's armies say," the bald witness said in a loud voice that needed no translation. I could see his mouth, and the sound of his words didn't match. And like everyone else in Camp Abilene, I was captivated by the scene playing out on the big screen before us. "Woe to you, Chorazin! Woe to you, Bethsaida! For if the mighty works done in you had been done in Tyre and Sidon, they would have repented long ago in sackcloth and ashes. But I tell you, it will be more bearable on the day of judgment for Tyre and Sidon than for you. And you, Capernaum, will you be exalted to heaven? You will be brought down to Hades. For if the mighty works done in you had been done in Sodom, it would have remained until this day. But I tell you that it will be more tolerable on the day of judgment for the land of Sodom than for you."

For a moment the officers in riot gear froze. The two

witnesses stood calmly before them. Then the leader shouted something in Hebrew that didn't get translated, and the group spread out. A dozen law enforcement officers in heavy armor with wooden clubs and plexiglass shields moved toward the two old men. Neither spoke a word. Their eyes were fixed straight ahead. As the police officer in charge shouted out to arrest the men, the two witnesses opened their mouths, and fire spewed out. It was like the scene of a fantasy movie. Every muscle in my body tensed. The refugees fell silent, but the police officers in Jerusalem screamed in agony as they were burned alive.

I'll admit—I felt a thrill. It was like watching your team score a touchdown in the final seconds of the game, running the ball all the way across the field, somehow avoiding the defenders and turning the tide, which only seconds before had seemed impossible. The fire came rushing out and consumed the policemen. It wasn't like a flamethrower. The law enforcement officers didn't thrash around as their clothes burned. And it wasn't like they were merely scorched either. The fire seemed to spread out around them, increasing in intensity as the men died. It poured out of them, like a paper doll burning up from the inside out.

The witness with shoulder-length gray hair said calmly, "Truly, truly, I say to you, we speak of what we know, and bear witness to what we have seen, but you do not receive our testimony. If I have told you earthly things and you do not believe, how can you believe if I tell you heavenly things?"

His partner joined in, "For God so loved the world, that he gave his only Son, that whoever believes in him should not perish but have eternal life. For God did not send his Son into the world to condemn the world, but in order that the world might be saved through him. Whoever believes in him is not condemned, but whoever does not believe is condemned already, because he has not believed in the name of the only Son of God."

The gray-haired man added, "And this is the judgment: the light has come into the world, and people loved the darkness rather than the light because their works were evil. For everyone who does wicked things hates the light and does not come to the light, lest his works should be exposed. But whoever does what is true comes to the light, so that it may be clearly seen that his works have been carried out in God."

Then they sat down on a fallen block that looked like it had been on the street for a thousand years. The video feed ended abruptly, and like everyone else who had seen the awesome display, I felt numb. Everything had changed in the blink of an eye. And I knew it was only a matter of time before Cat and I were put on the chopping block for our faith.

CHAPTER 29

HALF of the camp was energized and excited by the public executions. The other half was more subdued. Personally I was frightened, even though I knew it was coming. The Bible says, "When he opened the fifth seal, I saw under the altar the souls of those who had been slain for the word of God and for the witness they had borne." Lorenzo had taught that this judgment was in fact a great persecution of tribulation believers, but seeing it in real time was gruesome and hard to accept.

Returning to the warehouse I found myself haunted by the scene that had played out on the big screen and wondered when I would be called to account for my faith. Not everyone knew I was a believer. But enough people knew that I was certain to be called in and questioned. When that happened, I honestly didn't know what I would say.

When the work day ended I felt a slight sense of relief. If there was one thing that I could count on it was the fact that very little work got done after 5 PM. The administrators shut down their offices, and the debauchery began. I hurried back to my quarters to wait for Cat. We needed to get out of Camp Abilene. There was no sense in waiting any longer. I gathered all our things and got them ready on the cots we shared. It wasn't much. Just a backpack each, our sleeping bags, and our winter gear. Only Cat didn't return. There was a knock at the door, which was unusual. I felt a stab of fear, but there was no sense hiding. If it was my time to die, I decided to face it head on.

When I opened the door I found LB. He was alone and looked pensive. It was an unusual look for the big man, who normally had a smile on his broad face. It crossed my mind that if he had come to take me in he would have brought more people.

"What's wrong?" I asked, fearing that I already knew the answer.

"It's Cat," he said.

"What happened?"

"Try to stay calm, Hank," LB said. He gestured into the room. "You mind?"

"No, come on in," I said.

He stepped inside; I closed the flimsy door. "They're telling me she was attacked by one of the patients."

He raised both hands to calm me. I felt as though the ground had opened up beneath my feet to swallow me whole.

"She's not hurt, but..." he continued.

"But what?" I demanded.

"But the patient tore her hazmat suit," LB continued. "Ripped the air tube out and pulled off her headpiece. She's been moved to quarantine."

"Oh," I said, feeling numb.

"Yeah, like I said it's not anything to worry about. Not yet."

"Okay, but what are the odds?" I argued. "Dr. Padmal got sick because of a tiny crack in her suit."

"We don't know how he got exposed," LB argued. "We just know he's sick. Cat isn't sick, man. She may not get sick."

"Or she might get sick and die," I said, dropping on the end of the cot.

I had completely forgotten about our things piled onto the bed, and LB didn't mention them. He was a compassionate man who genuinely cared about the people who worked for him. I had never served under an officer that I liked more. And he cared about Cat too, was always friendly to her. LB wasn't a Christian, but he prided himself on being a disciplined, moral man. Perhaps it was a career in the Marine Corps that made him so emotionally strong, but he didn't usually drink himself into a stupor, or join in the sex parties that the Administrators threw on an almost nightly basis.

"She's strong," he said. "Healthy. This thing won't take her down. I'm sure of it."

"Can I see her?"

"Yeah, of course."

He led the way. It was dark outside and cold. The nights were harsh as winter held on. The wind was blowing hard, and the sounds of the refugee tents rattling in the gale was loud. A small trailer was set up just beside the big medical tent. It was a military grade prefab structure with an industrial air filter on top. We couldn't go inside, but the trailer had a window, and there were motion sensor lights on the outside.

LB knocked on the window, and we waited for a moment for the blinds to be lifted. And there was Cat, all alone in the quarantine trailer. Her eyes were puffy from crying.

"Hey!" I said. "Are you okay?"

She nodded.

"I'm so sorry," I told her.

She put her hand on the glass, and I put mine on my side. It was cold to the touch.

"I'm scared," she said, her voice barely passing through the flimsy trailer's walls. I had to read her lips mostly, but it was obvious what she had said. And I couldn't blame her for being scared. The Death Flu was terrible and a hard way to die. Of course, most of what I knew about it came from news stories online, and from Cat's firsthand accounts of how the refugees were struggling with the virus in the infirmary. I didn't wish it on anyone.

"You're going to be okay," I said. "I know it."

Of course I didn't know it, but I was hoping it. I had no power over sickness or disease, but I was confident in God's power.

"I'm sorry," she said, and I knew what she meant. She was sorry for being exposed of course, but what she was really saying was she was sorry that we couldn't leave.

"Don't be," I said. "Everything will work out. I know it. What can I do for you?"

"Nothing," she said.

"How long will you be in there?"

She held up two fingers.

"Two days?" I asked, feeling hopeful. Two days wasn't bad. We could leave when she got out. I would use the two days to get a few more supplies. It would take the camp a few days to enact any kind of mandate from NARA. I felt a little surge of hope.

But Cat shook her head. "Weeks," she said.

I didn't hear her voice and had to read her lips. She probably saw the disappointment on my face. It was a mental error on my part. I should have remained positive no matter what she told me, and I shouldn't have jumped to conclusions. Two weeks was much longer than two days. I wasn't sure what was going to happen in the camp in two weeks, not with the fifth seal judgment having been broken. There was no doubt in my mind that there would be violence against anyone who was even thought to be a Christian.

While I was trying to think of what to say that might encourage Cat, one of the security members approached LB. He was standing behind me, enduring the cold to show his support. Corporal Allie Mendolson was part of what we called the teams. There were three mobile security forces called the Alpha, Bravo, and Charlie teams. They went out on a regular basis, sometimes to look for refugees, and sometimes into Abilene to keep tabs on the locals who refused to join us. I couldn't blame the people of Abilene. The tent city was filthy, cold, and dangerous. But the city wasn't much better off. They had no power, no food or supplies, and no medicines. Gangs roved the streets, looting from the abandoned homes and businesses. There were gunfights almost every night.

"Nothing solid," I heard Allie say to LB. "But they're up to something."

"Good work," he said. "Have your team pull back. There's nothing more you can do tonight."

I turned my attention back to Cat. There were tears in her eyes. She spoke, but I couldn't hear her. I think that was on purpose. With LB distracted, she mouthed the words, "Don't wait for me."

"That's crazy," I said.

She drew a finger across her neck, then pointed at me. I knew what she was saying, but I couldn't leave her. Not even if it meant being killed for my faith.

"No," I said. "You'll get through this, and we'll be together."

"Maybe not," she said. "I might get sick."

"You won't," I insisted.

Cat was a practical person, and I knew what she was thinking. She wanted me out of Camp Abilene before things got dangerous. And she didn't want me sticking around when the odds were high that she was going to get sick. If that happened, she would never leave the infirmary. There had been no survivors of the Death Flu in Camp Abilene.

"Don't make this harder for me," she said.

"What?"

"Goodbye, Hank. I love you."

She touched her hand to her lips, then touched the glass. I did too. But then she lowered the blinds. I wanted to argue with her, but it was no use. LB put a hand on my shoulder.

"Come on, Hank," he said. "Let's go get drunk."

Somehow I ended up back in his office. LB had a desk with a big executive chair, but he also had a nice sofa. I knew he sometimes slept in his office and couldn't blame him. There were nights when the sound of carousing in the barracks made it difficult to sleep. His office in the security building was quiet, especially when there were no prisoners in the little jail section of the building.

He pulled out a bottle of whiskey from his desk. As you know, I'm not a big drinker. But that night I eagerly took a tumbler of the strong liquor from his hands.

"She'll make it," he said. "I know a survivor when I see one, Hank. Cat's got what it takes, brother. Ain't no doubt about that."

"Thanks," I said, partly for the words of encouragement, and partly for the drink.

I took a gulp. It was foul stuff and burned its way down my throat, leaving my tongue numb. But it also sent a wave of warmth from my stomach through my arms and legs.

"I hear they've got tacos in the mess hall," he said. "I can send for some, or we can just get wasted. Either option is fine by me."

"Can't eat," I said, turning the small glass in my hands. "I feel so helpless."

"And that's why we're going to wallow in self-pity tonight," he said. "But come tomorrow, we're shaking it all off and getting on with our lives. Cat will be okay. And there's nothing we can do but wait."

So we drank. I finished my first glass and had a second. LB had twice as many, but he wasn't as drunk as I was when he walked me back to my room. I managed to push our gear onto Cat's side of the bed and passed out on the other. LB pushed a waste basket next to the bed and put a bottle of water on the little table next to me.

The next morning I woke at dawn. Getting up in the mornings was never a struggle for me. Not that I didn't enjoy sleeping in on occasion, but after eight years in the Air Force my body was adjusted to rising early. I felt terrible, and not just physically. Cat was all alone and frightened. I thought that I should have been praying for her, but instead I got drunk. With my head pounding, and my stomach twisting, I managed to drink some water and prayed for the woman I loved. Then I took LB's advice. I showered, got dressed, forced myself to eat a piece of toast, then went to work.

It was the longest shift of my life. Part of me wanted to go see Cat before starting the day, but I hoped she was getting some rest. As soon as the clock hit 5 PM I shut down the warehouse and made a beeline for the quarantine trailer. Cat was waiting. And seeing her face filled me with hope.

"How are you feeling?" I asked.

"Fine. How are you?"

I could tell by the way she looked at me that I was a mess. Of course, people had commented all day that I looked terrible. I wasn't built for heavy drinking, and I wouldn't make the same mistake twice.

"I'm okay," I assured her. "Had some whiskey with LB last night. It wasn't a good idea."

That amused Cat. Her smile lifted my soul. And since there was no one around, so I asked the question that had been on my mind all day.

"Is there a way out of there?" I asked. "Maybe we could get out of here sooner rather than later."

Cat shook her head, the smile receding. "The only way in or out is through the infirmary. You can't go through there," she insisted. "I've seen how bad this gets, Hank. We can't risk it."

"I can't stand the thought of you being alone," I said.

"I'll be okay," she said sadly. "If I get sick, promise me you'll leave."

"I can't do that."

"I don't want you to waste your time on me," she said. "They won't let you see me if I get it. And I don't want you to get sick too."

Part of me felt like I would rather die than be without Cat. But I had to trust that God had a plan for me if that happened. I still had a purpose, even if I had forgotten about it for a while. Spreading Lorenzo's lectures and interviews was something only I could do. There were over a hundred gigs of video on the laptop that still hadn't been posted since the Rapture took place. Focusing on that kept me from slipping into depression as I contemplated the possibility of a future without Cat.

"Alright," I said. "I know God's going to keep you safe. I know his plan is for you and me together."

Cat's smile was forced. "I'm not so sure," she said. "I'm afraid."

"You can't be courageous without fear," I said. "I love you, Cat. I'll never give up on you."

Little did I know the choice was about to be snatched from my hands.

CHAPTER 30

THE MANDATE from NARA came through early the next day. Administrator in Charge Evelyn McComber sent out a memo that came through on my work computer. The camp had a wireless network system that worked about half the time. There was always an issue with one maintenance system or another. But the message popped up onto my screen as I was inputting the changes from the food stores that had been logged by the kitchen staff over the last few days.

Memo: AIC McComber

To: Camp Abilene Staff

Subject: New Zero Tolerance Policy

This straight from the North American Region Administration, all hate groups will be subject to treason charges, effective immediately. Any person or group found to be practicing divisive philosophies will be arrested and publicly tried for treason against the global governance board and the people of planet earth. Anyone seen or heard of teaching people to follow archaic religious belief systems are to be questioned and prosecuted. The focus of this mandate are specifically Christian Evangelicals, but applies to anyone trying to proselytize others.

I felt a sense of dread. Several people knew I was a Christian. My immediate superior LB being one of them. Our little group of Bible believers hadn't made a spectacle of ourselves. Most of the people in our group had known someone who had been taken in the Rapture. Many of them had little or no Bible knowledge, especially when it came to end times prophecy. And we didn't openly share our faith unless someone specifically asked. No one had asked me, although LB had shown a little interest. Still, we weren't a hate group, and we weren't trying to overthrow the government. The only logical reason why we should be targeted was that the global government, and more specifically, the evil entities behind it, feared us.

Somehow, despite the memo, I managed to keep working. Everyone had gotten the message, but as far as I could tell, like many bureaucracies, word from on high didn't get much traction. By that evening I was beginning to think everything would be okay. I ate a quick dinner with some friends, then went back out to visit with Cat. I didn't tell her about the memo. There was nothing she could do but worry about it, and I didn't want her worrying about anything.

A cold front had moved in. The days were gray, the nights dark and cold. I had no idea what the temperature was, but the wind chill was freezing. When I went back to the administration side of Camp Abilene my face felt frozen. I went to the mess hall, thinking of getting a cup of coffee to help warm me up. The mess hall was part of the recreation facilities for the staff that kept the camp operational. There was a small gym with exercise equipment, the dining area, and a recreational space with tables, games, and video displays. The latter was the scene of a nightly party that usually devolved into some sort of partner-swapping scheme. And everyone knew that AIC McComber and some of her staff regularly recruited refugees who were willing to participate in exchange for extra food and clothing. I was in charge of the camp's supplies, but I was pretty far down on the official command structure. When orders came from the top I was forced to obey them, even if that meant setting aside the best of whatever supplies we received for McComber's personal use.

I say all that to say that when I got to the mess hall there were still people in the building. Music was playing from the recreation room. I did my best to avoid that area. Everyone was invited to take part in the hedonistic parties, but I never did. In the dining area I got a cup of coffee and sat down for a moment at one of the tables. Who can say why things happen the way they do? If I had just gone back to my room perhaps things would have worked out completely differently, but instead I sat down in the mess hall, which led to me being seen by Assistant Administrator in Charge Miller. The heavy-set man with the thick mustache was a regular participant in the nightly parties and was the point man for recruiting refugees to take part. He was drunk when he burst into the mess hall and had a woman on his arm. She was only halfway dressed, and I started to look away, but then I recognized the woman.

"Hey! I know him," Ruth said, pointing at me. "That's Hank Downes."

"Yeah," Miller said, his voice slurring. "Should we invite him to play?"

"Oh, no," Ruth said. "He's a stiff. He'll be getting his head lopped off soon."

"What?" Miller said with a goofy grin.

I got up and started for the exit.

"You know," she continued. "He's a Christian."

I don't know what else was said. I can honestly say that Miller was drunk, and possibly high. THC, the chemical compound from marijuana, was part of the medical supplies sent in by NARA. It was on McComber's list of items that were to be set aside for her personal use. I went to my room, nervous at first, but then decided that Miller was too wasted to understand what Ruth was accusing me of. And no one had been arrested after the memo went out the day before, so even if Miller remembered the accusation, he might not care.

Sleep was hard to come by that night. I tried to pray, but I felt lonely. It was hard to be apart from Cat, and the enemy plagued me with fears. You may be one of those people who discount the work of Satan in our world. But let me assure you, there are demonic forces who are active and working to steal, kill, and destroy. That night I was forced to fight to hold onto my sense of security. Fear is an effective weapon to demoralize and paralyze a person or group. As I tossed and turned on my cot, I was plagued with fears of what might happen to me.

As it turned out, Miller may have forgotten, but Ruth didn't. Having found the memo, or perhaps being told about it, she made a complaint to the AIC. LB tried to tell me later that McComber tried to brush it off, but Ruth managed to get someone to put the accusation into the computer system. After that, McComber couldn't ignore it. I'm not sure when all that supposedly happened, because I was halfway through my breakfast when LB showed up with Allie Mendolson.

"Morning," I said. "You not eating, boss?"

LB looked sick, and I thought maybe he was hungover. The man rarely showed any signs of weakness and was almost always in a good mood. But that morning he was subdued.

"We need to talk, Hank," he said.

I got to my feet, thinking something had happened to Cat.

"Is it Cat?" I asked, a note of desperation in my voice. "Is she sick?"

"It's not Cat," LB said. "Far as I know, she's fine. You need to come with us."

For the first time I noticed that Allie Mendolson was armed. She had an M-16 across her back and a .45 automatic pistol on one hip. The pistol seemed too large for her, but I knew she was a dedicated soldier who knew how to use it. Not that I was planning to fight, at that point I hadn't even made the mental connection about what was happening.

"Okay," I said, picking up my tray of half-eaten food.

LB led the way out of the mess hall, and Allie followed behind me. I dumped my tray, put it and my silverware into the appropriate receptacle, and followed the major out of the building. We went straight to the security area, which was where I worked each day. By that point I knew what was coming, but still held out hope that maybe something had gone missing from the warehouse. Maybe there had been a theft and I was needed to help sort things out.

But we didn't go to the warehouse, or to LB's office. Instead, we went to the jail. It was empty, the doors open. Finally, LB turned around and looked at me.

"There was a complaint filed against you, Hank," he said. "Honestly, I think it's a bunch of bologna, but the call came down from the AIC. Nothing we can do but follow through."

"What was the complaint?" I asked, as if I didn't already know.

"Somebody accused you of being a Christian," he said. "Hell, I can't say that's a bad thing, but you got the memo, same as everybody else. The complaint was put into the system, and now we ain't got no choice."

"So, you're arresting me," I said.

"'Fraid so," he said sadly. "But it's just a formality."

The look in Allie Mendolson's eyes told me a different story. I didn't know her personally, although I was familiar with most of the security people. I knew she was a hard worker and dedicated. But there was a look in her eye that was more than just accusatory. If it were up to her I think she would have shot me on the spot.

"We'll have a hearing, and you can clear everything up there," he said.

"Sure," I replied, knowing that if clearing things up meant renouncing my faith, that things would only get worse.

"I gotta do it," he continued. "Shouldn't take long. If McComber doesn't drag her feet we can have the hearing this afternoon. It's a hell of time to be wasting our energy on this. There are real threats out there that need our attention, but you know how this kind of thing goes. Orders are orders. You need anything?"

"Would you find out how Cat is doing?" I said. "And don't let her know what's happening here."

"Yeah, I can do that," LB said. He held out his hand. "I hope there's no hard feelings."

"None," I said, shaking his hand.

Allie narrowed her eyes, her suspicions raised. I didn't want to get LB in trouble, so I backed up. He closed the metal door. It locked automatically with a loud clank, and I sank down onto the bunk. It was just a metal platform and the room smelled of chemical disinfectant, but I wouldn't have called it clean. In fact, it reminded me of a bathroom stall. Not just because there was a toilet in the corner, but because the walls had been scratched with all sorts of messages and crude drawings. The military issue gray paint on the walls was obviously soft enough to make leaving a message easy. There were names scratched into the surface, nasty messages, and lewd depictions. It's hard not to read what's written on the walls when you spend hours locked into a tiny cell like that. I did my best to keep my eyes closed, praying for wisdom and strength. I wondered if LB would put a gun to my head, or if they would try to decapitate me like the guards on the ziggurat in Babylon. Either way, my journey in this life would end soon. I thought about heaven. Everyone does at some point or other. It's impossible to contemplate death without wondering what comes afterward. I had read in the Bible that to be absent from the body is to be present with the Lord. And in the prophecy about the great persecution of Christians during the tribulation it says those martyrs are kept in a special place, close to the throne room of God. But I just couldn't picture it.

The minutes ticked by slowly. Eventually, a security team member named Tim Riley brought me a sandwich for lunch. It's hard to eat when you know that you're going to die. And I went through all the emotions too. Fear at first, then anger. Why, I asked, was God letting these terrible things happen to me? I had dedicated myself to him. I was fulfilling a purpose by posting Lorenzo's videos. But of course, I hadn't posted anything for a long time. Not since shortly after we first arrived at Camp Abilene. And I was far from innocent. There were times when I was selfish, rude, arrogant, and judgmental. Anger turned to hope. Maybe God wasn't done with me yet? Maybe by some miracle he would save me. McComber could change her mind after all. But hope was short-lived, and settled into a sad sense of acceptance. It was my time. I could feel that. Fear was still stabbing at me whenever I let my guard down. No one wants to die, even when we know that it leads to a new life in God's Kingdom. I didn't want anything bad to happen to Cat. And if she were to get sick with the Death Flu, I didn't want her to suffer alone. But all of that was out of my hands. And, a couple of hours after lunch, LB returned.

"Looks like we're gonna get this all wrapped up," he said. "They found a Bible in your room, but that's just a technicality. Ain't no law against having one. They want to see what's on your laptop, but it's locked and I've been pushing pretty hard to nip this in the bud."

"LB," I said, getting to my feet. "You know I'm a Christian."

"I don't *know* anything," he replied. "You ain't never tried to convert me. And I don't think we should be hounding people for what they believe. My grandmother believed she could talk to the dead, and my auntie sold mojo charms she made from animal bones and herbs. They lived all their lives, and no one locked them up for what they believed. This used to be a free country."

"But it's not anymore," I said. "It's not even a country, it's a region. The Bible predicted that, you know. The Bible predicted all of this."

"Hank," LB said in a quiet voice. "You need to stop talking like that. McComber's just another bureaucrat but there's some others here of stronger opinions."

"I know," I said, suddenly feeling my fears recede. "I'm ready to answer their questions."

"You keep Cat in mind," he warned me. "Don't you do nothing stupid, Downes, that's an order. Stick out your hands."

I did, and he put handcuffs on me, but left them so loose I could pull my hands free.

"We have protocols that say you have to be restrained," he told me. "But ain't nothing that says how tight I have to make 'em."

We walked from the security buildings to a little platform where the big screen had been set up. A crowd of refugees had already begun to form. They didn't know me, but something was going on, a distraction from the tedium of the day. The clouds seemed thick overhead, the day cold, but I didn't really pay it much attention. My focus was on my heart beating steadily in my chest, and the way each breath made me feel. Even the way my muscles moved my body. I had never really given those things much of my attention. As a kid I spent my free time reading books. In the Air Force I was always busy with a task. Since the Rapture I had been busy trying to stay alive, but there was no need to strive any longer. I felt my journey coming to an end–my destination was fast approaching. So I took the time to feel what it was like to live in my mortal body, while I still could.

The quarantine trailer was on the far side of the infirmary. I was grateful for that. I didn't want to stress Cat out, and I certainly didn't want her to see me die. LB sat me in a folding chair on the far side of the little stage, to wait for the AIC and whoever else would be judging me to come out.

"LB," I said softly. "Will you do something for me?"

"Depends," he said.

"You will tell Cat that I love her," I said. "Make sure she gets all my stuff, whatever she wants."

"Dude, shut your mouth," LB said. "This is just a circus. Ain't nobody dying today."

He couldn't have been more wrong.

CHAPTER 31

MCCOMBER CAME out with her assistant Miller and a woman I didn't really know. She had on thick glasses and was painfully thin. The three of them sat down at a narrow table. All the administrators gathered around close to the small stage. Behind them, the refugees pressed in, curious as to what was going on. There was a full team of security people too, and LB stayed close to me on the stage. His security people were all armed with machine guns. I saw Arnie from the armory, and Tim Riley from the jail, along with a few other security people who weren't armed with rifles. They mixed in with the administrative crowd, and there were maintenance workers there too. In fact, it seemed like everyone on staff at Camp Abilene, except for the medical personnel, had skipped out on work to see what would happen.

I recognized a few fellow believers in the crowd. They looked frightened, and I wished that I could reassure them, but I really had no idea what was about to happen. Then Allie

Mendolson appeared. She was escorting Ruth, who was cleaned up and in new clothes. She looked nervous, and part of me wanted to be angry with her. But another part just felt sorry for her. The poor woman's mother had told her the truth about God's love. And she had read the Bible for herself. In fact, we had read passages about Bible prophecy and talked about it together on her father's farm. But she hadn't truly believed it. I don't think she wanted to believe it. She wanted life to go back to normal, although, from what she told me, her life before the Rapture wasn't all that great.

"Alright, quiet down," Evelyn McComber ordered. "I call this hearing to order."

The loud speakers were gone, and the crowd fell silent. My body tightened, like a spring being compressed. I couldn't tell if it was from fear or excitement.

"This tribunal has been formed to deal with the accusation of treason against Lieutenant Henry Downes," Miller said in a loud voice. He was reading from his iPad. "According to the North American Regional Administration, and the Global Council for Peace, all persons adhering to and promulgating divisive ideologies are guilty of treason. We shall now hear the accusation by Ruth Emory."

I won't lie. It was painful to see someone I thought of as a friend speaking out publicly against me. Ruth looked completely different than she had the day before. Still too thin, the skin on her face looked brittle, but someone had supplied make-up to cover the dark circles under her eyes, and to give her pale, sunken cheeks some color. She stepped up in front of the three administrators, glanced nervously at me, and then spoke in a clear voice.

"Hank Downes is a Bible-believing Christian," she said, as if that fact were a horrible pronouncement of death. "After the vanishings he stayed with me and my father for a while at our family farm in Montana. He claimed the vanishings were the work of God, and that God was judging the entire world as sinful."

What she said was true to a degree, I suppose. I did believe that millions of people around the world suddenly disappearing, including all children, were the work of God. And I do believe that we are in a period of time called the tribulation in the Bible, a time when God judges the world for not believing him. But, the entire argument hinges on the fact that God's desire is that we will recognize our sins and his sovereignty, turn away from relying on ourselves, and put our faith in Jesus. Ruth sort of left that part out, even though I know we had many conversations about that very thing.

"He confessed to you that he believes in the Bible and in God?" Evelyn McComber asked.

"Yes," Ruth said, which really got the crowd murmuring. It also spurred LB into action.

"When I was a kid I believed in Santa Claus," he said so loudly that the three administrators couldn't help but hear him. "When I was a grown man I believed in the promise of my country, that we were the greatest beacon of freedom in the world. We've all held onto things that weren't necessarily true. But once we know better...well...that's the past. I would hope that no one would be punished for an old belief. If so, we better all line up and take our licks."

"Thank you, Major Burski," McComber said, obviously

trying to shut him up. "Is there anyone else here who has a grievance against Lieutenant Downes?"

"I do," Allie Mendolson said, stepping forward.

"Corporal," McComber said. "Please, give us your testimony."

Frankly, I was shocked. I hadn't, to my knowledge, even spoken to Allie other than to say hello a time or two. She was on Security Team Charlie, and our paths didn't often cross. She may have been on guard duty when a shipment of goods came into camp, but my attention was on cataloging the materials, not on who was holding a gun and standing guard around the truck.

Allie cut a striking figure. She wasn't as thin as Ruth but well-proportioned in her fatigues. The rifle over one shoulder and the massive pistol on her hip looked like they belonged in her experienced hands. Unlike Ruth, she didn't bother looking at me.

"I've seen Lieutenant Downes praying," she said. "We performed a search of his room and found several books on Christian prophecy, and a well-used Bible."

"Mendolson?" LB asked. "What are you doing?"

"My duty, sir," she snapped. "The lieutenant believes in a God who orders his people to slaughter the innocent. A God who judges you and me for every choice we make, every thought that passes through our head. I won't let that stand. We're building a better world, sir."

She suddenly started weeping. "I won't...stand for a God... who steals our children. And I'll never believe..."

"That's enough," McComber said, sounding embarrassed. "Thank you for that testimony, Corporal."

Allie cried hard and managed to nod before walking off the stage. Maybe I should have been angry, but instead I felt compassion for her. Who knew she had a child before the Rapture? Maybe I should have gotten to know her better and perhaps I could have helped her work through the pain. The anger that some people felt over having their children taken in the Rapture was something I hadn't thought to address before that moment. Not that there was time to make a change. The evidence brought against me was true, and I wouldn't deny it.

"Does the accused have anything to say in his defense?" McComber asked.

I stood up. The table with the three administrators was on my right. The crowd on my left. I cleared my throat, saw LB give me an encouraging nod, and thought to myself, what would Lorenzo say at a time like this?

"In my defense," I said. "I would like to clear up a few things."

"Go right ahead," McComber said.

I didn't get the impression she was for me or against me. She was the most neutral person I think I've ever encountered. Miller, to her left, looked at me with annoyance, the same way he had the night I arrived at Camp Abilene. The woman on her right leaned forward, anxious to hear what I was going to say.

"I do not believe that God is judging the world for sin," I said in a loud voice. LB visibly relaxed until I spoke again. "I believe His judgments are to draw us back to belief in him."

This stirred up the crowd, and it took McComber a moment to quiet them down. LB just bowed his head in defeat. I saw Ruth next to Allie. They were both staring at me, incredulous that I hadn't denied their accusations.

"Lieutenant Downes, are you aware that belief in religion is treason against the NARA?" McComber asked.

"I am aware," I said. "I'm also aware that the world being divided into three kingdoms is predicted in the Bible, as is this persecution of Christians."

"Heresy!" someone in the crowd shouted.

"Kill him!" someone else yelled, but I pressed on.

"If you want to execute me for what I believe, I won't try to stop you. In fact, I forgive you, just as Jesus did to those who crucified him. He is the one and only Son of God who died to take away the sins of the world. Anyone who puts their belief in him will be forgiven of their sins and live forever in his Kingdom."

"I think we've heard enough," McComber said. "Major, secure the accused."

He stepped up and put a hand on my arm. I fell silent so that he wouldn't have to shut me up physically. The three judges put their heads together as they contemplated my fate.

"Why'd you do it, Hank?" LB whispered.

"Because it's true," I said. "And I think you know it."

"You're crazy, man. Why not just tell them what they want to hear?"

"Because I can't deny him," I said. "Jesus loved me when I was unlovable. Saved me when I didn't deserve it. And gave me a mission. Please make sure that Cat gets my laptop and books."

He shook his head in disbelief. "You're serious?"

"Yeah, and it wouldn't hurt you to take a look at them. You'd be surprised what's really going on."

"I hate you for making me do this," he said in a tight voice.

"I'm sorry," I replied as McComber began to quiet the crowd.

When she had their attention she stood up. "As the Administrator in Charge of this facility it is my responsibility to ensure that the rules and regulations handed down to us from the NARA are carried out. Any individual who knowingly and willfully disregards those rules shall be punished. It is the verdict of this tribunal that Lieutenant Henry Downes is guilty of treason."

The crowd went wild. It was as if they were watching a football game and their favorite team scored a touchdown. I should have been scared, but I wasn't. Instead, I felt a sense of peace like I had never known before. I was calm, despite so many people screaming for my head.

"We further declare that Lieutenant Downes should be executed...immediately. Major Burski, please carry out the execution."

"I didn't bring a sword," he said. "Y'all know this is crazy, right? Hank ain't done nothing wrong. You can't kill a good man just for what he believes in."

Miller stood up. "Major, you will carry out our orders or you will be relieved of duty and charged with dereliction of said duties. You have a sidearm. Use it, or step aside."

LB looked at Miller like he might use his pistol on the administrator.

"It's okay," I said. "LB, it's alright, man. Don't get yourself into trouble on my account."

"This is wrong," LB insisted. "I'm doing this in protest."

"Just do it!" Miller growled.

I turned and faced the crowd. "Jesus loves you. He will forgive your sins and accept you if you call out to him."

"That's enough, prisoner," McComber said, but I ignored her.

"All you have to do is believe that Jesus is the Son of God and you will be saved."

LB took my arm. "Hank, please get on your knees."

He was crying, and that moved me. Tears flooded my eyes. I hadn't realized how much his friendship had meant to me until that moment.

"Sure," I said. "God loves you, LB. And so do I."

"Don't make it harder on me, bro," he said.

I got down on my knees, facing the crowd. They were an angry mob, some screaming and cursing for me to die. Others stared at me with morbid fascination. I made eye contact with a few from my group of believers. A couple were crying, but they all looked straight at me, as if willing me to have courage.

LB pressed his pistol to the back of my head. I could feel it shaking in his big hand. It was at that point that I realized I hadn't fallen apart or been a coward when faced with death for my faith. A sense of relief washed over me, and I actually smiled.

CHAPTER 32

THE FIRST SHOT didn't come from LB's gun. Someone in the back of the crowd chose that moment to open fire. A volley of bullets passed me by. One hit LB in the arm, spinning him around before he toppled to the stage. The three administrators took the brunt of the attack. Their bodies were riddled with bullets before they toppled backward in their chairs.

I flopped over, pulled my hands from the loose cuffs, and started crawling toward the back of the stage. Chaos had broken out. The crowd of workers and refugees alike panicked. They ran in all directions. Some of the security forces opened fire, shooting at anyone who looked dangerous. Unfortunately, there was a group of outlaws from town in the crowd, and the security officers on duty were the first people to be targeted and taken down.

LB was a big man. Pulling him across the stage was difficult, but I managed to drag him off the backside where we had a little cover from the shooting. He had dropped his pistol, and we had no weapons between us, but we were both alive. Fortunately, he was able to walk.

"Get to the security building," he said. "Can't stay here."

"Yeah, got it," I said, taking hold of his good arm and helping him.

We bent at the waist and ran toward the security buildings. We were lucky. Most of the outlaws were interested in the admin buildings and the mess hall of course, since most of them were starving, but also the private domiciles of the level one staff, which included the Administrator in Charge Evelyn McComber and her assistants. The security buildings looked like a jail, and the outlaws wanted no part of that, even though the warehouse with most of the camp's supplies was in the secure section. I got LB into the main building and past the reception area. The door to the armory was closed and locked, but like all the buildings at Camp Abilene, it was flimsy. I kicked it open easily, and we stumbled inside.

"I can't believe...they got inside," LB said.

"How bad are you hit?" I asked, ripping his sleeve to see the wound.

"Just passed through the muscle," he said. "Hurts like hell, though."

"We have to get out of here," I said.

"Why? This is the safest place in the camp."

Outside we could hear guns being fired. Some were fully automatic, which had to be the weapons the outlaws took from the security force members they killed. We all knew ammunition was limited, and it was standard operating procedure to keep the M-16s on semi-automatic to conserve ammo and ensure that we were aiming at good targets. LB was a friendly, jovial man, but he was a stickler for gun safety and discipline in the ranks.

"The camp is gone," I said. "We have to leave."

"And go where?" LB asked.

"We can decide that once it's safe," I said, wrapping a gun belt with a holster around my waist. I shoved the Beretta 9 mm into it, grabbed all the extra clips of ammo, and fed them into the loops on the belt.

"Here," I said, handing LB a .45 auto. He managed to check the slide.

There was a first aid kit on the wall. I yanked it off, pulled out the quickclot gauze and shoved it into the bullet wound on the big man's arm. He screamed in pain. It's odd to hear a man his size scream, and I thought he was going to crack my skull with the pistol I had just given him, but he merely leaned back, panting and sweating.

"That's one hell of a bedside manner, Downes."

"Sorry," I told him, as I slapped on an adhesive patch. "But it's the best I can do for now. Hang onto that."

He tucked the first aid kit under his arm. I pulled on a bulletproof vest with tactical webbing, and then picked my AR-15 with the bump stock out of the rack. It fired the same .223 ammunition as the M-16s. I slung one of them over my back and filled every loop in the vest with extra magazines.

"What's your plan?" LB asked.

"I'm sending you to get us transportation."

"Ain't none," he challenged me.

"There's a supply truck due in this afternoon," I replied.

"And you and I both know how spotty they can be. Odds are it won't get here for hours, if at all."

"Or maybe it's already here," I said. "Get to the ware-house. Pack whatever food you can, and if there's a vehicle, commandeer it."

"What are you going to do?"

"Get Cat," I said. "Rally the troops if there are any left."

"And don't get yourself killed," he said. "You hear me, Hank. No heroics."

"Roger that, Major," I said with a grin. "I'll meet you in the warehouse. Can you walk?"

"Yeah, I'm feeling good despite your lousy medical inter-vention."

"Good," I said with a big grin. "You were just about to blow my brains out after all. I guess we're even."

"I'll never understand you, boy," he replied. "But Hank, thanks for getting me off that platform."

"It was my honor, sir. See you in the warehouse."

"Oorah!" he said.

I had been fearless with LB's pistol pressed to the back of my skull, but I was terrified when I dashed out of the security building. There were bodies everywhere–some wounded, others already dead. People were screaming and shouting. The world was a chaotic mess it seemed. The only calm in the storm was the infirmary. No one wanted to go anywhere near it.

Running toward the quarantine area, I was confronted by an angry-looking refugee. I didn't know if he was out to get my weapons, or just crazed by the chaos, but when he got close I slammed the butt of my rifle into his face. He dropped; I kept running. I was almost to the infirmary when Allie Mendolson stepped into my path. She was armed, but had a gash on the side of her head. Blood was running from her hairline down across one cheek. Pointing her rifle at me, she ordered me to stop.

"I'm going to get Cat," I said.

"I don't care," she snarled. "You deserve to die."

"And you don't," I said. "LB is in the warehouse. We're rallying there. You have to go, Corporal. Move!"

"You deserve to die," she said, tears flooding her eyes.

"We all do," I said. "I'm sorry about your children."

"Don't," she snarled. "Don't you talk about my babies."

"I won't," I said. "But you can see them again. I know it's hard to believe, but you can. They're safe."

"They should be here with me!"

"Should they?" I asked. "How cruel would that be? Look around, Mendolson, things are terrible and will only get worse. Taking them away from this was an act of mercy."

Her weapon wavered and I moved close enough to put my hand on her shoulder. "Allie! Get to the warehouse. LB needs your help. Go!"

She went, her military training overriding her raw emotions. I couldn't blame her for the way she felt. I didn't have children, couldn't imagine having them and losing them, but I had been a child who lost his parents. That wound was still aching deep inside me.

I ran to the quarantine building and looked in the window. There were bullet holes in the building. The glass was already cracked from one. The blinds were mangled, and it was hard to see, but I thought I could make out a body on the floor. Fear gripped me harder than it ever had at that moment.

"Cat!" I screamed. "Cat!"

The body on the floor rolled over. I could see her. She started getting up. I smashed through the window with butt of my rifle.

"Cat! Are you hurt?"

"No!" she replied. "What's happening?"

"Long story," I said. "Outlaws attacked the camp. We're getting out of here."

Helping her out of the window was awkward, but we managed it. I pulled my pistol and gave it to her, then we started back through the chaos. Twice I had to put people down. The first was an outlaw with a hunting rifle and a big, bloody knife. He lunged at me; I shot him. The crack of the rifle's report was loud, but it seemed almost benign amidst the cacophony of the camp.

The second person was a big man attempting to rape a woman. He was on top of her, ripping at her clothes. Only a demonic entity would try to rape someone in the middle of a gun fight. There were bullets flying past us all the time. Not shot right at us, but just fired randomly through the camp. They made a cracking sound as the bullets broke the sound barrier in flight. We ran with our heads down, weapons ready. I saw the big man tearing at the woman's clothes in a frenzy. I bashed him in the side of the head with the butt of my rifle. He toppled sideways off the woman, and I realized with a shock that it was Ruth.

"No! No! No!" She was screaming as she writhed on the ground.

"Ruth!" I screamed in her face. "Get up. We have to move."

I grabbed her arm and pulled her off the ground. She didn't seem to understand me, but she didn't resist either as we dashed toward the security compound.

Some of the outlaws had discovered that the warehouse was the real treasure of the camp. They tried to get inside, but a group of security personnel were holding them off. I pushed Ruth and Cat inside the building with the jail and the armory. Then I opened fire on the outlaws with the AR-15. The bump stock transformed the semi-automatic weapon into full auto. I fired a sweeping barrage at half a dozen outlaws who were shooting toward the double metal doors that led into the warehouse. They went down in a cluster. And I dashed into the main security building.

CHAPTER 33

THERE WERE BODIES INSIDE. I took the lead, and Cat helped Ruth who had calmed down a little. We stopped at the armory. It was ransacked, but there were crates of .223 caliber ammo and cans with handles of .45 caliber bullets. Ruth took the crate, Cat got two full cans of .45 caliber rounds, and we hurried to the warehouse.

Of course I knew it couldn't be that easy. To run to the warehouse and ride off to safety in an armored truck would have been wonderful. Instead, we fought our way past the jail, where a couple of outlaws were hiding. They made the mistake of leaving the jail's metal door nearly closed while they shot at us through the pass-through slot. When I shot back, the impact of my bullets pushed the door closed. We were right by a broom closet. I grabbed a mop with a plastic handle, rushed forward, and wedged it into one end of the pass-through slot. The handle was almost exactly the width of the hallway. I managed to wedge the mop sideways so that opening the door was almost impossible.

Ruth and Cat had to crawl under the mop handle, but we made it past the outlaws without getting hurt. At the end of the hall there was a woman rummaging in LB's office. She had found his bottle of whiskey and had already taken a drink, maybe too. Her face was red. When I pointed my rifle at her she dove behind the desk. The last thing I wanted to do was kill her, or alert any other outlaws of my presence. So we ran past LB's office hoping the woman wouldn't come at us from behind. In the entrance to the short corridor that led to the warehouse, a group of outlaws were hunkered down. They didn't see us as we took cover behind a row of lockers.

"Stay back," I told Cat. "No matter what happens, don't try to fight."

"I'm not leaving you," she said.

"And I'm not leaving you," I replied. "But if I get killed, then you need to find another way out of camp."

I started to engage the outlaws, but Ruth grabbed my shirt sleeve and pulled me back toward her.

"I'm sorry!" she sobbed. "I'm so sorry."

Unfortunately, she was loud. One of the outlaws heard her.

"It's okay," I whispered. "I forgive you."

Cat looked mystified and a little jealous.

"Why would you?" Ruth sobbed. "I'm a terrible person."

"Everything will be—"

"Hold it!" a man snarled. "What have we here?"

I started to turn, and the outlaw swung his hunting rifle at me like a club. The butt end glanced off the side of my head, knocking me off my feet. I crashed into the lockers, but Cat had drawn her pistol. She shot the outlaw in his gut. He staggered backward, dropping his rifle.

"I'm hit!" he bellowed. "She's killed me."

I barely had time to bring my rifle to bear. There were four other outlaws in the room, and I was exposed. Cat and Ruth were tucked between two sets of lockers, but the only thing between me and the outlaws was the wounded man. I fired wild, the AR-15 rocking in my hands. The outlaws fired back, their bullets pinging the metal lockers and flying over my head. The battle, if it can be called that, lasted a few seconds. I emptied my magazine, and the outlaws died. A few of my bullets had hit the warehouse door, but it was made of metal.

"Hank!" Cat shouted.

"I'm okay," I said, surprised to still be alive.

"Are they..."

"Yes," I said. "Come on, we have to get out of here."

I scrambled to my feet. Cat and Ruth picked up the boxes of ammunition, and we hurried through the short corridor.

"Hey, in the warehouse!" I shouted. "This is Lieutenant Downes and two civilians. We're coming in."

The metal door swung open, and there was Corporal Allie Mendolson, bloody-faced and determined. Her rifle was pointed at me, and for a moment I sincerely thought she was going to kill me. In the public trial I was fearless, my heart surrounded by perfect peace. Even the prospect of death didn't frighten me. But in that short corridor, completely exposed and facing one of my accusers with a loaded rifle pointed at my chest, I felt intense fear. It took all my strength to hold back the sudden urge to pee, and my knees could barely hold me up.

"Come on," she finally said, lowering the rifle. "I had to be sure it was you."

"Yeah," I managed, although my mouth was suddenly painfully dry.

We came in and found a group tossing supplies out of a waiting supply truck. There were several wounded people on the floor by the big overhead door. I led the way to the truck. The driver was on his knees and looked angry. LB had his pistol out and was leaning against the wall.

"You made it," he said with relief. "I thought you were gone for sure."

"It's crazy out there," I said. "We need to go."

"The driver agrees with you so much he started to leave without us," LB said. "I changed his mind."

"What are you carrying?" I asked the driver.

"Clothes, a water processing unit, and canned goods," the driver mumbled.

"Perfect," I said. "What are we waiting on?"

"You," LB said. "I've got people in the camp. Can't leave anyone behind."

"But if we stay they'll surround us," I said.

"Which is why you are taking the wounded out of here," LB said. "Load up the truck, go ten miles due north, and wait for us."

"I should stay here," I said.

"Nah, what good is a logistics guy from the Air Force?" LB laughed. "Leave the heavy lifting to me."

I wanted to argue, but his plan made too much sense. Cat and Ruth handed over the ammo, which was promptly put to use by four other security personnel. LB ordered Allie to go with us.

"That truck needs protection," he snapped. "That's you, Corporal. Or do we have a problem with the chain of command?"

"No, sir," she replied.

"Good. There's a case with tools over there," he pointed across the warehouse. "Wheel that in back. You're the only one of us who can keep that thing running."

"Copy that," she said, turning to obey him.

Cat and Ruth were helping the wounded into the back of the supply truck. There were half a dozen people all with bullet wounds. Two were unconscious and had to be carried in.

"We're going to need medical supplies," Cat said. "Bandages, antiseptic, some way to slow down the bleeding."

"We'll get what we can," LB said. "Look for us by dawn. If we don't make it by midday, you head on to wherever you think is safest."

He stuck out his hand. I shook it.

"Hell of a thing you did today, Downes."

"I'm glad you made it, Major. Don't be a hero."

"The student becomes the master," he said with a chuckle. "My man. I'll see you at sunrise."

He led his band of soldiers toward the metal doors. A couple more security personnel were left to secure the building. We loaded as much food as possible into the truck, then took the rest of the ammunition and set out.

It was late afternoon, and heavy clouds brought on the darkness swifter than it would have fallen otherwise. We headed north on FM 600 straight north to See Bee Park on Fort Phantom Hill Lake. It was little more than a parking lot with a boat ramp into the lake, plus a pavilion. But it gave us easy access to the road north, and the water blocked off anyone coming from the east or south. On the open plains we could see anyone approaching from a long way, but there weren't any followers.

The truck driver wasn't too happy having his rig taken over, but we didn't have a choice. Cat and Ruth worked tirelessly with the wounded, but we lost both of the unconscious security officers before morning. The others had lesser wounds. We collected water from the lake and ate soup from the supplies in the truck. Ruth had picked up some extra clothing for herself, and there were loading blankets in the truck that made decent pallets for sleeping.

We were all exhausted, but we took turns standing watch and nursing the wounded. Cat and I took the first shift. I walked back and forth about forty feet from the truck near the parking lot entrance. Fatigue set in fast, and the wind off the lake was painful, but it kept me awake. Walking was the only way to stay warm. It was a miracle that the sky cleared that night. I really believe that. The clouds rolled back, and the stars twinkled above us. More importantly, a full moon lit the area, reflecting off the lake making the wide expanse around us visible in the gloom.

I woke Allie around one in the morning, and Cat roused

Ruth. Then we stretched out just inside the truck, wrapped ourselves in a moving blanket that smelled like sawdust, and fell asleep. Allie woke me just before dawn. I crawled out the truck, feeling so tired that I wanted to cry. It was cold, my joints ached, and my mouth felt gluey.

"What's that?" she asked me, pointing down the road.

All we could make out was a dark blob barely visible in the darkness.

"Don't know," I said. "It might be the major."

"Or it might be outlaws," she replied.

"We better make sure," I told her. "I'll go get a closer look. If you hear shooting, wake up the driver and get the truck out of here."

"What about you, sir?"

"I'll catch up, if I can."

There had been too many close calls of late. And while I felt good about being alive, I also felt terrible that I had lost the laptop with all of Lorenzo's interviews and conference appearances. Maybe I should have gone after it, but the truth was I didn't even know where the administrators had put it after searching my room.

I set off at a slow jog, doing my best to stay low. I doubt that I was out of sight, but I tried. There isn't much cover out in the west Texas plains. The sun turned the sky gray, then pale blue for just a few moments before the gray clouds rolled in again. I was glad I hadn't missed it, and was also glad at what the sunlight revealed.

LB was marching a column of armed men down the road. They were all carrying gear. I turned back as soon as I recognized them and ran back to the truck.

"Good news?" Allie asked, still worried.

"It's the major," I said. "They'll be exhausted. Let's get a fire going, heat some water for food."

There wasn't much in the way of fuel for a fire, but a couple of old supply pallets were broken up and got a couple of small fires burning by the time LB arrived. Cat set to work helping the sick with the medical supplies the group carried. They were mostly security officers from the camp, but also some maintenance workers and a few administrators. Everyone had a weapon of some sort, but fortunately they hadn't needed them on the road north.

We spent the day there at See Bee park. The driver moved the truck right beside the pavilion to create a windbreak. Once the tired group was fed, most of them found a place out of the wind to sleep. I sat with LB while Cat changed the bandage on his wounded arm.

"The outlaws didn't stay long," he explained. "They got what they could carry and fled. The refugees were the real problem."

"Especially when they saw how we were living?" I asked.

"Bingo," LB said. "Fortunately they didn't have guns, or we'd all be dead. I did manage to grab this."

He unzipped his backpack and pulled out a couple of books. I felt a surge of excitement. They were books on Bible prophecy and Lorenzo's old Bible.

"I'm of the opinion that we shouldn't censor people who have opposing points of view," he said. "I'm damn glad I couldn't pull that trigger up on that stage, Hank."

"What's he talking about?" Cat asked.

"Can we wait until she's done tending my wound before you explain it to her?" LB said, and we both laughed.

"Somebody better spill it," Cat frowned.

"I was accused of treason," I confessed. AIC McComber had a public trial."

"No!" Cat said. "She is such a horrible person."

"Was," LB said. "The outlaws took her down. Miller too. How do you think I got that scratch?"

"It's more than a scratch," Cat said. "It needs to be washed clean before it gets infected."

"Right front pocket," he said.

LB had on a camouflaged coat over his bulletproof tactical vest. I reached over and pulled out a flask.

"I'm not sure this is regulation rations," I said.

"Au contraire, mon frère," he replied. "That is essential to any officer in theater. Especially those down range in the thick of it. Just give me a sip, then you can use the rest on my arm."

He took a swig, grimaced at the taste, then sighed. He seemed genuinely happy until Cat poured the liquor into the wound on his arm. He groaned in pain and panted a little.

"That smarts," he said.

"Let's hope it kills the infection trying to set in," Cat told him.

"It'll cure or kill," he said.

"It's not funny, LB," she insisted. "You could lose your arm."

"I'll remember that, doc. And keep a check on the bandage. If it starts to smell, well, you'll just have to get out your saw and go to work."

Cat pulled me aside after she had seen to LB's arm, taping

the entrance and exit wounds with adhesive stitches and then wrapping the arm in gauze. She was tired. We all were. And we took the day to rest. I told Cat the entire ordeal in camp, from getting arrested at breakfast, to standing my ground on the platform in front of the crowd. I knew that if I hadn't been on my knees I would probably be dead, or at least wounded the way that LB was.

"But I'm not," I said after relaying the story. "I got LB off the stage. We made it back to the security center. I armed up and came to get you."

"You are the bravest man I've ever known," she said.

"It wasn't me," I told her. "God gave me peace through the whole ordeal."

"That's amazing, and I'm not downplaying it," she said. "But I was talking about you coming for me. No one's ever fought for me before."

"I always will," I promised her.

She kissed me, then pulled back. "I was so scared, Hank. I didn't know what was happening, and then people started shooting the trailer. All I could think to do was hide on the floor."

"It was the smartest thing you could do," I told her.

"But now that things are somewhat normal, and I've kissed you, I'm a little worried about getting you sick."

"Are you sick?" I asked, feeling a stab of terror.

Not that it would have changed anything. I really wouldn't have had it any other way. She was the love of my life. For those of you who read my first book, you may think I'm wishy-washy. And who knows, maybe I am. Maybe I'm the type of guy who falls fast and falls hard, but I felt so connected to Cat. If she had been sick, I would have nursed her myself, no matter the cost. Fortunately, she wasn't.

"No, just tired," she said. "But I didn't go the full two weeks of quarantine."

"The circumstances changed," I said. "But we need to make some decisions."

"About what?" she asked.

"About the future," I said. "LB's going to need to take these people somewhere safe. Somewhere official, where I'm not going to be wanted."

"I doubt anyone would tell the authorities that you were on the verge of getting executed for some stupid mandate about religious thought. I never imagined I would see the day that people are killed for thinking the wrong thing. I feel like I'm in a bad sci-fi movie."

"Tell me about it," I said. "They might not talk, but we can't depend on that. Besides, I've got a mission. Lorenzo's files may be lost, but his disciple isn't. I'm going to spread the word far and wide, Cat. I'm going to share the good news and call out evil."

"You're crazy," she said.

"Yeah, maybe so, but I know that's what I'm supposed to do. And I'm not a fool. I know it will be dangerous. That's why you might want to consider going back with the others."

"And leave my husband?" she said, pretending to be shocked at the idea.

"You could, you know," I said. "This is my calling. I'm willing to risk it, but you don't have to."

"I can't say I'm a hundred percent on board with your

theories," she said. "But I am completely, undeniably yours, Hank Downes. Nothing will ever change that."

"You don't know how happy it makes me to hear that," I told her.

"I have a pretty good idea," she replied with a grin before she kissed me fiercely.

CHAPTER 34

THAT NIGHT CAT and I sat by a fire with LB, Allie Mendolson, and a few other security officers. LB had put together a rotation of people to stand watch. He and I were scheduled to take the last turn of hours before dawn. I took the opportunity to tell them what was coming.

"The Bible describes the judgments as a series of events," I said. "The first was the appearance of Paul Eon."

"You're telling us the Bible lists a man by name?" Allie asked. Her hostility had died down a little, and she wasn't completely against hearing what I had to say. Certainly no one was keeping her in our little group. The fire was nice, but not warm enough to hold back the freezing temperatures near the lake.

"No, not by name," I said. "The Bible describes him as a rider on a white horse, who has a major influence on the world, including a treaty with many for seven years."

"The Near East peace accords," LB said. "Alright, I follow you."

"That was to be followed by war," I continued.

"The rider on the red horse," Cat said.

I nodded. "And that is followed by famine. The Bible says a loaf of bread would cost a day's wages."

"Man, I know that's how it was back home," LB said. "People were starving. I never thought I'd see bread lines in America, much less people dying of hunger."

"But hyperinflation often follows war," Allie pointed out. "They were paying for food with wheelbarrows of money in Germany after World War Two."

"And then the fourth judgment," I said. "The rider on the pale horse."

"And hell follows him," LB said.

"That's right. The Bible says a quarter of the world's population would die from war, starvation, disease, and wild animals."

"How close are we to that number?" one of the other people at the fire asked.

"One quarter would be two billion," LB said. "I don't know about the rest of the world, but we're way down here at home. I'd be surprised if one quarter was left."

"But again, and I hate to be the naysayer here, war leads to famine and to disease," Allie said. "It's not much of a prediction really. There's war, and a lot of people die."

"Maybe," I said. "If you look past the way things actually happened, you can doubt it. But we had the vanishings, which the Bible calls the Rapture. Then Paul Eon came on the scene—"

"And everyone thought he was the greatest thing since Elvis Presley," LB said. "It is surprising to consider that war would break out after we finally get peace between Israel and all her Muslim neighbors."

"Maybe," Allie said. "But this is the human race we're talking about. There's always been war."

"So let's press on," I said. "The fifth judgment would be a persecution of Christians."

"Get out," LB said. "The Bible says that?"

"It says that when Jesus opens the fifth seal John–that's who's writing the book–sees the souls of those who have been slain for the word of God and for the witness of their testimony. They were crying out for God to avenge them because of the injustice of their deaths."

"That's pretty on point if you ask me," LB said. "I guess that's where we are in the story."

"Exactly," I said.

"What comes next?" Cat asked.

I sighed, looking deep into the flames of the fire. "The sixth seal judgment is an earthquake, the likes of which the world has never seen before."

"Glad we ain't in Cali," LB said.

"There have always been earthquakes," Allie said.

"True, but here's what it says," I replied, opening Lorenzo's Bible and reading from the book of Revelation, chapter six. "When he opened the sixth seal, I looked, and behold, there was a great earthquake, and the sun became black as sackcloth, the full moon became like blood, and the stars of the sky fell to the earth as the fig tree sheds its winter fruit when shaken by a gale. The sky vanished like a scroll that is being

THE FOUR HORSEMEN   267

rolled up, and every mountain and island was removed from its place."

"Damn, God ain't joking around, is he?" LB asked.

"No," I said.

"It's horrific," Cat said.

"Wait, wait, wait," Allie jumped in. "I don't get it. How is it a judgment on the earth that the good guys get killed? I mean, you said the fifth seal is the persecution of Christians. Why would God allow that? Why would that be a judgment on the earth?"

"Great question," I said. "Scholars have debated that point for a long time. I personally think that it springs from our concept of judgment. We think of judgment like a convict being handed his sentence."

"No doubt," LB said.

"But that's not the way the Bible speaks of judgments. For instance, in Romans it says that because people didn't believe in him, and because they chased after sin, that he gave them over to the lusts of their hearts. He gave them over to dishonorable passions and a debased mind."

"I don't follow," Allie said.

"Think about it for a second," I said. "All the judgments so far have been a result of what people have wanted all along."

"People wanted war and death?" Cat asked.

"No, but they wanted to reduce the population. They wanted to shift the center of power. We all lived through the Covid pandemic. No matter your political persuasion or personal beliefs about where the virus came from, or why it was released on the world, you have to see that some people used the crisis to garner power."

"The world changed, and America changed the most," LB said. "That's for certain."

"But if you look into the elite, globalist organizations, from the United Nations to the World Economic Forum, you will see that they had plans for these things. And now they've carried them out."

"Maybe," Allie said. "But you're starting to sound like a conspiracy theorist."

"I don't know if you are aware of this, but my mentor was Lorenzo Maltza. He was an expert on the supernatural, from UFOs to ghost hunting," I explained. "He was also good friends with Arthur Doll."

"The UFO guy?" LB asked.

"The same," I said. "We went to his cabin in northern California a few weeks before the vanishings. He had been offered some serious money to promote the idea that in alien lore there is the idea of aliens performing a mass abduction. We're talking millions of people taken from Earth."

"I heard that," Allie said. "A lot of people said the aliens took the people during the vanishings."

"That was the official story. And Arthur was one of the experts who backed that story up," I said. "It sounds like a conspiracy, and it's hard to imagine that different people, from different cultures around the world, would collude to deceive the greater populace, but that's exactly what happened. And I can tell you why."

"Alright, alright," LB said. "The man can spin a yarn. You are welcome at my campfire any time, sir."

"It's not a story," I said. "It's an age-old explanation that we've been taught not to believe."

"What?" Allie asked.

"Evil," I said. "Specifically a group of powerful beings with malicious intent who have us trapped in the middle of their war with God."

"The devil," Cat said. She had heard all this before. I wasn't sure exactly how much she believed, but she knew what I was trying to communicate.

"Satan, the fallen angels," I said. "They have an agenda."

"And what's that?" Allie asked. "To enslave the world?"

"No, they don't care about us," I said. "They just want to hold off their own destruction for as long as possible. Haven't you ever wondered why so many people hate the Jews? Or more recently, why global leaders are targeting Christians? You see, the Bible says that before Jesus returns physically to the earth, his people, the Jews, will call out for him. Right now, they still don't believe that Jesus was the Messiah, but they are being won over."

"Like those two cats who breathed fire onto that squad of police trying to arrest them," LB said.

"Yeah, and by the way, those guys were predicted in the Bible too."

Allie leaned forward. "Seriously?"

"You tell me," I said, flipping a few pages in Lorenzo's Bible. "And I will grant authority to my two witnesses, and they will prophesy for one thousand two hundred and sixty days, clothed in sackcloth."

"That could be about anyone," Allie said.

So I kept reading aloud. "These are the two olive trees and the two lampstands that stand before the Lord of the Earth. And if anyone would harm them, fire pours from their mouth and consumes their foes. If anyone would harm them, this is how he is doomed to be killed."

"Holy shit!" LB said. "Oh, forgive my language, but that ain't the kind of thing you can sweep under the rug. That's for real, right there. That's in the Bible?"

I handed Lorenzo's Bible to him.

"Right there," I said. "Chapter eleven, verses three through five."

"I can't believe it," Allie said.

Cat was quiet. The other members of our little circle looked just as surprised.

"I was shocked by it all too," I said. "When Lorenzo showed me this stuff, I was rocked, but I didn't do anything about it. I just sort of thought it was all strange until the Rapture. I mean, Lorenzo didn't disappear right in front of me, but when a man with a broken hip is suddenly just gone, there can't be many explanations."

"That's when you got saved," Cat said.

"Yes."

"I lost my boys," Allie said. "I put them down for naps and opened a bottle of wine. When they didn't wake up I went to check on them."

Tears were rolling down her cheeks. Cat moved closer and wrapped an arm around Allie. I could see she had more to say, so I just waited.

"They were gone," she said. "I was a good mother. I wouldn't let anyone hurt them. I checked the doors, all the windows, there's no way someone took them. They just disappeared. And when I heard my neighbor talking about God and the Rapture. I flew into a rage. I nearly beat her to death.

THE FOUR HORSEMEN   271

That's how I ended up out here. I couldn't stay in the house where I lost them."

"They aren't lost," I said softly. "We're living in a time that God is calling on us to make a decision about who we're going to believe. It's a hard time, and things are only going to get harder. But it's a decision time, and God spared those who are too young to make that decision."

"Will I see them again?"

"They're with God," I said. "You'll see them again if you put your faith in him."

"What if she doesn't?" one of the others said. "Will God withhold her children from her? That doesn't sound very loving to me."

"If we don't accept the free gift of salvation that God is offering to us by believing in Jesus, then we'll go to hell when we die," I said calmly. "She won't want to see her children there."

"So if we don't join God's team he sends us to hell as punishment?" LB asked.

"No, see, we're all headed for hell. Every last one of us. But God loved us so much that he sent his Son to pay our debt, which he did on the cross. That opens the door. It's like we're in prison, but God opened the door. Now it's up to us if we want to remain in the prison, or if we want to walk through the open doorway and into freedom."

"Alright, that I can understand," LB said.

I nodded, happy to know I was getting through to people. I knew exactly how they felt too. When you know the truth, it's time to make a choice. What will you believe? It's the most important decision you'll ever make. But don't take too long to make it. We aren't promised tomorrow. God's patience with us won't last forever. That night, decisions were made. And I know that's why Satan and his evil companions want to shut us up. That's why writing this book was so important. We've all got to decide who we'll follow, who we'll serve. There's no Switzerland in this war–everyone is on a side. It's up to us to decide which side is the best one for us.

CHAPTER 35

THE NEXT MORNING the truck left, carrying most of the survivors from the attack on Camp Abilene–but not everyone. Cat and I stayed behind, along with Allie Mendolson and LB. Officially, we were deserters. NARA would call us traitors. But in reality we were freedom fighters, unwilling to continue serving a corrupt system that supported an evil, global dictator.

We walked north, avoiding towns. Eventually we found a Jeep Wrangler that Allie got started. Day by day, mile by mile, we moved up into the Great Plains. Resting wherever we could find water and food. Avoiding large groups of people, but helping those in need whenever we could. I didn't have the laptop with Lorenzo's files, but did find an iPhone and was able to upload videos of my own teaching.

We were somewhere near the convergence of Colorado, Kansas, and Oklahoma when the sixth seal judgment hit. Man, that was a wild, terrifying trip, and it completely changed everything. But that's a story for another time. I'll try to write if the opportunity presents itself. It's still a full time job just providing for our little group and keeping the people I care about safe.

Speaking of the people I care about, Ruth went on with the supply truck. She was pretty messed up by everything that happened. Accusing me and nearly seeing me executed had wounded her soul. You may think that by the letter of the law she did nothing wrong, but in most cases it's our motivation for why we're doing something that really counts. She wasn't trying to be a good citizen or to protect anyone. She was trying to get back at me, for whatever perceived slights she felt I had made to her. The fact that I had been the person who saved her during the attack was almost more than she could bear. As for me, I was just glad she was safe for the moment, and I was content to pray for her.

I have to admit, I'm proud of these two books, and thrilled that you have stuck with me through both of them. There's more ahead, and if I survive long enough I'll tell you all about it. Until then, may God bless you and keep you, until his glorious Second Coming! Maranatha!

AUTHOR'S NOTE

Thank you for reading the Four Horsemen. I honestly didn't have plans to write this book, but just felt compelled to. I've always pondered writing a book/series set in the seven year tribulation period that is to come. Hank gave me that opportunity and I'm so grateful. And yes, there will be more books.

If you are intrigued with the subject matter of this book, or the first book of the series *They Walk In Darkness*, I highly recommend that you look into the works of some other great writers, and scholars. First up, any of the end times books by Dr. David Jeremiah will give you great insight. He does a wonderful job of explaining things, and while there are many views and interpretations of Bible Prophecy, he is an excellent place to start. Another great introduction is Todd Hampson's *The Non-Prophet's Guide To The End Times*.

If you're looking to get deeper into the unseen spiritual reality that we live in, I highly recommend all of Derek Gilbert's books, but especially *The Second Coming Of Saturn*. If you want solid theology that outlines the Divine Council doctrine of the world being divided between many angelic beings (Deut. 32:8) who neglected their duties and instead set themselves up as gods to be worshiped, then you want to read Dr. Michael S. Heiser, specifically *Supernatural: What The Bible Teaches About The Unseen World And Why It Matters*.

As always, if you have questions you can reach me through my website: www.TobyNeighbors.com I wrote this book with a sense of urgency, and maybe there's a reason for that. And if you enjoyed it, but were hoping for more of the spiritual side of things, buckle up, because in the next book things get really, really crazy.

If you want to support me in my work, please just purchase my books (either for yourself or for others). And leaving a rating/review on Amazon and/or Goodreads.

If you are looking to keep up with what I'm working on you can follow me on Facebook, Instangram @TobyNeighbors-Author, and sign-up for my mailing list.

ALSO BY TOBY NEIGHBORS

They Walk In Darkness

Wizard Rising

Magic Awakening

Hidden Fire

Crying Havoc

Fierce Loyalty

Evil Tide

Wizard Falling

Chaos Descending

Into Chaos

Chaos Reigning

Chaos Raging

Controlling Chaos

Killing Chaos

Elder Wizard

Lorik

Lorik the Protector

Lorik the Defender

We Are The Wolf

Welcome To The Wolfpack

Embracing Oblivion

Joined In Battle

The Abyss Of Savagery

The Vault Of Mysteries

Lords Of Ascension

The Elusive Executioner

Gryphon Warriors

Regulators Revealed

Avondale

Draggah

Balestone

Arcanius

Avondale V

Third Prince

Royal Destiny

The Other Side

The New World

Luck Holds

Zompocalypse

Spartan Company

Spartan Valor

Spartan Guile

Dragon Team Seven

Uncommon Loyalty

Total Allegiance

Kestrel Class

Jump Point

Gravity Flux

Modulus Echo

Zero Friction

Planet Fall

Charter

Jack & Roxie

My Lady Sorceress

The Man With No Hands

ARC Angel

Battle ARC

Broken Crucible

Hidden Kingdom

War INC

Carthage Prime

Cronus Team

Skandia Seven

Mercurial

Magnificus Prime

Incursio

Merlin Appears

Runners

Survivors

Infiltrators

Resistance

Conquest

Occupation

Extraction

The Signal

Battle Orders

Base Of Fire

Hard Site

Recall

Evade

Assault

Space Fever

Staying Alive

Fractal Cut

Blast Zone

Action Zone

Covert Infil

Armor Brigade

www.ingramcontent.com/pod-product-compliance
Lightning Source LLC
Chambersburg PA
CBHW052032240626
47153CB00006B/2053